The
Beach House

Also by best-selling author Rochelle Alers

The Book Club series
The Seaside Café

The Inkeepers series
The Inheritance
Breakfast in Bed
Room Service
The Bridal Suite

"A Christmas Layover" in *The Perfect Present*

The
Beach House

ROCHELLE ALERS

www.kensingtonbooks.com

DAFINA BOOKS are published by

Kensington Publishing Corp.
119 West 40th Street
New York, NY 10018

All Kensington titles, imprints, and distributed lines are available at special quantity discounts for bulk purchases for sales promotion, premiums, fund-raising, and educational or institutional use.

Special book excerpts or customized printings can also be created to fit specific needs. For details, write or phone the office of the Kensington Sales Manager: Kensington Publishing Corp., 119 West 40th Street, New York, NY 10018. Attn. Sales Department. Phone: 1-800-221-2647.

The Dafina logo is a trademark of Kensington Publishing Corp.

ISBN-13: 978-1-4967-2188-4
ISBN-10: 1-4967-2188-8
First Kensington Trade Paperback Printing: June 2021

ISBN-13: 978-1-4967-2189-1 (ebook)
ISBN-10: 1-4967-2189-6 (ebook)
First Kensington Electronic Edition: June 2021

10 9 8 7 6 5 4 3 2 1

Printed in the United States of America

The Beach House

Chapter 1

Thirty years ago

Leah Berkley walked out of Dillard's holding two shopping bags with her mother's Christmas presents—a silk blouse and perfume. Buying the perfume was a no-brainer. Madeline coveted women's fragrances the way some women yearned for precious jewels to adorn their bodies.

Leah hadn't taken more than three steps when she bumped into a hard body, and the impact caused her to drop the shopping bag with the perfume. Her eyes filled with tears as she heard the bottle shatter on the concrete. It had taken her months of performing odd jobs on and off the Vanderbilt University campus to save enough money to buy gifts for her mother. Whether it was correcting and typing papers for other students or occasionally working the front desk at a nearby motel, Leah never thought a job, if legal, was too menial for her.

"I'm sorry."

Her head popped up when she heard the deep voice of the

man looming over her. "You should be!" she shouted angrily. "Why the hell didn't you look where you were going?"

"I'm sorry, miss."

"You should be," she repeated. Suddenly Leah was ashamed of her nasty tone. After all, it was an accident, and she should have been more alert instead of fantasizing about her mother's reaction to what she planned to give her for Christmas. "I'm sorry," she said, apologizing, "but that was something I wanted to give to my mother."

The man bent down to pick up the bag, which was beginning to leak, and he dropped it in a trash receptacle a few feet away. "I should be the one apologizing, because I wasn't looking where I was going. Come with me and I'll buy you another one."

Leah looked at him for the first time. Despite her dilemma, she saw he wasn't handsome in the traditional sense, but attractive. She liked his large hazel eyes that seemed to smile when his mouth wasn't. He claimed a head of thick, wavy, dark-brown hair, while his features were masculine but unremarkable. He did not give her a chance to reject his offer; he cupped her elbow and steered her back into the store. What she did notice was those on the sales floor staring, smiling and acknowledging him with a nod as he directed her over to the fragrance counter.

"This young lady just purchased a bottle of . . ." His voice trailed off, and he stared at Leah until she gave him the name of the perfume. "I'd like to purchase the largest bottle that you have. And please gift wrap it." The saleswoman bowed her head as if he were the member of a royal family.

Leah moved closer to his side. "I don't need the largest bottle." She knew her mother would give her a tongue-lashing about being extravagant if she gave her a gift costing . . . more than two hundred dollars! It was only months ago that her parents had moved out of an apartment and into a rental house, after her father had been promoted to head mechanic at a local used-car dealership. They tended to watch every penny because they were responsible for all repairs on the property.

"It's my way of apologizing."

His lips parted in a smile, transforming his features and making her catch her breath. There was something about the man that was devilishly charming—but it wasn't the charming with whom she felt comfortable. She was used to boys on campus staring at her because of her bright-red hair color, but to her they were boys that still hadn't exhibited the overt confidence of this man willing to spend money on a woman he'd just met.

Alan Kent felt as if he'd been gut-punched when he stared at a pair of brilliant topaz-blue eyes. He was so taken with the pale, lightly freckled face of the redheaded young woman that it wouldn't permit him to look away. There was something about her that called to mind Botticelli's *Birth of Venus*. He knew she was young, but not so young she might possibly be jailbait. The huskiness in her voice and the rounded firmness of her breasts under the pumpkin-orange twinset indicated she wasn't a girl but a woman. She had the face of an angel and the body of a seductress.

He lowered his eyes, reached into the breast pocket of his suit jacket, and took out a credit card. He held it in his hand rather than set it down on the counter, so his name wasn't visible to the woman standing less than a foot away. If she hadn't recognized his face, then he didn't want to give her the advantage of knowing his name before he was willing to disclose it.

Alan paid for the perfume, nodding to the salesclerk. He was familiar with the woman. On occasion he'd come to the store to makes purchases for different women, and she was always the epitome of discretion whenever he interacted with her.

They exited the store, Alan still holding on to the shopping bag. He stared at the young woman with whom he'd found himself enthralled the instant he felt the press of her body against his. Her warmth and clean, sensual scent had caused his flaccid penis to swell so quickly that he feared embarrassing himself, something he'd never experienced with any other women.

"Now that I've replaced your mother's gift, does her daughter have a name?"

Pale eyebrows lifted slightly. "And if I don't tell you my name, are you going to hold the perfume hostage until I give in?"

Well, I'll be damned, Alan thought, smiling. There was fire under her cool exterior. But then there was the stereotype about fiery redheads, and this was his first interaction with one.

Alan handed her the bag. She reached out, taking it from his hand, their fingers touching. And for the second time he felt a jolt eddy through his body, and in that instant he knew he couldn't allow her to walk away from him without knowing more about her.

"I'm sorry if you misconstrued my intent, Miss . . ."

"Berkley."

"Does Miss Berkley have a first name?"

"It's Leah."

Alan wasn't about to congratulate himself, because he wanted to know more than just her name. "Is it *Miss* Berkley?" She nodded. He extended his hand. "It's a pleasure to meet you, Miss Berkley. I'm Alan Kent." This time he did congratulate himself when her expression did not change; it was obvious the Kent name hadn't registered with her.

Her lips parted in a smile. "I know we started off on the wrong foot, but how can I thank you for your generosity?"

Alan glanced at his watch. "I'd like for you to have lunch with me."

Leah's smile faded. "I can't, because I promised my mother I would help her get the house ready for Christmas. Perhaps I can get a rain check."

"Of course," he said much too quickly. "When would you like to get together?"

"It can't be until next spring."

He successfully hid his disappointment. He didn't want to have to wait four or five months before seeing Leah again. "What's happening next spring?"

"I'm graduating from Vanderbilt University."

A slow smile lifted the corners of his mouth. Not only was Leah young and very pretty, but it was obvious she had the smarts to be accepted into the prestigious private university. "What's your major?"

"English literature. I plan to teach."

He smiled. "Nice." He reached into the pocket of his suit jacket and took out a monogrammed silver case and handed her a business card. "You can call me whenever it is convenient for you."

Leah took the card, and he could tell the Kent name suddenly registered. Alan was a partner at Kent, Kent, McDougal & Sweeny, Attorneys at Law. There were several Kents in Richmond, but it was Alan's family that had the clout and prestige. His father and uncles had continued the family tradition going back several generations of earning a judgeship.

Her lips parted in a nervous smile. "Thank you again for your generosity, and I will call to let you know when we can have lunch."

Alan angled his head. "Is that a promise?"

"Yes, it's a promise."

He held out his hand, and she stared at the well-groomed fingers for several seconds before she realized he wanted her to take it. His palm was soft as her own. At that moment she was aware of the differences between the man holding her hand and the men in her family, who were and had been farmers, sharecroppers, factory workers, and mechanics. Men who used their backs and hands to make a living, while Alan and his family sat behind desks or argued cases in a courtroom. Meanwhile, Leah had hoped to break the cycle once she married and, hopefully, had her own sons. And she was certain to let them know the sacrifice she'd made to become the first Berkley to attend and graduate college.

"Goodbye, Alan."

He gave her fingers a gentle squeeze. "Not goodbye, Leah. We will meet again soon."

Leah raced across the field where the families and friends of the graduates had gathered following the conclusion of the ceremony. Her parents had driven from Richmond to Nashville the day before to help her clean out her dorm room. They'd checked into a local motel for the night, and it had been the first time in months she, her mother, father, and brother shared a meal together.

Her steps slowed as a man approached her. Alan Kent looked quite elegant wearing a panama hat, a tan suit he'd paired with a taupe shirt with a white collar, dark-brown silk tie, and matching slip-ons. Her heart was beating a runaway rhythm in her chest under her gown.

"What are you doing here?"

His eyes narrowed. "How about, 'It's nice to see you, Alan?'"

For a long moment Leah stared back at him. There was a proprietary edge in his voice. "Hello, Alan."

He inclined his head. "Now, to answer your question as to why am I here." He extended the hand he'd held behind his back. "I came to watch you walk across the stage to receive your degree, and to give you this. Call me when it's convenient for you." Turning on his heel, he walked away.

Pinpoints of heat suffused her face, and it had nothing to do with the intense late-spring heat, when she peered into the decorative shopping bag to find a square box wrapped in silver foil and tied with black velvet ribbon. She knew instinctively that it was a piece of jewelry. "Alan, please wait!"

"Leah!"

She turned when she heard someone call her name and did not see Alan when he stopped and stared at her over his shoulder. Her arms went around the neck of the boy whom she'd dated off and on during their junior and senior years, and he picked her up and swung her around and around.

Leah met his brown eyes behind a pair of thick lenses. She and Philip Brinson had been inseparable once they'd become study buddies. He tutored her in math, and she helped with his English courses. Their relationship deepened over time, going from friends to lovers, with the realization they would not have a future together. She knew their sleeping together was a passing phase, and once they left college both would go their separate ways to live separate lives. She'd hoped to secure a teaching position in her hometown, while Philip would continue his education at Vanderbilt's School of Medicine.

Philip brushed a light kiss over her mouth. "Well, kid, this is it. Are you ready for the next chapter?"

Her smile was dazzling. "I'm more than ready. How about you?"

A slight frown furrowed her best friend's forehead. "I have to get ready if I'm going to continue the family tradition of becoming a doctor."

"That should be easy for you with a father and grandfather practicing medicine."

"We'll see." He nervously tapped his degree against his thigh. "I gotta go. I know my folks are looking for me."

"Same here," Leah said.

She watched the tall, lanky boy, with a profusion of thick, black waves falling to his shoulders, walk. He'd refused to cut his hair, to defy his very conservative parents. Philip wanted to be an engineer but yielded to pressure from his family to earn a medical degree and join the family practice. Luckily, she wasn't faced with that dilemma. As she was the first in her family to attend college, her parents were very supportive when she revealed she wanted to become a teacher.

She saw Alan standing where she'd left him. Looping her arm through his, she met his eyes. "I'm sorry about that. I needed to say goodbye to my friend. I also want to introduce you to my parents."

"You don't have to do that."

"But I want to."

"Don't forget you owe me a lunch date."

"I haven't forgotten."

She finally found her family among the throng greeting and congratulating graduates with bouquets of flowers and envelopes she knew were filled with checks or cash. Leah had never deluded herself into believing she could financially compete with her classmates despite attending on full academic scholarship. Her mother went to work at a dress factory not only to supplement her husband's salary but also to send her money for meals and incidentals.

Madeline waved to her as she clutched a bouquet of sunflowers in the opposite hand. Her mother had remembered her favorite flower. Leah had found a small patch of earth in the trailer park where she lived with her family before they'd moved to an apartment, and subsequently to a rental house, and planted sunflower seeds. They sprouted to become tall stalks with large flowers, and then without warning they died; she'd discovered a neighbor's cat was using her garden as a litter box.

"Oh, Mom, the flowers are beautiful." She pressed her cheek to her mother's. "I love you so much. Mom, Dad, I'd like you to meet Alan Kent. Mr. Kent, these are my parents, Larry and Madeline Berkley, and my brother, LJ."

Alan shook hands with Larry, Madeline, and LJ. "It's nice meeting everyone. You must be very proud of Leah."

Madeline's bright blue eyes shimmered with unshed tears. "We couldn't be prouder of Leah, Mr. Kent. Graduating with honors, no less."

Alan touched the brim of his hat. "I wanted to give your

daughter a little something for her special day. There's someone else I need to see. Perhaps we'll meet again soon."

"Now, where did you meet him?" Larry said when Alan
was out of earshot.

"I literally ran into him last year when I was home for
Christmas. I dropped the bag with Mama's perfume, and he
offered to pay for another one." She wasn't going to tell her
parents that Alan had paid twice what she'd spent on the
smaller bottle.

Larry narrowed his eyes. "He came all this way to give
you a gift?"

"Didn't you hear him say he was going to meet someone
else?"

"I just don't like the way he looked at you," Larry grumbled.

"Daddy, stop. There's nothing going on between us."

"Lawrence, don't!" Madeline warned. "Let's not ruin the
day because of your suspicions. In case you haven't noticed,
Leah is a grown woman, more than capable of choosing
whoever she wants as a friend."

Leah knew her mother was annoyed whenever she called
her husband by his given name. "I'm glad I made you proud,
Mama," she said softly, while hoping to defuse what was becoming an uncomfortable situation. It had been her mother's
wish since Leah had learned to read at three that her daughter would go to college—something that had been denied her
once she'd discovered herself pregnant six weeks prior to
graduating high school. Madeline married Larry Berkley,
moved with him to a trailer park, gave up her dream of going
into fashion design, and settled down to become a wife and
mother.

Leah turned to look up at her father. He was tall, with a
full head of red hair and soulful blue-green eyes; she adored
him and he in turn never hid his love for her.

"We did it, Daddy."

"*You* did it, princess. You've accomplished what no other Berkley has ever done, and that is get a college degree." He tapped his forehead with his forefinger. "Now you can use your head to make a good living instead of doing backbreaking work to put food on the table."

Leah knew her father was overly sensitive when it came to his family's attitude about not wanting to better themselves. Most were content with their blue-collar status, while living paycheck to paycheck. He was determined to reverse the trend. He'd preached to her that she should concentrate not on boys but books, because there would come a time in her life when she could have whatever boy she wanted.

"I couldn't have done it without you and Mom's support."

"There isn't anything I wouldn't do for my kids." Larry angled his head, smiling. "I see you got a gift, but there are more gifts for you once we get home."

"You didn't have to get me anything," Leah said in protest. "You've done enough." She was more than grateful that her parents had sacrificed what little they had to help her achieve her goal.

He kissed her forehead. "Enough jawing. It's time we head out before it gets too late."

Her sixteen-year-old brother stepped forward and hugged her. Larry Junior had grown several inches since she last saw him. If she was her father's daughter with her brilliant hair color, then LJ was the more masculine clone of his mother with his dark hair and blue eyes.

"Congratulations, sis. I can't wait to graduate high school and go to college."

"It's going to happen, LJ." She wanted to tell her brother that if he stopped "chasing skirts," as their father put it, and put that energy into his schoolwork, he would become an exceptional student. Not only did he like girls, but they also liked him. Madeline would complain about the amount of time he spent on the phone talking to them or when several would drop by the house unannounced to ask for him. Their father had sought to short-circuit his interaction with the opposite sex when he'd gotten permission from his boss to have LJ work with him over the summer recess.

Leah took off her cap and gown and left them on top of the boxes in the cargo area containing the items from her dorm room, and then slipped into the minivan and sat on the second row of seats behind her mother. She had mixed feelings about leaving Vanderbilt for the last time. She had taken AP courses in high school and enrolled in college as a sophomore. During the three years she'd spent at the venerable institution she'd never felt accepted, from the moment some of the girls discovered she'd spent the first nine years of her life living in a trailer park. It hadn't mattered that her parents had moved to an apartment, where she'd had to share a bedroom with her brother, and subsequently into a house where she finally had a bedroom to herself.

If it hadn't been for her dormmate, a beautiful black girl from Chicago who was also on academic scholarship, Leah's college experience would've ended in disaster as she'd contemplated dropping out and enrolling in a college close to home. Cynthia Edwards, the daughter of a dentist and social worker, told her they *didn't need to be accepted by the stuck-up bitches with the morals of alley cats who depended on their fathers' money to pay for their abortions*. It was a wakeup call for Leah not to try so hard to become a part of their social circle; her roommate provided her the emotional support she needed to mature and come into her own.

She and Cynthia bonded as sophomores, but things changed a year later when her roommate pledged a sorority and moved into the dorm with other students from Delta Sigma Theta sorority. Leah then had a revolving door of roommates, as they each decided to live off-campus or dropped out because of a myriad of reasons.

One semester she had the room to herself, and that was when Philip had begun spending more time with her; she hadn't deluded herself into believing she was in love with him because they were sleeping together. He'd become her first and only lover, and there wasn't a time when she did not enjoy their relationship.

Sighing, she slumped lower in the seat and closed her eyes. Her body wasn't as tired as her brain. She wanted to take at least a year off before pursuing a graduate degree, because she needed the time to step back from attending classes and completing assignments. Leah also planned to take at least a couple of weeks of doing nothing more than sleeping, catching up on reading for pleasure, and bonding with her family.

It was nightfall when Leah opened her eyes again, as her father maneuvered into the driveway to their home. She could not believe she'd slept during the six-hundred-mile drive from Nashville to Richmond. She and her mother went inside while her father and brother unloaded the half dozen boxes from the van, leaving them in the hallway outside her bedroom.

She smiled at Madeline. "I'm going to take a shower and then go straight to bed." It would be the first time in years that she didn't have to set the alarm on a clock to wake her up to make it to class on time.

Madeline kissed her cheek. "Don't you want something to eat?"

"No, I'm good."

"If that's the case, then don't bother to get up early. We all will probably be at work when you get up in the morning. The fridge is stocked if you decide to cook for yourself."

"I'll be fine, Mom. I just need to decompress and get used to sleeping in because I don't have to get up for an early class." She didn't tell her mother that she wanted to be alert, clear-headed, and confident to present well when interviewing for a teaching position.

Leah walked into her bedroom, closed the door, flopped down on the bench seat at the foot of the bed, and unwrapped Alan's gift. She let out a gasp when she saw a magnificent strand of pale-pink pearls with a sapphire-and-diamond clasp. Her hands were shaking when she picked up the gift card: *Congratulations on your graduation. A beautiful woman should always have pearls. ASK.*

She was aware of the pearls worn by many of the girls at Vanderbilt, which they'd inherited from their mothers and grandmothers, but they could not compare to the size and luster of these perfectly matched baubles. "What are you doing, Alan?" she whispered.

Leah wondered if he was trying to buy her affection. First it was the perfume for her mother, and now it was an extravagant graduation gift that was totally unexpected, and she had to remind herself that Alan Kent was not a college boy with whom she'd become familiar over the past three years, but a grown man whose family's name was cemented in Richmond's history spanning several centuries.

What she had to ask herself was, why her? What was there about her that had garnered his interest so that he would drive more than six hundred miles to witness her graduation? Why couldn't he have waited for her to return to Richmond and contact him for their luncheon date?

Leah knew if she had been one of those girls at Vanderbilt who wore cashmere twinsets with their mother's or grandmother's pearls she would've been flattered to have Alan express an interest in her. However, she wasn't looking for a husband, boyfriend, or even a lover at this time in her life. She wanted to teach and earn enough money to supplement her father's salary so her mother could quit her job at the dress factory. Leah put the pearls in a drawer under a stack of T-shirts. She planned to wait a few days before calling Alan to thank him for the gift and set up a date for lunch.

Her father's graduation present had been a used car. The ten-year-old Volvo sedan with more than one hundred thousand miles had a new engine, rebuilt transmission, four new tires, and new seats. The exterior was refurbished until it looked new. He said she would need her own car once she began teaching. Alan did not know she valued her parents' gifts more than his: they'd taken time from their busy lives to make something for her, while he'd walked into a jewelry store to pick out an expensive piece of jewelry. It wasn't that she did not appreciate his generosity, but the pearls were something she would only wear for a special occasion.

Chapter 2

L eah sat in the reception area of the well-appointed law firm, waiting for the receptionist to let her know when Alan would be available to see her. When she'd called him earlier, she was told he was on an overseas call, but she was to come to the office because he would block out several hours to meet with her.

She had taken particular care with her appearance, wearing one of the many dresses her mother had made for her during her spare time. Madeline's graduation gift was a closet filled with skirts, jackets, dresses, blouses, and slacks for when she embarked on her teaching career. Leah realized it had taken her mother innumerable hours to meticulously sew each garment, which were indistinguishable from those in department stores. Leah wondered if, under another set of circumstances, her mother would have been able to make a name for herself in fashion. Leah had washed and set her hair on large rollers and when dry had used a large-tooth comb to achieve a mass of waves falling around her face to her shoulders. Her makeup was perfect for daytime, with a hint of blush on her cheeks, muted shadow on her lids, and a tangerine-orange color for her lips.

"Miss Berkley, Mr. Kent will see you now."

Leah's head popped up, and she pushed off the armchair to follow a young woman down a hallway where the heels of her shoes sank into the plush carpeting.

Alan stood outside his office, watching Leah as she followed his secretary, successfully concealing a smug grin. He had not made a mistake coming to see her in Nashville. It had taken him weeks to decide whether to attend her graduation, and it was only then he'd contacted a friend with connections to Vanderbilt to get a ticket for the ceremony. He'd waited for Leah's name to be called and witnessed her walk before he got up and left. She had graduated magna cum laude. Beauty and brains. Those were the two qualities he admired most in a woman.

His gaze lingered on the length of her bare legs under a burnt-orange sleeveless sheath dress ending at her knees. She wore espadrilles with black ties that circled her slender ankles. He met her blue eyes, smiling, and extended his hand. "Please come in, Miss Berkley." He wasn't disappointed when she returned his smile with a polite one.

"Thank you for taking the time to see me, Mr. Kent."

Alan closed the door, cupped her elbow, and led her to a leather love seat. He stared at Leah. She'd styled her hair in a profusion of strawberry-blond waves framing her face. "I'll always take time for you, Leah."

She gripped the small leather clutch in both hands. "I'd like to thank you for your very generous gift. You really did not have to give me anything."

It was all he could do not to touch her. "I did because I wanted you to have something special with which to remember me."

Shifting, Leah turned to give him a direct look. "There's no way I'll be able to forget you whenever I wear the necklace. It is truly beautiful."

Alan smiled. It was his intent for her not to forget him. "I've made reservations for us to have lunch at a place where I usually take my clients. It's about thirty miles from here, so we'll have to leave now to make it there on time."

Leah rose, he also coming to his feet. He reached for his jacket, slipped his arms into the sleeves, and escorted her out of the office through a rear door leading to the parking lot. His secretary knew to take his calls. Opening the passenger-side door to the Mercedes sedan, Alan waited for Leah to sit before he rounded the car and slipped behind the wheel.

He maneuvered out of the lot, silently applauding himself for his patience in waiting for Leah to graduate. He didn't know what it was about the redhead that had him fantasizing about her when he least expected it. At thirty-five he'd dated a lot of women, and slept with some of them, but there was something about the woman sitting next to him that had him preoccupied with her. It was obvious she wasn't as sophisticated as the ones with whom he was familiar; however, that hadn't deterred him, because whatever she didn't know he planned to teach her.

"Now that you've graduated," he said, breaking the comfortable silence, "what do you plan to do?"

Leah met his eyes for a nanosecond. "I'm going to look for a teaching position before I go back to school for my master's degree."

"Have you selected a graduate school?"

"No."

"Why not?"

"I don't need to think about books and term papers for a while. And working will allow me time to save some money for tuition."

"Do you have any student loans?" Alan had asked yet another question.

"No. I went to Vanderbilt on a full academic scholarship."

"Good for you. That means you have a head start when so

many kids are burdened with student debt even before they begin working."

"I also need to work because I'd like my mother to quit her job at a dress factory."

"What does your father do?" Alan was asking a litany of questions to which he knew the answers, because he'd had the firm's investigator conduct a background check on the elder Berkleys. He did not want to get involved with a woman with parents who had run afoul of the law. Her family's working class aside, there was something about Leah that enthralled him as no other woman had. Perhaps it had to do with her not being impressed with his family's name and prominence not only in the state's capital but also through its history, to when Virginia and the rest of the thirteen colonies were still under British rule.

"He's the head mechanic at a used-car dealership. He's a genius when it comes to repairing cars."

"The only thing I know about a car is how to turn it on and off."

"What about pumping your own gas?" Leah asked.

"No."

"Are you afraid of getting your hands dirty?"

Alan clenched his teeth at the same time his fingers tightened on the steering wheel, and he struggled not to lose his temper. Did she really believe he was incapable of putting gas in his car? "It has nothing to do with getting my hands dirty. I don't pump gas because I can't abide the smell."

A flush suffused Leah's face as she averted her eyes. "I'm sorry I—"

"There's nothing to apologize for," he said, cutting her off. Alan did not want to start off on the wrong foot with Leah, because he didn't want this encounter to be their last one. This was their third meeting, and each time he noticed she had what he thought of as a sharp tongue. She wasn't reticent; she said whatever came to her mind. Women he became involved with were usually docile and accommodating, while

Leah Berkley was just the opposite. It would take her a while to come to the realization that he wasn't one to be submissive when it came to a woman. "I think it's time you stop referring to me as Mr. Kent."

"What do you want me to call you?"

"Alan."

Leah smiled. "Then Alan it is."

He also smiled. Other than her face and body, it was her voice that held his rapt attention. It was low, sultry, and very sexy for a woman. Decelerating, Alan left the main road and turned onto one with towering trees lining both sides like silent sentinels. It had been several weeks since he'd last visited the Bramble House. The inn catered to a select clientele with the social class and background and the ability to pay the exorbitant fees for various suites in which to conduct their liaisons. It was where well-to-do men entertained their mistresses, while the inn's staff was the epitome of discretion.

And in the ten years since he'd become a member of a select group of men held in high esteem by the residents of Richmond, Alan had been very discriminating when inviting a woman to accompany him to the Bramble House, because the women with whom he'd slept had as much or more to lose than he if word got out that they were engaged in an extramarital affair. His preference for sleeping with a married woman was because she could not afford to get pregnant and attempt to pass it off on her husband as his. And there was never a time when he did not use a condom, because he did not plan to father a child before marriage.

He was openly dating a young woman his mother had hinted he should marry, but Alan found her boring and undesirable. The last time they'd slept together he'd fantasized about making love with Leah, and he'd ejaculated so quickly that Justine had asked if something was wrong. He'd said no, but that was a lie.

Rumors were circulating that their engagement was imminent, and rather than embarrass Justine Hamilton or her family, he hadn't refuted it. She came from a good family, would become the perfect hostess, and once she pushed out a couple of Kents she would be content to become the dutiful wife.

He pulled into the parking area and shut off the engine. "We're here."

Leah stared out the windshield at a rustic two-story structure. A sign indicated it was founded in 1898. "How did you find this place?" she asked, undoing her seat belt.

Alan released his own seat belt. "A friend turned me on to it. I hope you're hungry, because the food is exceptional."

"I did have an early breakfast."

"Don't move," Alan said when she attempted to open her door. "I'll come around and help you out."

He opened her door and extended his hand as she placed her palm on his and he gently pulled her to stand. She looked up at the Tudor-design structure with stained glass windows. "How often do you come here?" she asked Alan, as he led her to double oaken doors with large brass doorknockers.

"It all depends," he said noncommittally.

"On what, Alan?"

"On the client. There are some I can interview in the office conference room, and then there are others that call for more privacy. I've discovered some people are willing to open up and become completely relaxed after a few drinks and a meal."

She waited for him to open the door and then stepped into an area with leather facing benches and gaslight-inspired wall sconces from a bygone era. A tall, slender man with shimmering white, expertly barbered hair came over to greet Alan. He was dressed entirely in black, which made him appear even thinner.

"Good afternoon, Mr. Kent." He nodded to Leah. "Miss."

Good afternoon, Lucien," Alan said in greeting. "Is it possible for us to be seated in the Yorktown Suite?"

Lucien smiled. "Of course, Mr. Kent." He motioned to a

white-jacketed waiter who practically ran over to him. "Please take Mr. Kent and his guest to the Yorktown Suite."

The young man, who did not look old enough to shave, bowed as if Lucien were royalty. "Yes, sir."

Leah stiffened slightly, and then relaxed when Alan rested his hand at the small of her back. She knew it would take her a while to become accustomed to him touching her. She wasn't going to delude herself into believing he wasn't interested in her the way a man was with a woman. His showing up unexpectedly at her graduation and gifting her with the pearls spoke volumes. However, at no time could she forget that he was a mature man with enough money to give a woman he'd met once and for less than an hour a gift with a price tag comparable to what her parents paid to rent their house for a month.

She followed the waiter up the staircase leading to the second story. All the suites were named for Revolutionary War battles. Leah smothered a gasp when the door opened and she walked into a space with furnishings that appeared to be antiques; if not, then exquisite reproductions. Her gaze lingered on a four-poster bed draped in a gossamer fabric before moving to a sitting area with plump armchairs and a dining area with table and chairs with place settings for two. Pinpoints of sunlight coming through the windows turned the glass into a kaleidoscope that resembled precious jewels. Alan led her over to the table, pulled out a chair, and seated her at the same time the waiter reached for two binders on the credenza.

He handed one binder to Alan, and then one to her. "Today's special is Dover sole meunière and broiled lobster with a buttery Pernod sauce."

Leah met Alan's eyes across the table. "Please give me a few minutes to look over the menu."

"Is there anything I can get you from the bar?" Alan asked her.

"I'll have a club soda with a twist of lemon."

His eyebrows lifted slightly. "Are you sure you don't want something a little stronger?"

She smiled. "Very sure."

"You, sir?"

"I'll have Jameson's and ginger with lime."

Leah waited for the waiter to leave the room before giving Alan her complete attention. "This place is really charming."

Alan angled his head, smiling. "I'm glad you like it. Whenever I come alone for lunch I will eat in the dining room, but sometimes it gets a little noisy because the televisions are tuned to sports channels."

"You prefer coming here rather than some of the more popular downtown restaurants."

"Yes. At least here I won't be interrupted while I'm trying to enjoy my meal."

"Please don't tell me I'm dining with a celebrity."

He lowered his eyes. "I'm hardly a celebrity."

"Your father was a judge, and you're a managing partner in one of Richmond's most prestigious law firms."

Alan went completely still. It was obvious she'd researched his family. "Is there something you want to know about me that you haven't uncovered on your own?" A rush of color suffused Leah's face with his query, and he did not know whether he'd embarrassed or angered her.

"No, Alan," she said softly. "I know all I need to know."

He wanted to tell Leah that there was so much about him she would never know. There was his public persona, and then there was the private one. What he did behind closed doors was a jealously guarded secret known only by a few close friends.

Alan felt as if Leah had withdrawn from him although they sat several feet across from each other at the small, round table, and that was something he couldn't permit to happen. Not when he'd planned to seduce her. "I noticed you didn't order anything alcoholic."

She blinked slowly. "That's because I can't drink."

"Does it make you sick?"

A hint of a smile parted her lips. "No. I'm not old enough to drink."

Alan recoiled as if someone had hit him in the nose. "How old are you?"

"Eighteen."

Slumping in his chair, Alan stared at Leah as if she'd grown an extra eye. He'd believed she was twenty-one or even twenty-two, but not eighteen. "At what age did you graduate high school?"

"Fifteen. I accelerated a grade twice, and I took a number of college courses in high school, so when I enrolled at Vanderbilt it was as a sophomore."

"You're a genius."

"No, Alan. I'm what folks would call an overachiever. By the way, how old are you?"

"Thirty-five." His age was one thing he never lied about.

Her mouth formed a perfect O. "You're almost twice my age."

"Does that bother you, Leah?" Alan questioned.

"No, because no one can control their age."

"What I mean is, does it bother you that a man almost twice your age would like to date you?"

Leah gave him a direct stare. "Yes. Only because you're practically engaged."

He leaned forward. "You heard about that?"

"Yes, Alan, I heard about that."

"It's not official," he countered.

"It doesn't matter. Everyone knows you're dating Justine Hamilton, and to me that translates into you're off the market."

"What if I break up with her?"

"Don't. Not on my account. Besides, I'm not interested in a relationship at this time."

"What about us being friends?" Alan realized he was close

to begging, but he would grovel if it meant seeing Leah again. Not only was Leah the youngest, but she was also the most difficult woman he'd attempted to get close to. When she smiled he discovered he couldn't bring his gaze away from her mouth. And it wasn't the first time that he had had to ask himself what was there about Leah Berkley that had him acting like a horny teenage boy with no control.

"I don't have a problem with us becoming friends."

He smiled. "Okay, then friendship it is." Alan felt a small measure of relief. At least she hadn't rejected him outright. Leah had referred to herself as an overachiever, and Alan knew she possessed exceptional intelligence. "Speaking of careers, you said you wanted to teach. Have you applied to any schools?"

"Not yet. I wanted to take a month off before I begin sending out my résumé."

"Public or private?"

"Public or private what, Alan?"

"Schools. If you want to teach at a private school, then I can help you out. I'm familiar with the headmistress and several members on the board of the Calhoun Preparatory Academy for Girls."

Leah did not realize she had been holding her breath until she felt slightly lightheaded. The Calhoun was one of the most prestigious schools for girls in the state, and she could not have imagined securing a position with the venerable academy.

"Do you think if I interview with them they will hire me?"

"I will make certain they hire you," Alan said.

"What do you want from me in return if they do decide to bring me on as faculty?" The question had rolled off her tongue before Leah could censor herself.

Resting his elbow on the table, Alan gave her an intense, penetrating stare. "Have lunch or dinner with me at least twice a month."

Her jaw dropped. Leah didn't know why, but she hadn't expected him to say that. "That's it?"

"Did you think I would ask you to sleep with me?"

She pulled her lower lip between her teeth. "It was a thought."

"A thought, or is that what you want, Leah?"

Her face flamed with heat she was helpless to control. She didn't know what it was, but a part of her did wonder how it would be to sleep with Alan. Philip had been her only lover, and the first time they'd shared a bed she'd cried herself to sleep because she had expected so much more. It was weeks before she would allow him to make love to her again, and after several months she was able to experience her first orgasm.

"It's not what I want," she lied smoothly, "because it would ruin our friendship, and I don't want to be responsible for you cheating on your fiancée."

"Unofficial fiancée, Leah."

"It doesn't matter whether she is or isn't, Alan. I don't intend to become a third party in someone's relationship."

"What if she's no longer in the equation?"

Leah's eyelids fluttered wildly as she stared across the small space at the man who continued to assault her emotions. It was as if he could reach inside her and read her mind, know what she was thinking. If she were truly honest with herself, Leah knew she wasn't completely immune to him. He was older, wealthy, prominent, attractive, and had enough influence and clout to help her secure a position with a private school at which every year one hundred percent of the graduates were accepted into prestigious colleges throughout the country. She knew it would be so easy to have a clandestine relationship with him and in turn reap benefits that would've been denied her if they'd never met, but not at the expense of her coming between him and another woman who'd planned to become Mrs. Alan Stephens Kent. She shook her head. "Don't, Alan. Please don't break up with her. Especially not because of me."

"It is because of you that I would be willing to stop seeing her."

"Why me?" Leah asked, her voice rising slightly. "This is the third time we've seen each other, and today is the first time we've spent more than a half hour together, and I can't believe you're actually considering tossing aside a woman whom you been dating long enough where people expect you to announce your official engagement, for an eighteen-year-old. It just doesn't add up, Alan."

His impassive expression did not change. "Why not you, Leah? Do you not believe yourself worthy to become involved with me?"

Leah counted slowly to ten to keep from spewing curses and completely ruining her chance of interviewing for a teaching position at the Calhoun Academy. If Alan was willing to use her, then she would use him to get what she wanted. She'd planned to send her résumé to several school districts, and she was confident that she would secure a position; however, she never would have considered the academy, because many of the instructors were former students, children of privileged parents, and that meant she never would have been considered for a job, despite her grades.

"I'm more than worthy, Alan, otherwise I wouldn't be sitting here with you. I may not have the pedigree of the women with whom you consort, but they are no better than me. I studied hard and worked my ass off to prove I was smarter than most of the uppity bitches at college that looked down on me because I spent the first nine years of my life living in a trailer park. I earned my grades, while they slept with their professors to pass a course. So, I resent you thinking I'm not worthy. In fact, I believe I'm better than you, because if I had a boyfriend or even a fiancé I would never consider ditching him for you." Alan was stunned and excited with Leah's outburst. Her face was flushed, her eyes were shooting blue shards, and he couldn't pull his gaze away from her heaving breasts under the polished cotton dress. And he knew he was wrong for implying she wasn't worthy, because she was. At eighteen she was everything Justine wasn't at twenty-six.

"I'm the one that isn't worthy of you." He knew he'd shocked her with the comeback when her jaw dropped. "You must think I'm cruel and unfeeling to stop seeing a woman I've been dating because I'm interested in one I'd like to get to know better."

"I didn't say you were cruel, Alan."

He placed a hand over his heart. "Thank you for absolving me of that notion."

Leah smiled. "Acting contrite doesn't become you."

"But I am contrite. I . . ." His words trailed off when the waiter returned with their beverages and set them down on the table.

"Sir, miss, are you ready to order?"

Alan opened the binder and pretended interest in the menu selections. He knew what he wanted because he tended to order the same dish for lunch. "I'll have the lamb chops, medium well, with mixed glazed vegetables, and a Caesar salad." He glanced at Leah as she bit her lip while studying the menu.

Her head popped up. "I'll have a Cobb salad with balsamic vinegar on the side."

Alan wanted to ask Leah if she was on a diet because she'd ordered a salad, but then decided not to say anything. He'd found it frustrating when he dined out with Justine that she took an interminable amount of time perusing menu selections, and then ordered a salad. The year before she'd announced that she was a vegetarian and planned to lose as much weight as she could before their wedding. Although he'd cautioned her not to talk to her family and friends about a possible date to announce their engagement, she'd ignored his warnings. It was as if she wanted to talk it into existence.

He reached for his highball glass and held it up. "Here's to friendship."

Leah picked up her glass, touched hers to his. "To friendship."

He took a sip, the whiskey and soda going down smoothly as warmth spread throughout his body; he stared at Leah over the rim and wondered if in her naïveté she was aware of the effect she had on him. Although she exhibited confidence and independence that belied her age, Alan still felt the need to take care of her. Enrolling in college at fifteen had forced her to grow up and mature faster than her peers who were still engaged in high school activities.

"Do you have a résumé?" he asked her.

"Yes. I have a number of copies and several official transcripts. I got the additional transcripts to save time having to send away for them."

Once again Alan was impressed with Leah's sense of preparedness. "I need you to give me your résumé and transcript, and I'll pass them along to the headmistress. She'll probably contact you for an interview, and then you'll have to wait for her to submit your documents to the board for approval. If there is a vacant position, you'll be appointed for the coming fall term."

Leah's eyes shimmered with excitement. "Please let her know I'm willing to accept a position as a permanent substitute. And because I don't believe in putting all of my eggs in one basket, I'm still going to send my résumé to other school districts."

Alan forced himself not to panic. He didn't want Leah to teach in another county where he wouldn't have close access to her, or where she would be given the opportunity to meet someone with whom she could have a relationship.

"I'd like you to wait at least two weeks before you send out your résumé. I'll call Mrs. Kelly when I get back to the office and ask her to set up a time for an interview. When we get back I'd like you to drop off your résumé and transcript

at the office in an envelope marked personal and confiden-
tial. My secretary knows not to open anything marked personal. I'm also going to give you the numbers to my home
and the private one at the office. If I don't pick up, then leave
a message on the answering machine."

"You don't know how much I appreciate you doing this
for me."

He successfully hid a smug grin when he took another sip
of his cocktail. "It's all about friends helping friends."

Leah stared at him from under lowered lids. "Maybe one
of these days I'll be able to return the favor."

And you will, he thought. Alan still did not give up on the
possibility of his sleeping with Leah. And his wanting to
make love to her bordered on a craving that was akin to
something he'd never experienced before. He'd always had a
strong libido, but it had gone into overdrive, and he was
forced to get out of bed and masturbate whenever her image
invaded his erotic dreams. Although satiated, he'd experienced shame because he hadn't had to pleasure himself since
coming into puberty at thirteen.

Their food arrived, and they spent the next hour discussing and debating local and national politics. Alan discovered Leah was a Democrat and was excited that she would be
voting for the first time in the coming November elections.
He admitted being a registered Republican, which put them
at odds when it came to support of their respective candi-
dates. However, they were respectful of each other's opinion,
and unknowingly she had gone up several more points on his
approval scale; Alan knew Leah would make the perfect
wife. Of course, he would wait until she was twenty, because
he didn't want her to be labeled a teenage bride.

Once lunch was over, Alan drove back to Richmond and
waited with Leah while she got into her car. She promised to
go home and return with the documents he wanted. She
shocked him when she moved closer and kissed his cheek,
thanking him for lunch and their time together.

Alan stood in the parking lot, watching the taillights of Leah's car as she drove away, then turned and entered the office through a rear door. He walked into his office, closed the door, and picked up three telephone message slips. One was from his mother, asking him to call her back, and the other two were from clients. He planned to call the clients, then his mother. The only time Adele Kent called him at the office was when she and her husband had had an argument. Now that his father was deceased Alan was relieved that he no longer had to get involved with his parents' squabbles, because one day they would be at each other's throats and the next acting like newlyweds.

He slipped out of his suit jacket, hung it in the closet, and sat down behind his desk. He thumbed through a leather-bound address book to K. First things first. He needed to call Constance Kelly. The phone rang twice before he heard her voice.

"Hello."

"Hello, Constance."

"Alan. How are you?"

"I'm well, thank you. I'm calling because I'd like to ask a favor of you."

"Anything for you. What do you want?"

"I'd like you to interview and hire a young woman as an English teacher. She just graduated from Vanderbilt with honors."

"She sounds like someone we need, because one of my English teachers is leaving. Her husband's company just assigned him an overseas position and she's decided to go with him."

Alan pumped his fist. Talk about perfect timing. "She's going to drop off her résumé and official transcript to me this afternoon, and I will try to get it to you either tonight or tomorrow morning."

"You can come tonight. I'll be here until eight because I'm meeting with the scholarship committee to choose the recipients for the next school year."

"Thank you, Constance."

"I should be the one thanking you, Alan. The scholarship committee was overwhelmed with your more than generous donation."

"Anything for a good cause. I'll see you later."

Smiling, he ended the call. He'd had to wait five months for Leah Berkley to graduate college, and he knew once he dropped her résumé and transcript off with Constance, and she interviewed Leah, Leah would become an immediate hire. Getting the board to approve her wouldn't be as easy because some of the members would question Leah's family's background, but in the end her name would be added to the incoming faculty of the Calhoun Preparatory Academy for Girls.

Chapter 3

Leah had just finished emptying the dishwasher when the doorbell rang. She'd spent the entire morning cleaning the house from top to bottom. She'd stripped beds, changed the linens, put up several loads of wash, cleaned the bathroom, dusted all flat surfaces, and vacuumed the floors. Everyone was up and out of the house before seven, which gave her at least five hours to get everything done by noon. Since returning home, she'd assumed the cooking duties, which freed up her mother to relax and enjoy her dinner.

It had been three weeks since she'd shared lunch with Alan at the Bramble House, and she'd returned to his office to drop off what he needed to give to the headmistress. Three days later she received a call from an administrative assistant at the Calhoun Academy to set up a time and date for an interview with Mrs. Kelly. The very prim and proper woman did express her concern about Leah's age because she was the same or close to the age of their senior students, but it wasn't a factor that would cause her to reject her application.

When she'd told her parents that she was applying for a

position at the private school, both said she shouldn't get her hopes up that she would be hired. Because Alan had reassured her she would get the position, Leah refused to let their doubts dampen her enthusiasm.

She peered out the window to find the letter carrier and opened the door. "Good morning."

The woman held an envelope. "I have a certified letter for Leah Berkley, and I need a signature."

"I'm Leah." She took the pen, signed the card, and returned the pen. "Thank you." Turning over the envelope, she saw the return address. It was from the Calhoun Academy.

Leah hadn't realized her hands were shaking as she closed and locked the door. Flopping down on the living room sofa, she opened the envelope and let out a high-pitched scream. She was going to be a teacher at the Calhoun Preparatory Academy for Girls. Her eyes grew wide when she read the starting salary. It was more than what Mrs. Kelly had quoted during the interview.

Tears of joy and relief filled her eyes and flowed down her face. Walking into the kitchen, she picked up the receiver off the wall phone and dialed Alan's private number. "They hired me," she whispered into the mouthpiece.

"Congratulations. Didn't I tell you they would?"

"Yes, you did," she agreed.

"We're going to have to celebrate."

"When do you want to get together?" Leah asked.

"Are you free this weekend?"

Leah wanted to ask him if he planned to see his girlfriend yet did not want to pry. This weekend would be perfect for her, because her father had planned to go to a car show several hundred miles from Richmond to look at cars he wanted to buy and restore, and this year her mother and brother had decided to go with him. They wanted to leave Saturday at dawn, stay overnight, and return Sunday evening.

"Yes."

"What are you doing Saturday?" he asked.

She folded her body down on a stool. "I'm free all day."

"Would you mind going back to the Bramble House? On Saturday nights guests are treated to live music between the hours of nine and midnight."

"I'd love to."

"I'll make a dinner reservation for seven. That will give us two hours to eat before we go downstairs to listen to music."

"What time are you picking me up?"

"Six."

Leah smiled. "I'll be ready when you get here."

"Congratulations again, darling."

"Thank you, Alan."

It wasn't until she hung up that she recalled his endearment. She wasn't his darling, sweetheart, or babe, and he needed to save the sweet talk for his girlfriend. Leah hadn't seen Alan since their lunch at the Bramble House. When she'd returned to his office to drop off the envelope with her résumé and transcript, the receptionist had asked whether she wanted to see Alan again, but she told the woman she was only there to leave some documents for him. She'd curbed the urge to call him after her interview with Mrs. Kelly, believing the woman would follow up with him as to her impression of his recommended applicant.

And Leah did not want to think of their Saturday meeting as a date. They were just friends getting together over a celebratory meal.

Leah came down off the porch when Alan stopped in front of her house. He was out of the car and had opened the passenger-side door by the time she reached the sidewalk. Everything about her screamed sophistication from her head to her feet. She'd styled her hair in a twist with jewel-tipped pins, and the long-sleeved, scoop-neck de rigueur little black dress ending at her knees hugged every dip and curve of her slender body. Sheer black stockings and four-inch, black satin-covered heels drew his attention to her long, shapely legs. He couldn't stop grinning when he saw the pearls around her neck.

He moved closer, one hand going to her waist. "You look incredible." She was wearing more makeup than when he last saw her, and if he hadn't known her age Alan would've taken her for a woman in her early twenties.

She demurely lowered her eyes. "Thank you."

He waited for her to sit and swing her legs around before closing the door. Leah was thanking him, when he should've been the one thanking her for allowing him to be seen with her. She looked and smelled wonderful. He rounded the sedan, fastened his seatbelt, and reversed direction. The Berkleys lived in a working-class neighborhood with one- and two-story homes each with a patch of grass doubling as a front lawn. Most were well kept, and the streets were free of litter and debris. Posted signs indicated there was a neighborhood watch.

Alan recalled Leah saying she needed to work because she wanted her mother to stop working at a dress factory, and once Constance told him she planned to hire Leah, he was able to convince her to increase the starting salary with a promise he would forward a check to cover the difference.

"How have you been?" he asked when he came to an intersection with a four-way stop sign.

"Good. I've been keeping busy taking care of the house and cooking to give my mother a break."

"Who taught you to cook?"

"It began with my maternal grandmother, who'd moved in with us after Grandpa died."

"How old were you when you had your first lesson?"

"I think I was about six. The first thing she taught me to make was biscuits, and then bread. She passed away a year before we moved out of the trailer park and into an apartment. By then I was tall enough to look over the stove, and I'd help Mom with Sunday dinner. It continued until I left for college."

He gave a sidelong glance. "Are you saying you're a passable cook?"

Leah landed a soft punch on his shoulder. "I'm more than passable. I happen to believe that I'm a very good cook."

"I won't be able to confirm that unless you decide to cook for me."

"No, Alan. That's not going to happen, because that's something you should do with your fiancée."

Alan swore under his breath. His uncle was putting pressure on him to give his colleague's daughter a ring because Justine had complained that most of her girlfriends were either engaged or married. He was able to belay her anxiety once he told her he wanted to wait for her late-October birthday to make the official announcement. It was enough to temporarily pacify her so that she'd stopped asking for a ring at least once a week. And if he had one wish it would be to marry Justine and have Leah as his mistress.

"You're right," he mumbled.

Not only couldn't Justine cook, but he knew he would have to hire a cook once they were married. As an only child she'd been pampered by her parents, something he'd decided not to continue. Whenever he refused to do what she wanted, she would resort to tears, which annoyed him, and that was one reason he'd asked himself why he continued to see her. However, he knew the answer. He was thirty-five, was the managing partner in a successful law practice; Justine's father was a judge, while his own plans included a judgeship like his father, uncles, paternal and maternal grandfathers, and his future father-in-law. He turned the radio to a station featuring movie soundtracks, and he knew the tense moment between them was over when Leah rested her left hand over his right on the steering wheel.

"I'm sorry that I snapped at you."

Alan reversed their hands, giving her fingers a gentle squeeze. "There's no need for you to apologize. It was insensitive of me to ask you to—"

"Don't say any more, Alan. I don't want to ruin the evening talking about other people. Tonight, it's going to be just us celebrating thanks to you what will become a new beginning for me."

Alan lifted her hand and pressed a kiss to her fingers when it was her lush mouth that he'd wanted to kiss. "I want this to be a night that both of us will remember for a long time."

"I know I will," Leah said, smiling.

He stared out the windshield, concentrating on the road in front of him rather than dwelling on the woman sitting only inches away. Everything about her was appealing, and as much as he tried, he wasn't able to penetrate the wall she'd erected to keep him at a distance.

Leah noticed when she'd come to the inn with Alan for lunch the parking lot was only half filled with vehicles, but not tonight. It was Saturday—date night—and red-jacketed valets were busy parking cars. Couples in business suits and chic evening dresses exited vehicles and were strolling toward the Bramble House's entrance. When she'd gone through her closet to decide what to wear, Leah hadn't been certain whether her dress would be appropriate for dinner because she felt it was better suited for a dressier affair. It had become her first and only big-ticket item during college after Philip invited her to accompany him to Denver for his parents' thirtieth wedding anniversary. The salesperson at the Nashville boutique had reassured her that when she put the dress on she would turn heads, and she had. The simplicity of the garment and the décolletage that revealed a hint of breasts each time she took a breath had garnered lustful stares from men and glares from women. She hadn't heard from her friend since graduation and she didn't expect to; however, she would always have wonderful memories of what she'd shared with him.

"Is it always this busy on weekend nights?" she asked Alan.

"The few times I've come it wasn't. But that was in the winter. I suppose it's the warm weather that brings folks out."

Not only was it a very warm summer night, but a light breeze had managed to offset the intense daytime heat and humidity that made it unbearable to remain outdoors for long periods of time. Alan tucked her hand into the bend of his elbow when the greeter held the door open for them. The lights were dimmer than they'd been when they'd come for lunch, and the interior was noticeably cooler.

The woman at the hostess station gave Alan a key card, and instead of taking the staircase to the second floor, they entered a small elevator in an alcove. Another couple was in the car, and Leah felt the muscles in Alan's arm tense under the sleeve of his suit jacket when the other man stared directly at Alan, leaving her to believe that they possibly knew or recognized each other. The woman gave her a saccharine smile before focusing her attention on the man holding her close against his side. Leah noticed that only the man wore a wedding band.

Suddenly it became clear to her. The Bramble House, located at least thirty miles away from Richmond, was an establishment where men were able to conduct their affairs with impunity. The hostess gave Alan a key card without checking the desktop's monitor. He'd told her it was where he'd entertained clients, and she wondered if that invitation also extended to women. However, it was of no import to her, because Leah had told herself it would be the last time she would accompany him to the inn although she'd promised to dine with him at least twice a month. While she was more than appreciative of his assistance in her securing a teaching position, they would celebrate her success and then, like her association with Philip Brinson, she would go on with her life while Alan would announce his engagement and marry his fiancée in a high-profile event befitting a Kent. She had no intention of becoming the other woman.

Alan slipped the key card in the slot on the door to the Yorktown Suite, waited for the green light, and then opened the door. He stood aside, waiting for her to enter, and Leah could not believe the sight unfolding before her eyes. A bouquet of roses in every conceivable hue, an ice bucket with a bottle of champagne, a platter of antipasto, flutes, small plates, and silverware covered the dining area table. The only illumination came from flickering candles in wrought-iron holders, and the sound of a popular love song filled the space from hidden speakers.

A small gasp escaped Leah when Alan scooped her up in his arms and deposited her on a love seat, his body following hers down. "I wanted to make the night special."

Leaning into him, she pressed her mouth to his, aware that she'd shocked him when he went still. "You have. Thank you, Alan," she whispered against his parted lips.

He smiled. "There's no need to thank me, Leah. There isn't anything I wouldn't do for you."

Maybe she was too caught up in the moment and failed to register the passion in his voice. Leah never would have thought of Alan as a romantic. She had never had anyone wine and dine her on this scale; she felt like the princess in a fairytale. Tonight, Alan had become her prince and she his princess.

"When did you plan all of this?"

"Right after you called to tell me you'd been hired. I knew then the occasion called for something very special."

Leah rested her hand on his smooth-shaven jaw. "It is."

"I know you said you don't drink, but will you have a small amount of champagne?"

She nodded. "Yes."

The first time she'd drunk champagne was at Philip's parents' anniversary party. It had only taken a couple of sips of the bubbly for her to decide if she was going to drink, then it would be champagne. It was slightly sweet, but not as sweet as pop, and before the celebration ended she'd finished the flute.

Alan stood, removed his jacket, and extended his hand. "Come with me to the table, and I'll serve you."

He seated her, lingering over her head before pressing a kiss to her hair. Leah smiled up at him over her shoulder before her gaze shifted to the table. There was a tin of caviar, ramekins with marinated olives, pâté, a bowl of parmesan cheese straws, herbed pita crisps, toast points, and a trio of avocado-lime, mango and chutney, and salsa dips. Tiny parmesan shortbreads were topped with parsley pesto and goat cheese and roasted cherry tomatoes and feta.

"This is really a lot of food."

Alan wrapped a towel around the bottle of champagne and expertly removed the cork with a muted pop. "I didn't know what you would or wouldn't eat, so I asked for a variety of hors d'oeuvres."

"Everything looks delicious, and I intend to sample everything on this table."

He filled two flutes, handing her one before hunkering down next to her. "May you remember this night for years to come."

Leah touched her glass to his, her eyes meeting his in the flickering glow of candlelight. In that instant she wished things could have been different; that Alan wasn't promised to another woman.

"I'll never forget you or this night."

Leah lost track of time as she ate, drank, and danced with Alan, unwittingly falling under the spell he'd carefully orchestrated so she wouldn't forget him or the night. After her third glass of champagne her limbs felt like al dente spaghetti. Her arms went around his neck as she pressed her breasts against his chest, languishing in the strength of his hard body.

She moaned, but the protest appeared ineffective to her own ears when he picked her up and carried across the room to the bed. Time stood still, her senses drowning in sensual heat.

Long, heated moments later, Alan rolled off her body and onto his back, stunned. It was the first time since becoming sexually active that he hadn't used protection, and he prayed she was on some form of birth control, because he couldn't afford to get her pregnant. Not when he was expected to propose to Justine.

Shifting slightly, he tried making out her face in the wall sconce outside the bathroom. "Are you on the pill?"

It was a full ten seconds before Leah said, "No. My period has always been irregular, so I can't tell if we picked the wrong time to make love." She sat up. "I never should've done this."

Alan pulled her down to lie beside him. "Don't, darling."

"Don't call me that, Alan, because I'm not your darling."

He wanted to tell her she could be his darling if only she was amenable to becoming his mistress, and she would want for nothing. He would set her up in her own condo and buy her whatever she wanted or needed. The first thing would be a new car.

"I'm sorry, Leah."

There was another pregnant pause. "Did you plan all of this?" Leah asked. "The flowers, champagne, romantic music, and a candlelight dinner with the hope that I would fall for your seduction?"

Alan knew it was hopeless to lie to her. "Yes."

"Thank you for being honest. And now that we're baring our souls, I did want you to make love to me, but not without protection."

He dropped a kiss on her mussed hair. "I'm sorry about that, but once I tasted you I couldn't stop and put on a condom."

"You have condoms here?"

"Yes. I have some in the bedside table drawer."

"Make certain you use them the next time."

His breath caught in his throat. "You want me to make love to you again?"

Leah looped one leg over his. "Yes, because this will be the last time we'll be together like this."

Alan's heart sank like a stone. He couldn't believe that a girl half his age had bewitched him as no other had and probably ever would again, and for that he hated her. And in that instant he decided not to make love to her again no matter how tempting the offer.

"What time do you have to be home?"

"I can leave anytime you want."

Twin emotions of desire and hate warred within him, and yet Alan wasn't ready to let her go. "Let's get some sleep, and once we wake up I'll take you home."

Leah managed to forget about Alan as she spent the summer experimenting with new recipes, going over the syllabus for the upcoming school year, and attending a series of new-teacher orientation sessions. With the approach of fall, she felt more fatigued than usual. She was in bed at nine, slept with the ceiling fan on all night, and woke drenched in sweat.

Leah shuffled into the kitchen early Saturday morning in October and flopped down on a chair at the table. Her mother, who had taken down a mixing bowl from an overhead cabinet, stared at her.

"Are you feeling okay?"

"Not really. I've been dragging my behind for a couple of weeks now."

Madeline came and placed a hand on her forehead. "You don't feel warm." Her blue eyes narrowed. "When was the last time you had your period?"

"I don't know. I've never been regular."

"That's not good, Leah. Maybe you need to see my gynecologist so she can put you on something to regulate it."

"Does she have Saturday hours?"

"Yes. I think she's there until two."

Pushing to her feet, Leah walked over to the refrigerator. Madeline had attached a magnetic board on one of the doors with a list of telephone numbers. Picking the receiver off the wall phone, she punched in the number. The receptionist told her there had been a cancellation and she could come in at one.

She hung up. "I have a one o'clock appointment."

"Do you want me to come with you?"

"No, thanks, Mom. I'll be all right."

Two hours later she lay across her bed sobbing as Madeline attempted to comfort her. Leah had almost fainted when the doctor told her she was almost three months pregnant. And she had been quick to admit she'd had unprotected sex with Alan Kent.

Madeline rubbed her back. "Sweetheart, you're going to have to calm down and call Alan Kent to let him know that you're carrying his baby."

Leah sat up quickly. "Why, Mom? It's not as if I'm in love with him. And besides, he has a fiancée."

"Which is why the sonofabitch should not have taken advantage of you!"

She knew her mother was angry, because it was on a rare occasion that Madeline Berkley cursed. Leah blotted her eyes with a crumpled tissue. "He didn't take advantage of me."

"The man's twice your age, Leah, and we both know you're not the first woman he's slept with. Why didn't he protect you?"

"I don't know. You'd have to ask him."

"You bet your ass that's exactly what I'm going to do."

Leah panicked. "Stay out of this, Mom!"

"Why should I? The man seduces my eighteen-year-old daughter and you say I shouldn't get involved?"

"What's all of the yelling about?"

Leah shifted on the bed to find her father standing in the doorway, massive arms crossed over his broad chest.

"Your daughter is going to make us grandparents," Madeline said as she slipped off the bed and walked over to her husband. "She slept with Alan Kent."

Larry lowered his arms in slow motion, both hands in fists. "I'm going to kill that bastard for taking advantage of my girl."

"Daddy, no!" She didn't know why her parents believed Alan had taken advantage of her. She'd been drinking, but she wasn't so under the influence that she couldn't have told him no. She'd wanted him to make love to her as much as he had.

Larry's eyes gave off blue and green sparks. "I knew that sneaky bastard was up to something when he came to your graduation. And I told your mother he wasn't going to stop until he got what he wanted. But I'm willing to bet he didn't intend to get you pregnant, not when the word is he's going to marry Judge Hamilton's daughter."

Leah had heard enough. "Mom, Daddy, please let me handle this my way."

"Are you going to tell him about the baby?" Madeline asked.

"Yes. He has a right to know he's going to be a father."

"When are you going to call him?" Larry questioned.

"I'm going to wait until Monday."

Alan could tell something was wrong when he saw Leah's face. She was leaning against the driver's-side door of her car when he pulled up. She'd left a message on his private line that she wanted to meet him in the parking lot adjacent to the high school. He hadn't seen her in months, and he'd finally gotten over her. Constance called to tell him Leah had become a pleasant addition to the faculty. She'd become a favorite with the students, and even teachers and support staff were impressed with her intelligence and easygoing personality.

"How have you been?" he asked, not knowing what else to say.

"Pregnant."

His knees buckled slightly. "Did you say you're pregnant?"

Her expression did not change. "Yes, Alan. I'm carrying your baby."

He closed his eyes and sucked in a breath. "What do you intend to do?"

She stood straight. "Have it, of course."

Alan felt like an animal caught in a trap. He'd planned to give Justine a ring at the end of the month; meanwhile a woman with whom he'd slept once was telling him that he was going to be a father. "What if I pay you to get rid of it?"

"Fuck you, Alan! You can't give me enough money to kill my baby."

He recoiled as if she'd struck him across the face. "Don't you realize you're fucking up my life, Leah!"

"No, Alan. You did that yourself when you fucked me without wrapping up your cock!"

"Nice talk for an English teacher."

"Go to hell, Alan!" Turning on her heel, she opened the car door, got in, and drove away, leaving him staring at her taillights.

"Fucking bitch!"

Just when he'd finally convinced himself that marrying Justine was the right thing to do after dating her for a couple of years, Leah telling him she was carrying his baby changed everything. First, he had to tell Justine about the baby. If she was still willing to marry him knowing he had an outside child, then they would go through with their plans. If not, then he and Leah would have to decide how they planned to raise the child.

Leah sat between her parents in the parlor in the Kent family mansion, known to locals as Kent House. The magnificent structure was listed on the National Register of Historic Places. It had been two weeks since she'd announced that she was pregnant, and all hell had broken loose. Justine Hamilton broke up with Alan; and his mother had insisted he and Leah marry as soon as possible.

Adele Kent glared at Leah. "I can't believe that with all of the contraceptives on today's market you would allow yourself to get knocked up."

"Watch your mouth, Mrs. Kent," Larry warned. "My daughter did not make this baby by herself. And your son is a grown-ass man that shouldn't be sleeping with a girl half his age and not protect her."

Judge Ronald Kent held up a hand. "There's no need for name-calling or insults. Leah is carrying my grandniece or nephew, and I believe we both want the same thing. I've spoken to Alan, and he's willing to marry Leah. That is, if she's willing to accept him as her husband."

Leah suddenly felt like a specimen on a slide under a microscope with everyone staring at her. The exception was Adele, who continued to glare. A follow-up visit with the gynecologist and a sonogram had revealed she was carrying twins, and she could not imagine raising two babies at the same time on her own.

She didn't love Alan, but with time perhaps she would. But his reaction to her revelation she was pregnant was imprinted on her brain like a permanent tattoo. Her father hadn't hesitated when her mother revealed to him she was pregnant, while Alan had suggested she have an abortion.

She would have her babies, love them unconditionally, and although their surname would be Kent, she planned to raise them as Berkleys.

Leah gave Alan a long, penetrating stare. "Yes. I will marry you."

Pushing to his feet, Alan crossed the room, took her hand, and eased her off the love seat. Reaching into his pocket, he took out a ring with a large cushion-cut emerald surrounded by brilliant blue-white diamonds and set in platinum, and he slipped it on her left hand. He angled his head and brushed a kiss over her parted lips and then turned on his heel and walked out of the parlor.

Leah stared at her hand, wondering if it was the ring Alan had planned to give to Justine Hamilton. She'd heard rumors that Justine was so devastated that she wasn't going to be Mrs. Alan Kent that she had left Richmond and moved to Florida to live with her older sister.

"It's not the one Alan was going to give Justine," Adele said, reading her mind. "That ring belonged to my mother. The one you're wearing was my grandmother's. She also gave birth to twins. Your mother and I will arrange your wedding to be held here at Kent House. Of course, it will be a private affair with only our immediate families in attendance. My brother-in-law will be the officiant, and once you're married you and Alan will move into a wing of this house, because his condo has two bedrooms and one doubles as a library. Once you're more advanced in your pregnancy I will hire a nurse to look after you, and a nanny after the babies are born." She gave Madeline a weak smile. "I don't want you to worry about Leah. I'm going to make certain she's well looked after."

Madeline glared at her. "I have no doubt you will, Adele, because I'll be coming by to check on her. Of course, I'll call first."

Leah closed her eyes, wishing she could also close her ears. Her future mother-in-law didn't care a whit about her but was obsessed with the babies in her womb, only because she was carrying the next generation of Kents.

Chapter 4

"What the hell is this!"

Leah opened her eyes to find Alan holding the rental agreement for the summer bungalow on Coates Island. She couldn't believe she'd slept so long that Alan had returned from his golf outing. Her eyes shifted to the clock resting on a shelf of the bookcase. It wasn't the next day. She had fallen asleep and dreamed about her life before she'd married the cruel, unfeeling man sitting in the chair glaring at her.

She'd tried to love him, but it was if he did everything in his power to make her hate him, while his mother's influence had been so strong that whatever affection he'd ever felt for her vanished. After a while she'd stopped trying and concentrated on herself. She adored her sons, enjoyed her position as headmistress for the Calhoun Preparatory Academy for Girls, and was looking forward to vacationing in North Carolina during the upcoming summer recess.

"What are you doing here?"

"Have you forgotten that I live here, Leah?"

"That's not what I mean, and you know it," she snapped. "I thought you were going to spend the weekend in Florida."

"It was canceled because of rain."

"You knew it was raining in Florida before you left."

"It was predicted to stop, so we figured we would get in a few rounds."

Leah wanted to laugh in his face. Alan had used the ploy that he was golfing with his buddies whenever he spent time with other women. Even at sixty-seven he hadn't stopped whoring. And he didn't think she knew it, but she'd discovered he now had to take a pill to achieve and sustain an erection.

The tall, slender, charming man she'd met what now seemed eons ago hadn't aged well. He was balding, his face was bloated, he'd gained a lot of weight; the broken capillaries in his nose indicated he drank too much, and as much as he attempted to conceal it, his hands shook uncontrollably.

"That's too bad," she drawled facetiously.

Alan shifted his bulk on the delicate chair. "Why can't you have more comfortable chairs?"

Leah wanted to tell him the chair wouldn't be so uncomfortable if he lost at least fifty pounds. "I happen to like that chair." He crumpled the paper in his hand, and Leah sprang up to take it from him, but he held it out of her reach. "Give me that."

"Not until you tell me what this is all about."

Her temper flared as she stood. "You're a lawyer, Alan. I'm sure if you read it you understood the legalese."

"I understood every word, but what I want to know is why are you renting property in North Carolina."

A sardonic smile parted Leah's lips. She never told Alan that while he'd toured countries in Europe and Africa with their sons the prior summer she had spent the most glorious time on Coates Island, North Carolina.

"Because I plan to spend the summer there."

Alan balled up the paper. "No you're not."

"Yes I am," she said softly.

He stood up. "I forbid you to go!"

Leah took a step, bringing her close to him. "In case you've forgotten, let me remind you that you're not in your courtroom where you tell folks what they can and cannot do. I am going, and there's nothing you can do about it."

"You think I won't stop you."

"You can't stop me, Alan."

Leah did not have time to react before she felt excruciating pain on the left side of her face when Alan slapped her. He hit her again, and this time his fist connected with her jaw. They'd argued in the past, but he had never attempted to hit her. She tasted blood where he'd split her lip. Temporarily stunned because no man had ever struck her, not even her father, she swung but missed him as he sidestepped her.

Leah knew she was physically no match for a man who outweighed her by at least a hundred pounds. "I'm leaving you."

"No you're not!"

"Watch me, Alan Kent!" She walked out of the suite, heading for the staircase to get ice from the kitchen to put on what she was certain was her rapidly swelling lip. Not only was she leaving him, but she also planned to file for divorce. If he hit her once and she did nothing about it, Leah knew he would do it again, and she did not want to become a statistic as a battered wife.

She'd just reached the top of the staircase when he grabbed the back of her shirt. Blows rained down on her as she put up her hands to protect her face, and then his fingers snaked around her throat, cutting off her breath. Her eyes bulged and she felt a roaring in her ears, and she knew if she didn't get away from him he would strangle her to death. Leah went into fighting mode, kneeing Alan in the groin. He bellowed in pain, and then she felt herself falling when he shoved her down the staircase, the carpeting burning her exposed skin. Her face bounced off the parquet flooring, and her whole world went black.

"Mrs. Kent, please try to open your eyes."

Leah's eyelids fluttered wildly as she struggled to open her eyes. She knew she was in a hospital when she heard beeping from the machines monitoring her vitals. "How . . . how . . ." The constriction in her throat made it hard for her to get the words out. She did manage to open her eyes to find a white-coated doctor leaning over her.

"Mrs. Kent, I'm Dr. Brady. You're at St. Luke's Memorial Hospital. Your husband reported that you'd fallen down a flight of stairs in your home. He's been here every day to check on you."

"How long have I been here?" she whispered.

"Eight days. You had some swelling on the brain, so we put you in a medically induced coma to wait for the swelling to go down."

She raised her left hand to touch her forehead. "Will I be all right? My brain?"

"Tests indicate you won't have any lingering effects. You may experience headaches, but I recommend you follow up with a neurologist if they prove debilitating."

Leah sighed. "Okay."

"You were banged up pretty badly when the EMTs brought you in. The bruises will fade after a while, and once you're discharged we'll send you home with pain meds. I recommend that you take it easy for the next two to three weeks."

"Did my husband tell you how I'd fallen?"

Dr. Brady flipped through several pages in her chart. "He said he came home and found you unconscious at the foot of the staircase."

"He's a liar."

The young doctor's large brown eyes grew wide behind the lenses of his glasses. "Are you sure, Mrs. Kent?"

"I'm very sure. Dr. Brady, do you know what my husband is?"

"No, I don't, Mrs. Kent."

"He sits on the bench of Virginia's Court of Appeals. Judge Alan Kent beat me and pushed me down the stairs." The young doctor sat on the chair beside her bed. "I want you to take down everything that I'm going to tell you. I know you're mandated to report incidents of assault to law enforcement, but not this time. What I want is documentation of my injuries to use as leverage in case my husband decides to contest our divorce."

Her voice was low and steady as she told him everything the man to whom she'd been married for nearly thirty years had done to her and the doctor wrote it in her chart. Movement caught her eye, and she smiled when she saw her sons filling the doorway. It was apparent Alan had called them.

She nodded to the doctor. "That's all of it."

Closing the file, he stood up. "I'll be back later to check on you. A nurse should be in shortly to change the IV and check your catheter."

She held out her free arm to hug Aron and then Caleb. Although they were identical twins and most people couldn't tell them apart, it had never been difficult for Leah. Not only were their personalities different, but it was their body language. Aron, older by three minutes, was laid-back and fun-loving, while Caleb was serious, more intense.

They were tall, several inches above six feet, and athletically built. Both were extremely health conscious. They'd limited their intake of sugar and fat and worked out at a Manhattan health club. They'd inherited Alan's hazel eyes, had dark hair with glints of red whenever they spent too much time in the sun, and her features. People usually took a double take when seeing them together. Leah had stopped asking them whether they were involved with a woman, respecting their right to conduct their private lives however they wanted.

Caleb pulled over a chair and sat, while Aron took the one Dr. Brady had vacated. She noticed there were dark circles under their eyes. "When did you two get in?"

Caleb rested his hand over hers. "We came the day after Dad called to say you had an accident. We've come every day, but you were in what the doctor said was a drug-induced coma and he said he would contact us once they brought you out."

"How do you feel, Mom?" Aron asked.

A dreamy smile flitted over her features. "I'm not feeling anything because there are probably pain meds in that IV. How do I look?"

"I know you don't want to hear it, but you look like you've gone several rounds with an MMA fighter," Caleb said, frowning.

Leah closed her eyes, recalling the beating she'd endured at the hands of her husband. "I did. And his name is Alan Stephens Kent."

"What the fuck!"

"No!"

Aron and Caleb had spoken in unison.

Caleb ran his fingers through his hair as he shook his head. "Are you saying that Dad did this to you?" Leah nodded. "I'm going to kill the sonofabitch!"

"No you're not," she countered. "I don't want either of you to say or do anything to him, because I'm divorcing your father. As soon as I'm able to leave this hospital bed I'm driving down to North Carolina to stay with a friend until I'm ready to file for a divorce."

Aron slumped back in his chair. "You know Dad is going to contest it, because he doesn't like losing."

"I know that. The doctor wrote down my account of the

so-called accident and if needed I'll produce it in court. And then we'll see how long he'll be on the bench when he's been accused of spousal abuse."

Caleb covered his face with both hands. "I just can't believe he would hit you," he said through his fingers.

"Your father and I haven't been getting along for years. The day you guys left for college was when I moved out of our bedroom. Alan and I haven't slept together for more than ten years."

Her sons exchanged a look. "I knew something wasn't right when we came here for Christmas," Aron said. "When I asked Dad why you two weren't sleeping together he mumbled something about his snoring worsening since he's gained a lot of weight."

"He lied about snoring."

Caleb slowly shook his head. "Why didn't you tell us things weren't right between the two of you, Mom?"

"I didn't say anything because I did not want to involve my children in something that could possibly upset them."

"Upset us!" Aron spat out. "We're grown men, Mom, not little kids who want to see their parents stay together even if they're at each other's throats at every turn. If I'd known he was capable of doing this to you I would've put the bastard in the ground and taken my chances with the law."

Leah didn't want to believe her cool-headed, softhearted son was talking about killing his father. "That's why I didn't say anything to you. We've had our verbal battles over the years, but this is the first time that he hit me."

"And it will be the last," Caleb stated firmly. "I won't say anything to him about what you've just told us, but we'll stay long enough for you to be discharged and leave for North Carolina. And if Dad tries to stop you, then I hope you have enough money on hand to bail me out of jail after I beat the living shit out of him."

Leah's eyes filled with tears. All of her life she'd protected her sons, and now the tables were reversed as they promised to protect her. "Why don't you see if you can find Dr. Brady and ask him if and when he can okay my discharge."

Aron stood up. "I'll do it."

"How long can you be away from your job?" she asked Caleb after Aron left the room. He'd recently secured a position clerking for a criminal court judge.

"I told the judge that I had a family emergency, and he said to take as much time as I need."

"What about Aron?"

"He's applied to the Kings County DA's office for a position as an assistant district attorney, and he's currently waiting to hear back from them."

Both her sons had passed the New York bar exam the previous year and were ambivalent whether they wanted to return to Richmond to join the practice their great-grandfather had established. Fortunately for them, because of their trust funds, they could afford to pay the exorbitant New York City rents while seeking employment.

"You still don't want to move back here and take over the family firm?"

Caleb stared out the window, sighing. "I'm really up in the air about leaving New York."

"Is it because you're involved with someone?"

He met her eyes. "How did you know?"

Leah smiled. "You weren't that subtle when you were here for Christmas. Whenever you left the room to take a phone call and came back, there was this sparkle in your eyes that said whoever you were talking to made you very happy."

"I can't put anything past you, can I?"

"I'm certain there are a few things, but remember I am your mother and I did raise you."

"I really like this girl, but there may be a slight problem."

"She's married?"

"No."

"What is it, Caleb?"

"She's mixed-race. African and Korean American."

Leah blinked slowly. "You think her race is a problem?"

"Not for me," he retorted.

"And you think I would be opposed you falling in love and marrying a mixed-race woman?"

"I don't know, Mom."

"Dammit, Caleb! It's apparent you know nothing about me. Have I ever told you or your brother who you should date?"

Caleb managed to look contrite. "Well, no."

"Then why would you anticipate my not accepting someone you love?"

"I don't know, Mom. Can you forgive me if I've prejudged you?"

"I'll think about it."

"You're kidding."

"No, I'm not," she snapped. Leah did not want to believe her sons would think she was a racist. It was their father's family and not hers that had bought and sold human beings on which they'd built their wealth.

"I'm sorry, Mama."

Her annoyance vanished quickly. It had been years since either of her sons had called her that. "When am I going to meet your girlfriend?"

A smile spread over Caleb's refined features. "Probably not for a while. This is her last year in medical school."

Leah's smile matched his. "So, she's going to be a doctor."

"Yup. She wants to be a pediatrician."

"Good for her. And I'm happy for you, Caleb. You tell your girlfriend that your mother would like to meet her whenever she has a break and that she'll always be welcome in my home."

"I'll definitely let her know." He sobered. "Are you still going to live at Kent House during the divorce?"

"I doubt it, Caleb. It holds too many unpleasant memories for me. I'll probably buy a small house with no more than three bedrooms and a couple of bathrooms in case my sons and their friends decide to visit. And I want enough property so I can put in an herb and flower garden."

She didn't want to tell her son that living under the same roof as her mother-in-law had been akin to torture. Adele Kent had sought to monitor every phase of her life from child rearing to how to run a household or host a dinner party. Once the woman was moved to a skilled nursing facility, she felt as if she could exhale for the first time in years.

Aron returned to the room. "Dr. Brady said that he's going to examine you later and if everything checks out then he'll sign discharge papers for you to leave in two days. You don't have to worry about anything because Cal and I will be here to take you home. Once you're feeling better, we can help you pack what you need for your trip. I'm going to keep the rental car and drive down with you before flying back to New York."

"You don't have to do that, Aron," Leah protested. "I'll be all right driving down by myself."

"What about pain meds, Mom?" Caleb questioned. "Won't you still be on them?"

"I won't take any before I leave. Coates Island is only about three hundred fifty miles from here, and I usually make the drive in around six hours."

The brothers looked at each other, and then Aron met her eyes. "Okay. But you have to promise to call either me or Cal when you get there."

She smiled. "I promise." Leah's smile faded when she saw Alan walk into the room. "Get him out of here."

Caleb and Aron turned at the same time and approached their father. She didn't know what Caleb said to him, but he turned and left. "We're going home with Dad," Aron said over his shoulder. "We'll be back later tonight."

Please don't hurt him, the voice in her head pleaded. She didn't want her sons to do anything to Alan that might result in them getting arrested. They'd always been as protective of her as she had been of them. However, she'd allowed them

the freedom and independence to strive that Adele had denied Alan. It wasn't until she'd married him and moved into
Kent House that she saw another side of her husband's personality, and it frightened her. He was as spiteful and vindictive as his mother; the older woman turned a blind eye to her
son's tomcatting as she had with her own husband. But Leah
didn't care who he slept with as long as he didn't touch her.

Then, like quicksilver, he would come to her pleading for
forgiveness with a promise he would be faithful. There were
two years during which he did change, coming home every
night, and she got to experience a modicum of happiness and
joy as a wife and mother. He was a wonderful, selfless lover
who taught her what to do with her body to bring them both
ultimate pleasure. However, it was short-lived; Adele sabo-
taged their newly discovered passion when she told her son
that she had to fire the landscaper because she'd overheard
Leah flirting with the man.

Alan flew into a jealous rage, accusing her of wanting to
know what it would be like to sleep with a man closer to her
own age. Not once during their marriage had she ever brought
up the seventeen-year difference in their ages, and she told
him she wasn't responsible for his insecurities. That had been
the wrong thing to say, and he left the house and didn't come
back for a week. Meanwhile Adele had accused her of driving her son away and said that Justine would have made a
much better wife for him because not only was she better
born but also better bred.

Her sons had just celebrated their eleventh birthday when
she first thought about divorcing Alan. She'd threatened to
leave and demand full custody of the children if his mother
continued to interfere in their lives. Alan knew she was serious, and he agreed because he was being considered for a
judgeship and did not want his personal laundry aired in
public.

She closed her eyes and smiled. In a matter of days, she

would be free to live her life by her own leave. What Leah did not understand was why she'd stayed in a toxic marriage for as long as she had, and she knew if Alan hadn't assaulted her she probably would've stayed even longer.

She had a few things to do before leaving for Coates Island that included taking an extended leave of absence from Calhoun Academy. Leah would spend the spring and summer on the island, and when she returned to Richmond it would be to purchase a house and file for divorce, and not necessarily in that order.

The scent of saltwater came through the open windows of Leah's Audi as she drove over the bridge linking Coates Island to the mainland. The sun was so bright that she had to pull down the visor because the lenses of her sunglasses weren't filtering out the rays. The bruises on her body hadn't faded completely and she ached all over, but she'd refused to take a pain pill because she feared it would impair her driving.

She'd rented the bungalow for the summer once she discovered Alan and her sons would be out of the country for a couple of months. It had been an impulsive decision, and she had no idea how it would change her life. Leah had bonded with the co-owner of the Seaside Café and a young woman who had taken an extended leave from a childcare center. She, Kayana Johnson, and Cherie Thompson all shared something in common: books. They'd formed a book club and met every Sunday afternoon to eat, drink, and discuss a predetermined title. The two women were as close as she could get to having sisters. They didn't agree on everything, which made their meetings stimulating and interesting. She'd emailed Kayana once since leaving and that was to let her know she'd contacted the agent to begin the process of renting the same bungalow where she'd stayed the prior summer.

Because it was the off-season Leah knew the Café offered a buffet brunch from ten to two o'clock Monday through Saturday. She'd left Richmond at dawn in anticipation of reaching the island before the restaurant closed. She stopped for an hour in Charlotte to eat and stretch her legs before heading east toward the Atlantic Ocean. Leah glanced at the clock on the dashboard. She had another twenty-five minutes before the Café closed for the day.

She parked her car in the restaurant's lot and made her way around to the entrance. During the summer season, as a vacationer, she wouldn't have been able to drive along the local roads because of congestion. Either she would walk, bike, or take jitneys to get around the island.

When she walked in she noticed there were three elderly couples in the main dining room. There were only four hundred permanent residents living on Coates Island, but the numbers swelled to more than a thousand between the Memorial Day and Labor Day weekends. Most of the vacationers renting bungalows and checking into boardinghouses and bed-and-breakfasts were returnees or, as they referred to themselves, repeaters.

Kayana had just walked out of the kitchen when Leah waved to her. She had to admit her friend looked incredible. Her flawless brown complexion radiated good health and her once chin-length chemically straightened hair now brushed her shoulders.

"Hey, stranger."

The cook stared at her. "Leah?"

"In the flesh."

Seconds later, they were hugging and jumping up and down like a couple of schoolgirls. Kayana eased back, holding her at arm's length. "What brings you down here off-season?" Leah removed her oversize sunglasses, and Kayana gasped. "What the hell happened to your face?"

The contusions she'd suffered when Alan punched her had been black and blue but were now a yellowish-green, and she knew it would probably take another week before all of the bruises faded completely. The first time she looked into a mirror and seen her face she nearly fainted. And once she observed her naked body in a full-length mirror she'd covered her mouth to muffle a scream. There were bruises and abrasions from her face down to her feet. Caleb was right. She looked as if an MMA fighter had punched, kicked, and pummeled her into submission. Leah had left the bathroom to get her phone and take photos of her nude body from every angle, which would serve as visual documentation to Dr. Brady's medical report.

"My husband beat me," she said as she concealed her eyes with the glasses.

"Holy shit! I hope you had the bastard arrested."

"I left him but didn't report it to the police. I'll tell you everything later. I'm here because I had to get away from Richmond to heal and get my head together before I go back and begin divorce proceedings."

"How long do you plan to stay?"

"I'm going to rent a room at the boardinghouse until I can move into a bungalow for the summer season."

"You don't have to do that, Leah. You can stay in the upstairs apartment."

She knew Kayana had a two-bedroom apartment above the restaurant with one bedroom she'd converted into a reading room. "I don't want to intrude on you."

"You can't intrude because I don't live here anymore."

"Where are you staying?"

Kayana held out her left hand. It was Leah's turn for her jaw to drop when she saw the narrow gold band on her third finger. "You're married?"

"Yes. Graeme Ogden and I were married last Christmas. We're living in his house here on the island, so the upstairs apartment is yours for as long as you like."

Leah recalled the tall, middle-aged man with large gray eyes who'd taught math and economics and had come into the restaurant practically every day. He was always staring at Kayana, but Leah never suspected they were seeing each other.

"Congratulations, Mrs. Ogden."

Kayana lowered her eyes. "Everyone still calls me Kay Johnson, so it's going to be a while before I get used to being called Mrs. Ogden. By the way, have you eaten?"

"I stopped in Charlotte and had breakfast."

"Do you have any luggage?"

"Yes. I've loaded up the trunk of my car with clothes I'll need for the next six months." It was the end of January, and she planned to stay on Coates Island until the third week in August.

"Give me your keys and I'll have Derrick bring your bags up. Meanwhile, do you want to eat down here or upstairs?"

"I think I'll hang out down here. I just need to use the restroom to wash my hands."

"I'm going to lock the front door before anyone else decides to drop by. As soon as these folks leave I'll sit and eat with you." Kayana walked to the entrance door, locked it, and turned over the sign indicating the restaurant was closed.

"You're going to have to tell me why you decided to change your mind about playing in your own sandbox," Leah said. Kayana had stated emphatically that she would never get involved with any customer who frequented the Café.

Kayana rolled her eyes upward. "I can't believe you remember me saying that."

"I remember a lot of things we said to one another last summer. Have you heard from Cherie?" Leah and Cherie had had a few verbal confrontations until they were able to work through a few misconceptions.

"Yes. We exchanged Christmas cards, and she enclosed a note saying she has been working overtime to accrue enough hours to extend her three-week vacation to five."

"I hope . . ." Whatever Leah was going to say died on her

lips as she stared at Derrick Johnson as he entered the dining room. He wore a white chef's jacket, black-and-white-striped pants, running shoes, and had covered his head with a painter's cap.

If Graeme Ogden had stared longingly at Kayana, then Leah was guilty of staring lustfully at Kayana's older brother whenever they occupied the same space. Tall, dark, with an incredibly toned body, she thought him to be the most beautiful man she'd ever seen. Kayana and Cherie had teased her that as a married woman she shouldn't be gawking at men.

"You're salivating, Leah," Kayana whispered in her ear.

Waves of heat eddied up her chest to her face, and Leah was relieved she was wearing the dark glasses because she didn't want Derrick to see the fading bruises on her cheek and around her eyes.

"He's gorgeous," she mumbled, not moving her lips. There was something about Kayana's brother that made her feel things she did not want to feel because she knew nothing would come of it. Legally she was still married, and although she knew he was widowed with a teenage daughter. Kayana had admitted Derrick refused to get involved with a woman until his daughter was older, and she didn't know if he would even be remotely interested in her.

Kayana approached Derrick and looped her arm through his. "Derrick, do you remember my friend from last summer?"

Derrick smiled, and a matched set of dimples creased his lean jaw. "Leah Kent."

Her pulse quickened. It was obvious he hadn't forgotten her. "I'm surprised you remembered my name."

"It was hard to forget my sister's book club friends. I must admit I was really impressed that y'all were willing to spend your vacation reading and discussing books."

Leah met Derrick's large, dark eyes, smiling. "And we plan to start up again this coming summer."

"We've already selected our titles," Kayana told her brother. "I hope it's all right with you if Leah lives upstairs until she can move into a vacation rental."

"I don't mind, but she will have to earn her keep."

"I'm willing to pay—"

"Don't even go there, Leah," Derrick said, interrupting her. "I was just teasing about you earning your keep. There's no way I'm going to charge my sister's friend to live here."

"Right now, I'm recuperating from an accident, but as soon as I'm one hundred percent I'm willing to help out here in any capacity you want or need."

Derrick gave her a direct stare. "How are you in the kitchen?"

"Are you asking if I can cook?"

"Yes and no. But more importantly, are you familiar with what goes on in a kitchen?"

"A restaurant kitchen?" she asked.

"Any kitchen."

Leah was stunned by his questioning. What was there about her that had people questioning whether she could perform tasks women all around the world did every day? When they'd met for their first book club meeting Cherie had made disparaging remarks about the size of the diamonds in her wedding band and earrings, and that's when she'd had to inform her that marrying a wealthy man wasn't something she should aspire to.

"I am more than familiar with a kitchen, and I *do* know how to cook."

"Stop messing with her, Derrick," Kayana interjected.

"I can bus tables and double as a dishwasher. I—"

"Enough, Leah," Derrick said, laughing. "I'll figure out a way you can make yourself useful if that's what you want."

"It is what I want."

"I guess that settles it," Kayana stated. "You'll live upstairs and help out any way you can. Derrick, can you please do me a favor?"

"What is it?"

"Bring Leah's bags in from her car."

Derrick disentangled his arm from his sister's and held out his hand. "Leah, I'm going to need your key."

Reaching into her crossbody, she gave him the fob. "It's the Audi with Virginia plates." She headed for the restroom, while Kayana reminded the remaining diners that the restaurant was closing in ten minutes.

Leah closed and locked the door behind her and then removed her glasses. Each time she saw her reflection in a mirror she felt like crying. She didn't know why, but she blamed herself for staying in a marriage that she knew would never get better. There was the excuse that she didn't want to leave Alan because her sons saw him as their role model, once they'd decided they also wanted to become lawyers. Alan had worshipped and spoiled his sons from birth, and it did not take Leah long to realize he was a much better father than a husband.

She'd come to Coates Island rather than go to Kentucky to be with her family to heal her body and her soul because it was the only place where she'd felt free for the first time in her adult life. It was where she could bare her soul to Kayana, because she was a former psychiatric social worker, so she knew she could trust her not to be judgmental. Her sons knew their father had assaulted her, but she refused to divulge more intimate details of their marriage. That information she would reveal to the attorney she would hire to handle her divorce. Leah still had to decide who she wanted to represent her before Judge Alan Kent was served with divorce papers. And while Alan could countersue and charge her with abandonment because she'd moved out of their home, she would level the playing field with medical documentation of his vicious assault.

Leah washed her hands, dried them on a paper towel, put back on the glasses, and left the restroom; she saw Derrick with the straps of a quilted weekender and large tote, with her laptop, looped over each shoulder while he wheeled the Pullman and a carry-on. It would've taken her two or three trips to bring the bags up the staircase to the second story while he would accomplish it in one.

"Thank you, Derrick."

He winked at her. "You're welcome, Leah. And I'm sorry about teasing you."

"Not to worry. I'm not that thin-skinned." Leah wanted to tell him she had to have a thick skin if only to endure the hellish years she'd lived at Kent House.

"That's good to know. I'll leave your bags in the bedroom."

Leah sucked in a breath as pain shot through her body. She had delayed taking a pill because they caused drowsiness, and now her ribs were hurting.

"Are you all right?"

She turned slowly to find Kayana staring at her. "Not really. I need to take my pain medication."

"Come and sit down. I'll bring you a glass of water."

She sat down, her eyes filling with tears. Reaching into her crossbody bag, she took out a tissue and blotted them before they fell, and then opened the pill bottle and shook one out. Each time she inhaled she felt as if she was being stabbed with a sharp object. Dr. Brady had prescribed the medication for her to take every four hours as needed, but she usually waited twice that long because she feared becoming dependent on the opioid.

Kayana handed her a glass of water, and she swallowed the pill. It would take a few minutes before it took effect. "Thank you."

"Don't move, Leah. I know you like my brother's lasagna, and there happens to be some left."

"This is definitely my lucky day." The first time Leah ate Derrick's lasagna she'd overindulged; she'd looked forward to Sundays to eat, drink potent concoctions, and discuss books while bonding with her new friends. She did not want to believe she'd had to wait until she was nearly fifty to meet women that not only shared her interests but also treated her as their equal. The throbbing in her side eased, and she knew the medication was working its magic. After eating, she planned to take a nap before unpacking and settling into her temporary home.

Chapter 5

"Leah. Leah!"

She opened her eyes when she heard someone calling her name and stared at Kayana sitting across the table from her. "I must have dozed off."

Kayana removed the white bandana from her hair. "You need to go upstairs and lie down before you fall on over."

"It's the pain pill."

"Are you in a lot of pain?"

"It comes and goes," Leah admitted.

"I still can't believe your husband hit you."

Leah took a sip of water, staring at her friend over the rim. "Believe it, because the bruises on my body look like inkblots."

"What the hell happened?"

"I told him I was coming down here for the summer."

"Say what?"

"Although Alan and I were unofficially estranged, we still took vacations together. The exception was last summer. We'd check into some exclusive resort with adjoining rooms, and I would spend a couple of weeks doing whatever I wanted while Alan usually went golfing or fishing. We rarely ate together, and once we returned to the States I'd go to my wing of the house and he would retreat to his."

"So, he took exception when you said you weren't going away with him and he decided to use your face as a punching bag."

Leah nodded. "It's when I kicked him in the balls that he pushed me down the staircase." She saw the look of horror on Kayana's face when she told her that she'd spent more than a week in the hospital and when she awoke from a drug-induced coma she'd revealed the details of her so-called accident to her doctor. "I decided not to report the incident to the police because Alan is a judge, and with his connections I didn't want them to conveniently lose the evidence. I'm going to use the medical report as clout if Alan decides to fight the divorce."

"What did your sons say?"

"They were ready to hurt him, but I pleaded with them not to get involved. I don't know what they said to him, but when they brought me home from the hospital Alan was nowhere in sight. I think they warned him to stay away until I left."

"Good for them," Kayana countered, smiling. "They remind me of Derrick. He takes protecting his sisters to another level. He went to see my brother-in-law after he left my sister, and he said he was ready to kick my ex's ass once he found out James had cheated on me."

"He sounds like my father."

"Does your father know what he did to you?"

Leah shook her head. "No, and I would never tell him, because Daddy would kill him. My father didn't like Alan when he showed up unexpectedly at my graduation to give me pearls as a gift. Even then Daddy thought he was too old for me."

"And he still is," Kayana stated firmly. "The man is seventeen years older than you, and that's the perfect recipe for jealousy and control. You're not even fifty, and meanwhile you tell me he's fat and—"

"Losing his hair and he has to take a pill to get an erection," Leah said, cutting her off. "He's not aging well and drinks too much."

"He's probably using alcohol as a form of medication."

"What he needs to drink is holy water to wash away his sins," Leah spat out.

"He'll get his in the long run, Leah. When karma comes to visit him, standing on his chest and breathing her hot breath in his face and recounting all the shit he has done to folks, he better pray that he'll have time to repent before she snatches his ass."

Leah couldn't help laughing. "I hope to be rid of him before that happens."

"Do you plan to live in Richmond once you're divorced?"

"Yes. I've taken a medical leave for the remainder of the school year. If I'm going to stay on as headmistress, then I'll need to live in Richmond."

"Enough chitchat, Leah. I'm going to leave a set of keys to the apartment and the code to the security system on the table in the living room. And if you get hungry after everyone's gone, you're welcome to raid the fridge. Right now, Derrick and I alternate working two weeks on and off. This is the first of Derrick's two weeks, so you'll be stuck with him until I come in just before closing to clean up so he can prep dishes for the next day. I would also like to pick you up Sunday and bring you home so you can meet Graeme."

"Okay."

"Leave your plate and go upstairs before Derrick has to carry you."

Leah pushed back her chair, reached for her crossbody, and slowly rose to her feet. She felt a little unsteady. "Give me a sec to get my bearings."

"Are you sure you can make it up the staircase on your own?" Kayana asked.

"I'm good."

And she was if she didn't try to move too fast. Leah managed to walk into and through the kitchen to the door leading to the staircase. She held tightly onto the handrail as she slowly made it up to the second floor without falling.

Heat wrapped around her like a warm blanket when she opened the door and walked in. The first time she'd come to the apartment she'd been thoroughly charmed with the space with the living room with a working fireplace, bedroom, reading studio, and minuscule bathroom with a vanity, commode, and shower stall. She opened the narrow closet next to the bathroom to find a stackable washer and dryer. She entered the bedroom and saw her luggage set against a wall.

Leah wanted to take a shower, but doubted whether she would remain upright because the full effects of the pain pill had kicked in. She removed the sunglasses, her running shoes, jeans, and pullover sweater. Clad only in her underwear, she pulled back the comforter and lightweight blanket and got into bed. The mattress was firm, just as she liked it, and within minutes of her head touching the pillow she'd fallen asleep.

Derrick unlocked the rear door, disarmed the security system, and then closed and locked the door behind him. He went through the ritual of turning on lights and exchanging his street clothes for a chef's shirt, pants, a pair of running shoes he only wore at the restaurant, and a bibbed apron. He tucked a towel under the ties of the apron, and then put on a painter's cap.

When he pulled into the parking lot, he saw Leah's Audi. He'd wanted to ask his sister why her friend had come to Coates Island during the off-season but then changed his mind. Kayana always resented his attempt to get into what she called her business. When he'd mentioned Graeme Ogden was interested in her, she had nearly bitten his head off. Derrick knew the man liked his sister because of the way he would stare at her. But he had to admire Graeme, because he'd gone after what he wanted, and now they were brothers-in-law.

Maybe Leah was surprised he remembered her, but there weren't that many women who'd come into the Café wearing an eternity wedding band with diamonds large enough to choke the proverbial horse. It was the same with the diamonds in her ears. He'd noticed the day before that her fingers were bare and small gold hoops had replaced the studs.

He had no qualms about her living in the apartment until she could find a vacation rental. He'd used the upstairs for storage until Kayana returned from Atlanta following her divorce and converted it into an apartment.

Derrick opened the walk-in commercial refrigerator-freezer and removed trays with marinated chicken and baby back ribs to bring them to room temperature before putting them in the smoker. He enjoyed cooking once the vacationers departed because the Café only offered one meal a day. He came in at six and left the restaurant after it closed at two, leaving him many more hours in the day to work out in the gym he'd set up in his home, watch the baseball and basketball games, and view films from his extensive movie collection.

His cell phone chimed a familiar ringtone. It was his daughter Deandra FaceTiming him. Wearing a headscarf and pajamas, she was still in bed, he noticed. Derrick knew he would never forget his late wife because his daughter was her mirror image.

"What's up, honey bun?"

"Daddy, I need you to send me some money."

"I just deposited money in your account a couple of days ago." His daughter, who had spent last summer with her aunt and grandmother, had decided to live in Florida for her senior year to establish residency before applying to several local colleges.

"I know, but Mikala's mother is taking her on a five-day cruise to the Bahamas for the Easter break, and she wants to know if I can go with them. I would have asked Grandma to give me the money, but I hear her tell people that come around trying to sell her something that she doesn't have any money because she's on a fixed income."

Derrick's impassive expression did not change, because he didn't want his daughter to see his reaction to his mother's constant rejoinder about a fixed income. Anna Johnson had worked long hours cooking and serving regular customers at the Seaside Café for years until she retired, and she'd preached to anyone who would stand still long enough to listen that she did not intend to give away her hard-earned money to folks looking to hustle her.

Mikala lived across the street from his sister Jocelyn's house, and she and Deandra had become thick as thieves. He'd met the girl when he'd driven down to Gainesville several months ago and discovered that she was a positive influence on his daughter, unlike some of her friends on Coates Island's mainland.

"I have to talk to Mikala's mother before I agree to anything."

"Okay, Daddy, but I really want to go, because I've never been on a cruise."

"I know, sweetie. Tell her mother to call me later tonight."

"All right. I have to go now because I have to get ready for school."

"Love you, baby."

"I love you, too, Daddy."

Derrick set the phone on a shelf over a stack of towels before turning on a radio and tuning it to a station featuring cool jazz. He studied the day's menu on a chalkboard. Under meat he'd listed barbecue chicken, ribs, crab cakes, and sausage and peppers. Veggies were string beans with white potatoes, baked beans, mini corn-on-the cob, glazed carrots, and wilted spinach. Cognizant there were approximately four hundred permanents residents and with a small number of people from the mainland coming to the island to eat, he'd begun preparing only enough to fill half rather than full trays. And once the specials of the day sold out, he did not replenish them. Those frequenting the Café knew at this time of the year it was first come, first served.

Derrick opened the door leading to the rear of the building with an electric smoker where he cooked brisket, pork shoulder, ribs, pork belly, and chicken. He had also installed a wood-burning oven where aged steaks were grilled to order. The large smoker, with four racks, was spacious enough to smoke up to a hundred pounds of meat at a time. He had on hand a supply of hickory and mesquite, apple, and pecan wood chips, which added a unique, milder smoked flavor. He loaded the wood tray with apple and pecan wood chips, filled the water pan with water and apple cider vinegar, and then preheated the smoker to 225 degrees. When the thermostat registered the programmed temperature, he placed the chicken on the top rack and slabs of ribs on the third.

Leah woke up disoriented; she hadn't drawn the shades before going to sleep and got out of bed to check the time on her cell phone, realizing she'd been asleep for more than ten hours. It'd been too early to get up and go downstairs, so she decided to unpack her bags. She filled dresser drawers with underwear, socks, tees, pajamas, and nightgowns, and hung slacks, jackets, skirts, and blouses in the narrow closet. Her shoes were lined neatly on the closet floor.

Leah set the books she'd put into the carry-on on a dropleaf table. The smaller bedroom in the apartment had been set up as a reading studio, with a convertible love seat, comfortable armchairs with footstools, and built-in bookcases on two of the four walls were packed tightly with Kayana's treasured books; framed prints of James Baldwin, William Shakespeare, Toni Morrison, John Steinbeck, and Zora Neale Hurston covered the remaining two. The shelves weren't as tightly packed as when she'd joined Kayana and Cherie in the room to discuss Octavia Butler's *Kindred*; she assumed Kayana had taken some of the books to her new home. Leah knew it would become the place where she would spend most of her time reading, relaxing, and healing.

Millions of stars in the nighttime sky had disappeared with the dawning of a new day by the time she made the bed and headed toward the bathroom to shower and shampoo her hair. Normally she would have used a blow dryer, but today she decided to let her hair dry naturally. However, she had taken an inordinate amount of time in the bathroom when she peered into the mirror over the vanity to apply two layers of foundation to her face to conceal the bruises. She'd stared at her reflection for more than two minutes, then applied a makeup remover, following with a moisturizer specially blended for her skin type. Anyone looking at her would be left to draw their own conclusions as to how she'd been injured.

Leah left the apartment, closed the door, and flipped the wall switch. A sconce provided enough light for her to navigate the stairs. Since falling, she'd become slightly paranoid when walking down a staircase. It was as if she was reliving a feeling of helplessness as she tried holding onto something—anything to stop the excruciating pain when her body bounced off the carpeted stairs. It had stopped when her head bounced off the wood floor and her entire world had gone black. She held tightly to the railing until reaching the bottom.

She noticed the security keypad had been disengaged, and then saw a sliver of light coming from under the door leading into the restaurant's kitchen. Leah opened it, smiling when she saw Derrick at one of the industrial sinks rinsing something in a large colander. It was apparent he hadn't heard her come in over the sound of the music coming from an audio component.

Derrick turned around when he realized he wasn't alone in the kitchen. Leah must have come in so quietly that he hadn't detected her presence. With wide eyes, he stared at her face. She wasn't wearing sunglasses, and he forced himself not to gawk at the discoloration around her eyes, so his gaze lingered on a pale-blue, long-sleeved polo she'd paired with slim-fitting jeans and black ballet flats; a narrow navy-blue headband held damp, dark red hair falling off her face to inches above her shoulders. She appeared fragile, almost waiflike. When he'd first met her last summer, although slender, she weighed noticeably more than she did now.

"Good morning, Leah."

She smiled. "Good morning, Derrick."

"Do you usually get up this early?"

"Not normally. I took a pill for pain, went to sleep, and lost track of time. When I finally woke up it was four o'clock. There was no way I was going back to sleep, so I decided to get up."

An expression of concern flittered across his features. "Are you in a lot of pain?"

Derrick recalled asking his late wife the same question whenever she tried to put on a brave face after she'd been diagnosed with stage-four pancreatic and bile duct cancer. He'd questioned Andrea so often that she'd refused to reply to what was so obvious. She had been in excruciating pain, and he'd hired a private duty nurse to make certain she was comfortable until she passed away at home in her sleep with her loved ones looking on.

Leah crossed her arms under her breasts. "Not as much as before. The doctor said I could take a pill every four hours for pain, but I try to go twice that long before I'm forced to take one."

"There's no need to be a martyr, Leah."

"I'm hardly a martyr," she countered. "If I keep myself hopped up on pain meds, then I won't be able to ascertain when I'm getting better."

Derrick knew she was right. He'd known a teammate when he played college football who had short-circuited his chance to be drafted into the NFL because he'd become addicted to his pain medication. "I was just going to make some barbecue baked beans, but I can put it off until later if you want breakfast."

Leah sat on a stool at the prep table. "I can wait for breakfast if I could have a cup of coffee." She pointed to the single-serve coffeemaker. "Do you mind if I make it? I do happen know my way around a kitchen."

He lowered his eyes when he recalled asking Leah if she was familiar with a kitchen, because there was something in her bearing that indicated she'd grown up with household help that included housekeepers and cooks.

"Point taken."

She slipped off the stool. "Where do you keep your coffee?"

Derrick wiped his hands on the towel tucked under the apron ties. "Come with me and I'll show you the pantry." He inhaled the subtle scent of Leah's perfume when she stood next to him. The fragrance was as light, delicate, and feminine as its wearer. He flicked on the light in an expansive space with walls lined with built-in shelves filled with canned goods and glass, plastic, and tins labeled with their contents. He opened a large jar filled with coffee pods, took out two, and handed them to Leah.

"We grind coffee beans for the urns because it makes for a fresher, richer taste."

"Do you offer coffee during brunch?"

"Only on request. But during the summer we go through hundreds of pounds of beans for our buffet breakfast."

"What beverages are available during off-season?"

"Sweet and hot tea, water, and occasionally someone will ask for pop. Some folks will even request wine or a cocktail, but those aren't included in the fixed price."

"You said you're making barbecue baked beans. Don't they take hours to cook?"

He gave her a sidelong glance. It was apparent she wasn't bothered with him seeing her injured face now that she was no longer wearing the oversize sunglasses.

"I soaked the beans overnight to soften them up. I'll put them in a covered pot, bring them to a boil, and reduce the heat and let them simmer until they are almost tender. After draining the water, I'll add my ingredients and put the beans in an aluminum pan in the smoker."

"Can I watch you make them?" Leah asked.

"Sure. Maybe if you're good I'll make you my sous chef."

"Good enough to become your sous chef and baker?"

Derrick gave her a direct stare. He ordered all of their baked goods, meat, and fresh fish from vendors on the mainland. "What do you bake?"

"Anything using flour and yeast. My grandmother taught me to make biscuits and an assortment of homemade breads. To this day I rarely eat store-bought bread. I don't bake too often because baked goods are my Achilles heel. Once I start eating it's hard for me to stop."

"I love biscuits, but I never learned to make them," Derrick admitted.

"I can make a small batch if you're willing to share them with me."

"How small, Leah?"

"Four."

"Make it six and you're on."

"Buttermilk?"

"Of course."

"With or without white gravy?" she asked.

"Damn, woman," Derrick drawled. "Are you trying to sabotage me?"

Her pale eyebrows lifted slightly. "What are you talking about?"

"I work out every day for at least an hour, but with you in the kitchen I'll have to increase my routine by at least another half an hour."

"Where do you work out?"

"I've set up a gym in my home because the nearest health club is almost twenty miles away and I don't want to have to drive that far after standing on my feet cooking for hours. I just want to go home, work out, shower, and then relax."

"You're like my sons. They claim they work out every day at a health club that's open twenty-four-seven."

"They must live in a big city?"

"They do. Both have apartments in Manhattan."

Derrick recalled the time when he lived in the city that never slept, but that was a lifetime ago: when he was married and before he'd become a father. "Do they like living in the city?"

"They love it. Both are young, unmarried, aren't burdened with college loan debt, so they're having the time of their lives."

Leah mentioning her sons suddenly piqued his interest. Judging from the jewelry she'd worn last year and the starting sticker price on her top-of-the-line luxury Audi sedan, and her renting vacation property on the island with the average fee beginning at more than a thousand a week, it was a blatant indication that Leah Kent lived well.

"What do they do?"

"Both are lawyers. My sons are identical twins."

"Nice. You got two for the price of one."

"It was more like one and done."

Derrick registered the finality in Leah's statement. "What do you want for breakfast?" he asked, deftly changing the topic of conversation.

"Scrambled eggs with bacon or sausage."

"No grits?"

Leah closed her eyes and sighed. Her expression and moan was so erotic Derrick couldn't stop staring at her. The swelling and bruises did little to diminish her delicate beauty. And there was something about the redhead he found captivating and knew it had a lot to do with confidence and her easygoing personality. Kayana had mentioned she'd taken an instant liking to Leah once they started up their book club, while admitting it was more difficult to bond with Cherie Thompson, probably because of their age difference. She had referred to Leah as "good people," which meant the schoolteacher had earned Kayana's seal of approval.

Leah opened her eyes. "If I have grits *and* biscuits I'll be the one fighting you for your workout equipment."

Derrick angled his head. "Forgive me if I've crossed the line, but you don't look as if you need to lose any weight." The slim-fit jeans fit her waif-thin body like second skin.

She smiled. "There's nothing to forgive. I used to have a weight problem. I'd gained more than seventy pounds when pregnant and instead of losing the weight after I delivered my sons, I gained even more, tipping the scale at more than two hundred pounds. It took hypnosis, a nutritionist, and a personal chef for me to learn how to eat healthy. I don't count calories or weigh my food, but I've identified the triggers that make me overeat."

"Bread products?"

Leah nodded. "They're like crack. I just can't have one slice or piece. Whenever you put out the mini corn muffins for breakfast, my brain sends me a 'do not touch' signal and I pass them by."

"You shouldn't deny yourself bread, because after all it is considered the staff of life. However, you're welcome to come by and use my gym anytime you want."

She smiled. "I may take you up on your offer one of these days, but that can't happen until I'm pain-free."

"What happened to you?"

"I fell headfirst down a flight of stairs."

"Ouch!"

"Word," Leah whispered.

"I'm going to get you what you need to make your biscuits, then I have to put the beans on the stove to simmer. It's going to take about an hour before I have to put them into the smoker."

"Are you serious about staying on the island until the end of the summer season?"

Leah's head popped up, and she gave Derrick a direct stare. Cooking with him had become a completely new experience for her. The stone-ground grits were delicious, scrambled eggs fluffy, and strips of applewood smoked slab bacon were grilled to perfection. The buttermilk biscuits were light and buttery, and there was enough heat from crumbled spicy sausage in the white gravy to tantalize her palate. She couldn't tell Kayana's brother that although she'd been married for nearly three decades, not once had she ever cooked for her husband.

"I know for certain that I'll be here until the week before the Labor Day weekend." She had to return to the school in time for new teacher orientation. "Why did you ask?"

"These biscuits are the best I've ever eaten, and I want to know if you'd be willing to become the Café's baker?"

She was momentarily speechless, unable to accept or reject his suggestion. Granted, she'd told Derrick she was willing to work to offset living rent-free in the upstairs apartment, but she was only teasing when she'd suggested becoming the restaurant's baker. Leah's eyes searched his for a hint of teasing. "You're kidding, aren't you?"

A hint of a smile tilted the corners of his mouth, and her gaze was drawn to his dimples. Why, she mused, did he have to be so damn perfect. Perhaps if he'd had a bump on the bridge of his nose where it had been broken at some time, or a small scar marring his smooth mahogany complexion, she believed she wouldn't have been so mesmerized by his face.

Then there was his body: tall, broad shouldered, and muscular. He had an athlete's physique, which he no doubt kept well toned with daily workouts.

Why, she asked herself, was she drooling over a widower with a teenage daughter like a lovesick adolescent? However, she didn't need to lie on a therapist's couch to be told that she hadn't had a normal adolescence. At fifteen she should've been a high school freshman hanging out with her girl-friends, flirting with boys, going to basketball and football games, and getting dressed up for fall and spring dances, and not on a college campus interacting with students old enough to vote and drink alcohol.

She'd graduated at eighteen, become involved with a man old enough to be her father who had gotten her pregnant the first time they slept together and had given birth to twins a month after she'd celebrated her nineteenth birthday.

Resting both elbows on the cloth-covered table, Derrick slowly shook his head. "No, I'm not. Every year I contract with a bakery in Shelby for their baked goods, but I'm willing to pay you to make an assortment of breads."

"You don't have to pay me," she protested.

"Yes, I do, Leah."

"Have you forgotten that I'm living rent-free on your property, and that you'll be supplying the ingredients for whatever I make. So, if you mention paying me again I'll pack up my stuff and move the hell out of here."

He sat straight. "Whoa! There's no need to go for my throat. I mentioned payment because I don't want to take advantage of you."

"That's not going to happen, Derrick."

"What?"

"I won't permit you to take advantage of me."

She'd spent too many years biting her tongue and agreeing to do things that went against everything she believed. Her parents had raised her to respect her elders, and that had kept her from confronting and cursing out her mother-in-law, and she held her venom in check until Alan did something that annoyed her, then she let loose with invectives whenever they were out of earshot of everyone.

"What would you want me to bake?" she asked. Her tone had changed, becoming softer and more conciliatory.

"I'll leave that up to you."

Memories of her baking with her mother and grandmother came rushing back as a sense of strength and renewal swept over Leah. "What if I bake a few samples, and you and Kayana can let me know which ones you like. I prefer to make a mini muffin rather than standard size to eliminate waste. Folks can take a couple of bites of a larger muffin and not finish it. But two bites of a mini and it's gone. It will be the same with loaf bread."

"How many muffins can you get out of a mini muffin pan?" Derrick questioned.

"Twenty-four. Mini Bundt pans will yield half a dozen cakes, and I know of another pan that cooks up fifteen bite-sized brownies."

"I'll give you access to the restaurant's website so you can order whatever you need."

Leah extended her hand. "You've got yourself a baker."

Not only would she order cookware but also different types of wheat and non-wheat flour, low-gluten and non-gluten flours, leavens, sugars, and salts. Baking would fill up the hours when she wasn't reading or meeting with Cherie and Kayana to discuss books.

Derrick took her hand, cradling it in his much larger one. "Thank you."

"No, thank you."

Leah knew she had made the right decision to come to Coates Island rather than travel to Kentucky to recuperate and heal from the emotional abuse she'd endured for more than half her life. Kayana, though shocked to see her show up without warning, had welcomed her with open arms while offering to let her live in the apartment.

She hadn't been on the island twenty-four hours and she had moved into a charming apartment, and she had made a commitment to provide baked goods for the restaurant. Going to bed with the smell of saltwater coming through the screens on the windows and waking up to the sight of the beach and ocean filled Leah with the knowledge that she was beyond abuse and intimidation. Alan may have sought to break her spirit, but the instant he raised his hand to hit her he'd given her strength to say no more. No more baleful glances, no more exchange of acerbic accusations, and no more pretense that they were a loving couple whenever they attended social soirees.

Chapter 6

Leah retreated to the apartment before Derrick opened the restaurant to the public. After they had finished eating breakfast she'd watched him combine chopped onion, light brown sugar, ketchup, red wine vinegar, molasses, Dijon mustard, chili powder, minced garlic, cayenne pepper, and kosher salt in the aluminum pan with the drained navy beans. The mouthwatering aroma of spices was tantalizing even before he'd placed the pan on the bottom rack of the smoker under a rack of marinated baby back ribs. He explained that the ribs would shed most of their fat during the first few hours and give the beans the benefit of the pork flavor without too much fat.

Leah had listened intently when he said brining chicken overnight and marinating meats for several days before smoking them low and slow made them Seaside Café customer favorites. She noticed he'd moved around the kitchen with a minimum of wasted motion for a man his size as he grilled crab cakes, sausage and peppers, and cooked string beans with white potatoes, mini corn on the cob, glazed carrots, and wilted spinach in under three hours, and filled the warming trays that had been set up on the buffet table the night before. Although Kayana did not cook during her two weeks off, she did come in after closing to assist Derrick prep dishes, clean the dining room, and set up the buffet table for the next day.

Leah was sitting on the love seat in the living room watching an afternoon talk show when she heard a knock on the door. She got up and opened it to find Kayana smiling and holding a tray covered with a cloth napkin. "I decided to come by early to check on you. Derrick told me to bring this up because you hadn't eaten since early this morning."

"Please come in. I was just watching a talk show," she said, taking the tray from Kayana. "Tell Derrick I appreciate the food." And she did. Leah had decided to remain upstairs while the restaurant was open for business.

Kayana walked in and folded her body down to the sofa. "You look a lot better today than you did yesterday."

Leah set the tray on a side table before sitting on the love seat; reaching for the remote device, she turned off the television. "I must admit I'm feeling a lot better than I did yesterday. I'm trying to get through the day without taking a pill. What I'll probably do is take it before going to bed so I can at least get a restful night's sleep."

"I was really surprised when Derrick told me you'd volunteered to make the baked goods for the Café's buffet breakfast."

Leah stared at the bundle of herbs on the fireplace grate. It was apparent the brother and sister had discussed her, and she wondered what else Kayana had confided to Derrick. "I made a small pan of buttermilk biscuits for breakfast, and he raved about them. And when I told him I knew how to make bread he asked me if I would bake for the Café."

"All right, all right, all right," Kayana drawled, grinning. "Be careful, girl, that you don't find yourself moving down here permanently like Graeme."

"Graeme had a good reason for relocating. You."

"And you don't, Leah?"

A slight frown furrowed Leah's forehead. "What are you talking about?"

"Derrick Edward Johnson."

Her stomach did a flip-flop with the mention of his name. "There's nothing going on between me and your brother."

"I'm not talking about anything romantic, Leah, because my brother still hasn't gotten over losing his wife." She pointed to the tray. "You really impressed him with your cooking skills, and he couldn't stop raving about your biscuits and sausage gravy. Why don't you start eating before everything gets cold."

Leah had misconstrued Kayana's mentioning her brother. She removed the napkin to find spareribs, a chicken thigh, baked beans, and wilted spinach. A plastic lid covered the mason jar filled with sweet tea. "Aren't you going to share this with me?"

"Nah. I had a late breakfast, and Graeme has promised to make dinner."

"He cooks?"

"He's become quite accomplished since we've been married."

"Good for you."

"Now start eating because you need to put some weight back on your bones. My brother happens to like women with some booty."

Although Kayana knew she was attracted to her brother the way a woman was to a man, Leah was realistic enough to know her association with Derrick would never go beyond friendship. "That's where you're wrong, Kayana. I'm in no position to have a relationship with any man for a while until I'm able to heal emotionally. It's impossible for me to wipe away the last thirty years like someone erasing a chalkboard. Plus, I'm willing to accept some of the blame for the shit Alan dumped on me because at any time I could've walked away."

"But didn't you tell me you stayed because of your sons?"

Leah picked up a knife and fork and cut into the tender chicken. "That's what I told myself when they were boys, but when they left for college I should've left with them. But I stayed for another ten years hoping things would change, and it got even worse. By then Alan didn't even care if I knew he was screwing around with other women, when before he'd attempted to hide his affairs.

"It never dawned on me that I was an abused wife until Alan hit me. In my naïveté I'd believed a man had to physically assault a woman for it to be considered abuse. And when it came to arguments we would engage in verbal confrontations that usually ended without a resolution."

Kayana leaned forward, resting her hands on her knees. "I don't envy you, because I don't have the temperament to have ongoing verbal confrontations with my partner. I say it once or maybe twice, then I'm done with it."

Leah chewed and swallowed the perfectly smoked meat. "Did you argue a lot with your first husband?" She knew Kayana had married a prominent Atlanta doctor who'd cheated on her with his colleague and got her pregnant.

"No. James and I would occasionally have our disagreements, but they never escalated to shouting matches."

"What about Graeme? Are you saying that you and Graeme agree on everything?"

"No, Leah. We understand that we happen to be two very different people that love each other but are willing to respect the other's opinion."

Leah stared at the contents on her plate. "The problem was and still is that Alan never respected me. I believe it boosted his ego to find a much younger woman fawning over him and he used that to his advantage when he set out to seduce and failed to protect me from an unplanned pregnancy."

"But you married him," Kayana argued softly.

"He only offered marriage because I refused to have an

abortion, and he didn't want his family's name sullied by becoming an unwed father."

"He'd asked you to get rid of his baby?"

"Yes. He was only weeks away from announcing his engagement to another woman and claimed I was fucking up his life."

"Why didn't he wrap up his meat?"

Leah laughed. "That's the same thing I told him."

Kayana stretched out her legs. "What I can't understand is why men tend to blame women for getting pregnant, when they refuse to wear condoms."

"I don't know, Kayana. Although I regret giving Alan so many years of my life I will never regret sleeping with him because of my sons. For some reason I always saw Caleb and Aron as boys and not as grown men until they dropped everything in New York to fly down to see me. I'd always protected them, and then the roles were reversed when they sought to protect me from their father."

"Good for them. I've had clients whose sons couldn't care less about their mothers who have sacrificed everything for their worthless behinds."

"Does Graeme have children?" Leah asked her friend.

"No. He and his late wife never had any, and that means we'll never become grandparents."

"Don't forget that you're an auntie. And we aunties are notorious for spoiling our nieces and nephews."

Kayana reached up and tightened the bandana covering her hair. "I hear you. I remember when Derrick's daughter was born, and now all she talks about is going to college."

"Has she selected a school?"

"Yes. The University of Florida."

"Isn't it in Gainesville?" Leah asked.

"Yes. It's my sister's alma mater, and it's where she met her husband. They'd settled in Gainesville after she got a teaching position at one of the public schools, while Errol went into law enforcement. They had three kids—two boys and a girl—before my ex-brother-in-law decided he wasn't cut out for marriage. When Derrick confronted him, he claimed he and Jocelyn couldn't agree on how to raise their children. My mother went down to Florida to live with her, and last summer Deandra went down for a visit and decided to stay and finish her senior year. Derrick really didn't want her to stay because she's his last link to her mother, but after a while he gave in. I told him she's growing up and becoming more independent and there's going to come a time when he has to let his little bird leave the nest."

Leah knew Kayana was right. She'd gone through separation anxiety when her sons announced they had applied to colleges in New York, Massachusetts, and California, and not Georgetown University, where generations of Kent men had attended and graduated. When they'd received their acceptance letters from New York University and Yale, both decided on NYU. Alan had made certain to rent an apartment for them in a building where visitors would have to be announced by a doorman and deposited enough money in their bank accounts so they wouldn't resort to eating ramen noodles like many college students who'd run out of money.

Leah had tried not to be the anxious, overbearing mother who called her children every week to find out what they were doing and waited for them to contact her. She and Alan drove up a few times, checked into a Manhattan hotel, and met with their sons for dinner and occasionally attended a Broadway play. It was during those visits that she'd felt as if they were truly a normal family. However, the charade was short-lived once she and Alan returned to Richmond. That was when Dr. Henry Jekyll turned into the evil Edward Hyde.

They managed to live separate lives while sharing the same roof, and for Leah it was more than okay. The year the twins turned six, after earning her graduate degree, she returned to the Calhoun Academy to teach, and twelve years later she was appointed headmistress. She knew she never would've gotten the position if she hadn't been Mrs. Alan Kent.

"My sons have left the nest, and I believe they don't want to return."

"They're planning to live in New York permanently?"

Leah nodded. "That's the vibe I've been getting from them."

"Didn't you mention that your husband's family has a law firm in Richmond?"

"Yes. His uncle's sons are now managing partners."

"Are they Kents?" Kayana asked.

"Yes. They are Kents down to the marrow in their bones."

Kayana gave her a quizzical look. "Why do you say it like the name Kent is a deadly communicable disease?"

"Because anyone I met claiming Kent blood treated me as if I had a contagious disease or had the audacity to talk about me where I could overhear what they were saying. My mother-in-law has done an excellent job of maligning me because I wasn't her first choice as a daughter-in-law."

"And the woman Alan had been dating came from the so-called right family?"

"Bingo. Justine Hamilton looked like Liz Taylor with her dark hair and violet-colored eyes. Men gawked at her because she had natural double D's. And it helps that her family is old money."

"Was she as young as you were when you first met Alan?"

"No. She was in her mid to late twenties. And I'd overheard someone saying that she was pressuring Alan to marry her."

"If Alan was in his thirties, then when he met you it couldn't have been that he was just into young girls. Look at yourself, Leah. You're no slouch in the looks department, and you're extremely bright. How many people do you know that graduate high school at fifteen and then get accepted into one of the country's elite colleges on full scholarship?" Leah searched her memory about the girls she'd taught and met at her school.

"Only one, but she was sixteen and was accepted into Harvard."

"There you go, Leah. Alan probably saw you as a novelty. You were young, vivacious, stimulating, and probably very sexy."

Leah blushed. "I've never thought of myself as sexy."

"And why not? Because your husband chose to sleep with other women?"

"I don't know the answer to that, Kayana. Alan is what I call a serial cheater."

"I've counseled beautiful, intelligent women who were dating or married to men who cheated, and when I tell them their significant other is insecure they don't want to believe me. I try to get them to see that if he was able to get them, then his ego tells him he can get others. And when I use the analogy comparing human behavior to those in the animal kingdom, that's when they get it. Remember last year when I said women will go after one another over a man, when in the animal kingdom it's the males that fight each other over females.

"Hypothetically, think of the alpha male lion with a pride of ten lionesses or an alpha wolf in a pack with the same number of females. They will fight to the death to keep all the females if they're challenged by another male, although they can only mate with one at a time. Even if Alan had married his Liz Taylor lookalike, he still would've cheated on her, while expecting her to be the dutiful little wife willing to have his children, host his dinner parties, and turn a blind eye to his peccadillos."

Leah couldn't control her burst of laughter. She smiled at the cook, silently admiring her flawless, nut-brown complexion with orange undertones, large brown eyes and delicate features in a small, round face and knew why Graeme Ogden hadn't been able to take his eyes off her.

"Have you been reading Cherie's historical romance novels?"

"No. Why?"

"Because that's where you'd probably read about peccadillos."

Kayana made a sucking sound with her tongue and teeth. "I could've been less delicate and said fuckin' around."

Leah laughed again. "That's exactly what they do, Kay. They fuck around until they get caught." Then without warning, she sobered. "When I went with Alan to what I later found was his love nest, I had no intention of sleeping with him. At the time I didn't drink, but after three glasses of champagne I was so out of it that I couldn't have protested even if I wanted to."

"Were you a virgin?"

Leah shook her head. "No. I'd slept with one boy in college. When I look back in hindsight I have to admit it was the best lovemaking I'd ever experienced up to that time."

"That's because Alan wasn't some bumbling college kid."

"You're right about that. It was the first time I had multiple orgasms."

"It's called baby-making fucking," Kayana said, grinning.

Leah's eyebrows lifted slightly when she recalled Alan's unbridled lovemaking. It was the first and last time he'd made her lose herself in the throes of ecstasy. "You're right about that."

"I'm going to ask you a personal question, and you don't have to answer it if you don't want. But did you and Alan have a normal sexual relationship after you were married?"

"It all depends on what you consider normal. He never touched me throughout my pregnancy. And I'd gained so much weight and even more after I delivered the babies that I'd moved into another bedroom after Alan called me a fat sow. I had to increase my daily caloric intake because I was breastfeeding two babies. Not only was I dealing with the extra weight, but also my so-called loving husband's insults, and postpartum depression. One day I was watching a daytime talk show and the topic was about women who wanted a makeover because they felt their husbands no longer found them attractive. There was footage of six months of before and after, and that's when I decided I needed to change my life, not for Alan but myself. It took months, but I finally lost the weight, joined a health club to work out, and I took one of Alan's credit cards and maxed it out when I filled two walk-in closets with new clothes, shoes, and accessories."

"Did he complain about you spending so much money?" Kayana questioned.

"No. With Alan it was never about money but family honor. He was only concerned about image and how people viewed and related to him. We were invited to a fund-raising event, and people were talking about my transformation, and that's when Alan realized other men were looking at his wife. A couple of days later he came into the bathroom while I was taking a shower naked and fully aroused. Although I was ovulating and horny as a mink I told him I wasn't in the mood."

"Talk about payback," Kayana whispered.

"No shit," Leah said, grinning from ear to ear. "I made him wait four months before I moved back into his bedroom. In the interim he'd leave gifts under my pillow. They could be a pair of earrings, bracelet, or necklace. If he was going to treat me like a mistress, then I was willing to play the part, because I knew he was still sleeping with other women. When he asked me what I wanted for our third anniversary I told him I wanted a pair of diamond earrings totaling four carats."

"Were those the earrings you wore when you came here last year?"

"Yup."

"Did you give him some?"

"Not right away. He probably thought I didn't like the earrings and then came through with the diamond eternity band. After eight carats of diamonds I figured he'd earned at least a couple sessions with the woman whom he'd married."

"No! You actually held your pussy hostage until he delivered the goods?"

"Yes! But only after I was fitted with an IUD. I'd asked for jewelry because if I left him I'd be able to sell them for top dollar. And knowing how vindictive Alan can be, I wouldn't put it past him to take my name off his credit cards."

"Did you sell them? Because I notice you're not wearing your bling."

"A couple of days before I left Richmond I cleaned out the safe in my bedroom suite and put everything in the safe deposit box in the bank where I have an account. I plan to leave them there until after my divorce. If my sons ever get married I will gift some to my daughters-in-law. And if they have girls, then my granddaughters will get the rest. I've told Aron and Caleb one of the conditions of my divorce is I intend to resume using my maiden name."

"Why does it sound as if you're ready to exorcise Alan Kent from your life?"

Leah closed her eyes. She'd just disclosed things to Kayana she'd never told another soul, and that included her mother. She opened her eyes and sighed. "If I'd had more good years with Alan than bad, I probably would still be with him. But once he put his hands on me it was all she wrote."

"Good for you, Leah. You can't imagine how many women stay with men that use them as punching bags to vent their frustrations or insecurities."

A beat passed, and she noticed Kayana staring at her. Picking up the napkin, she dabbed her mouth. "Do I have spinach between my teeth?"

Kayana blinked as if coming out of a trance. "No. It's your hair."

Leah ran a hand over her hair. "What about it?"

"Did you get a perm? Because last year it was stick straight."

"No. When I was a little girl I had naturally curly hair like Orphan Annie. Once I reached adolescence the texture changed, and now it's wavy. After I wash my hair I always blow it straight."

"It looks nice wavy."

"Thank you, ma'am."

Kayana's compliment was what Leah needed to make her less conscious of her face. Once the bruises faded completely she planned to forgo makeup and put her freckles on display. Twenty-four hours ago, when she opened the door and walked into the Seaside Café it signaled a rebirth of her new life as the adult Leah Berkley. "I know I haven't said it, but I want to thank you and your brother."

"There's no need to thank us, Leah. Even though not many locals live on the island we tend to look out for one another."

"You forget that I'm not a local."

"If you live here before the Memorial Day weekend and/or after Labor Day, then you're a local."

"I'm definitely here before Memorial Day, so I guess that makes me a local."

"Own it, girlfriend." Kayana stood up. "Derrick's probably wondering what happened to me."

Leah picked up the tray. "I'm going down with you. I can clean off the tables and sweep up the dining room while you guys do what you do in the kitchen."

Kayana took the tray from her. "No, you're not. You need to stay up here and out of the way, because I have to move tables, chairs, and sweep and mop the floor."

"You do all that?"

"Who do you think is going to do it, Leah?"

"But . . . but don't you have help?"

Kayana rolled her eyes upward. "This is not the Kent mansion where we employ help twenty-four-seven."

Leah recoiled as if she'd been slapped. "You didn't have to go there, Kayana."

"Yes, I did, Leah. Derrick and I operate a business where we depend on the good will of those who live on this island to choose to eat here when they could just as easily prepare their own meals. So, nine months out of twelve we're on austerity. And that means no waitstaff. We still must buy food, pay for utilities, send out laundry, make repairs, and perform janitorial duties. We don't expect to make much of a profit between September and May, but we also don't want to rack up losses."

"What if you close down during the off-season?"

"The Seaside Café has only closed during the off-season for holidays and special family events. Derrick closed for two weeks late last year to attend my wedding in Massachusetts and then to spend time in Florida with his daughter. Derrick and I have talked about closing Saturdays *and* Sundays, but we're still up in the air about that. Even though we're now closed on Sundays, it's always been a tradition with the Johnson family going back to Grandma Cassie to close on Easter Monday."

"If you're having a problem with cash flow, have you thought of getting investors?"

"We don't have a cash flow problem, Leah. It's about . . ." Her words trailed off. "Maybe one of these days Derrick will explain it to you. After all, he's the financial genius with degrees in accounting and finance. I'm leaving now, and I'll see you tomorrow. I hope you feel better."

Leah realized she'd just been dismissed when Kayana turned on her heel and walked out. She'd registered a change in her friend's voice and body language when she'd mentioned investors. There was no doubt she'd insulted her.

She wanted to tell Kayana that it was an honest question because she'd mentioned being on austerity for the nine months vacationers did not come to the island. Most resorts, whether in warm or cold climate, depended on vacationers to keep them viable. Her sons had gone to Park City, Utah, to ski during the Christmas holidays. If there wasn't enough natural snowfall, owners were forced to make snow to keep the resorts open in order to maximize profits.

Leah was aware that the Café was a family-owned restaurant that had to compete with fast food and chain establish-
ments in the nearby town of Shelby. However, for anyone
vacationing on Coates Island, the Seaside Café was their go-
to place to eat where they were guaranteed delicious, home-
cooked meals, large portions, and friendly, courteous service.
Although she'd rented a bungalow with a kitchen when she
was last here, she'd found herself coming to the Café to eat
breakfast and dinner. She would occasionally order several
takeout meals she planned to reheat in the microwave whenever she needed to finish reading a book before an upcoming
book club meeting.

The one time she took the jitney into town and then called
an Uber to take her to the twenty-four-hour supermarket in
Shelby to purchase the ingredients she needed to host a club
meeting, it'd felt strange to take a number at the deli counter
and wait to be called. Since becoming Mrs. Alan Kent, she
did not go to supermarkets to shop for groceries, because
Adele had assumed the responsibility of planning all meals
with the live-in chef. Even after her mother-in-law was trans-
ferred to the nursing facility, the live-in chef and housekeeper
remained on staff.

Once she was off the pain meds and clear-headed, she had
to research a lawyer willing to represent her when she sued
Alan for divorce, knowing it was going to become a herculean feat to get an attorney willing to challenge Judge Alan
Kent. Leah didn't want alimony or even a settlement. She just
wanted to be legally uncoupled and have the right to resume
using her maiden name.

Fortunately, she'd been able to save ninety percent of her
salary from the Calhoun Academy and had deposited the
funds in a separate account, but that would change once she
returned from her medical leave. Leah knew she would have
to withdraw money from the account to purchase a small
house or condo. She smiled. Life as Leah Berkley would be
vastly different from her life as Mrs. Alan Kent, and she was

looking forward to the time when she could go around Richmond as an independent woman in charge of her own destiny.

She closed the door, locked it, and headed for the reading room. Before she left the island last summer she, Kayana, and Cherie had selected the first three books they wanted to discuss. Leah had chosen to lead her discussion with *Memoirs of a Geisha*. Kayana's choice was *Love in the Time of Cholera*, and Cherie had chosen *The Alienist*.

Although many titles were available in electronic formats, Leah still preferred holding a physical book. And if she wanted to reread a section, she would slip strips of paper between the pages. Picking up Caleb Carr's best-selling title, she decided to read *The Alienist* first because it covered forty-seven chapters in five hundred pages, and it would take time for her to jot down notes. Cherie had mentioned it was a dark period piece set in New York City at the dawn of the twentieth century, when Theodore Roosevelt was the New York City Police Commissioner.

She settled into an armchair with a matching footstool and opened the book and was hooked from the very first sentence. It was January 8, 1919, the day of Theodore Roosevelt's funeral. Leah had to give Cherie kudos because the printed words on the page pulled her and refused to let her go until she had to stop and turn on a table lamp. The afternoon had slipped by so quickly that she'd lost track of time.

Placing a bright-pink slip of paper from a stack she carried when reading, she closed the book and set it aside. The mini fridge in the apartment was stocked with bottled water, juice, and wine. Leah knew drinking wine was out of the question because she was taking prescribed medicine that made her drowsy. She opted for water instead.

It was only seven and much too early for her to go to sleep, so she decided to watch television for a while. She found herself moving slowly after sitting for hours, but the discomfort wasn't enough for her to take a pill. She'd just settled down to watch an all-news cable channel when her cell phone rang. Leah smiled. The programmed ringtone indicated a call from her mother.

"Hi, Mom."

"Hello, baby. I was just calling to find out if you're coming to Kentucky during your Easter break."

Leah bit her lip. How had she forgotten that she'd promised her family she would come to Kentucky when school closed for the Easter week? But there was no way she wanted them to see her looking like she did, because there was no guarantee all the bruises and abrasions on her body would've disappeared by that time. Perhaps if her complexion were darker they wouldn't be so evident.

"I can't, Mom."

"Why not, Leah?"

"Because I had an accident."

There came a pregnant pause before Madeline asked, "What kind of an accident?"

"I fell down the stairs." Leah knew it was a half lie. She'd fallen down the stairs because Alan had deliberately pushed her.

"What! When?"

"It happened almost two weeks ago. I tripped and fell and hit my head. I was in the hospital for a little more than a week before the doctor discharged me."

"Why didn't you call me or your father? Why didn't Alan call us?"

"Because Alan wasn't home at the time," she lied. "The housekeeper found me unconscious and dialed 911." Leah lied yet again. It was something she hadn't done in the past with her parents, yet at forty-nine she had become quite proficient at hiding the truth.

There was no way she was going to tell her mother what had happened because it wouldn't end well for Alan. It wouldn't matter to Larry Berkley that his son-in-law was a judge; he would do more to the man than push him down a flight of stairs. What Leah should've done was call her par-

ents as soon as she was released from the hospital and downplay the seriousness of her ordeal.

"There is no excuse why he couldn't call us, Leah."

"I supposed he panicked. But he did call Aron and Caleb."

"Are they there with you now?"

"No, Mom. They had to go back to New York. I'm in
North Carolina staying with a friend. I've taken a medical
leave from school because I don't want my staff and students
seeing their headmistress looking as if she's been in a brawl."

"Are you on the island where you spent your vacation last
year?"

"Yes. It's perfect to relax."

"Your friend doesn't mind putting you up?"

"Not at all. I plan to stay here through the summer and
then go back to Richmond in time for teacher orientation."

"What is Alan saying about this?"

"He has no say in where I choose to go."

There came another noticeable pause. "Are you and your
husband getting along?"

Leah shook her head although Madeline couldn't see her.
"Not really. I'm seriously thinking about asking him for a divorce."

"Do you actually believe he's going to go along with
that?"

"I really don't give a damn, Mom. My sons are out of the
house living their own lives, so there's nothing keeping me
with him."

"You know I never wanted to interfere in your life from
the time you told me that you were pregnant with Alan
Kent's baby, but if you had hinted that you didn't want to
marry him, your father and I would've given you our full
support. I'd rather you'd had your twins without marrying. I
would've quit my job to babysit them while you furthered
your career. But what Alan wasn't going to get away with
was not giving you child support. He would've paid through
his ass or I would've gone to every newspaper in the state to

report that a man in his mid-thirties had taken advantage of an eighteen-year-old girl."

Leah's mouth opened when she heard her mother's proposed threat. And if she'd gone to the press Leah knew it would've ruined Alan's chance of getting a judgeship. "Everything worked out all right, because if it hadn't been for him I never would've been appointed headmistress of the school." Other than fathering her sons, Alan using his influence to get her hired and subsequently rehired at the prestigious private school where she'd eventually become headmistress was the best thing to come from her marriage.

"It was the least he could do to boost his wife's social standing among those other phony people who believe their shit don't stink!"

"Mom! When did you start cussing?"

"I've been cussing for a long time. I just don't let my kids and grandkids hear me. When I turned forty something inside me changed. Things I used to ignore I couldn't anymore. I have to assume it's the same way with you now that you're in your forties."

Leah wanted to tell her mother that she'd begun cursing Alan even before she'd married him, and it had continued for nearly three decades. "You're right. I'm ready to as they say live my life by my leave. I'll come and go when and wherever I want without having to check in with a husband."

"You're luckier than a lot of women, who believe they're stuck in marriage with no way out. Every mother that has a daughter should preach to them to get an education so they can have a career where they don't have to depend on a man to take care of them. I was luckier than a lot of girls in my school that found themselves pregnant and the boys they were sleeping with ran faster than a cheetah to leave town, because your father and I talked about getting married when we were both juniors."

"That's because Daddy is one of the good guys." Leah chatted with her mother for another ten minutes as Madeline brought her up to date about what was going on in the lives of her grandchildren. They'd become the sun, moon, and the stars to the older woman.

Once she ended the call she felt bad about lying but knew it was necessary. She would lie again if it meant concealing the truth as to how she'd sustained injuries serious enough for her to spend ten days in a hospital. But if Alan decided to fight her, then all hell would break loose once she had the hospital release her medical records. And if need be, she knew her sons would also testify against their father. However, she hoped it wouldn't come to that, and they could end their marriage amicably.

Chapter 7

Derrick had set two bags of soiled linen outside the back door and returned to the kitchen when Kayana walked in with the tray he'd fixed for Leah. A text from the laundry service confirmed the driver was expected to come before three to pick them up and drop off clean restaurant linens.

"Did you enjoy your book club meeting?"

Kayana scrunched up her nose. "Very funny. You know we're not going to start up again until Cherie gets here."

He took the tray, frowning. "She didn't eat half of what I fixed for her."

"I'd noticed she didn't eat much yesterday. After being fed intravenously for more than a week she probably has to get used to eating solids again."

Derricks lifted one inky-black eyebrow as he angled his head. "She was in the hospital that long?"

"Yes. She really hurt herself when she fell down the stairs."

"Fell or pushed," Derrick said, as he scraped the plate into a large, plastic-lined garbage can.

"Why would you say that?"

He gave his sister a direct glance. "When Leah told me she'd fallen headfirst down a staircase I didn't believe her."

With wide eyes, Kayana stared at him. "Why don't you believe her?"

"Because of the faint bruising around her throat. Someone choked her, Kay."

"Did she tell you that?"

"No, and I don't intend to get into her personal business. But if I had to hazard a guess, then I'd say it was her husband. When she came down here last summer she was wearing a wedding band, and now there's no ring. She's your friend, Kay, and you should let her know that we don't want any trouble if her husband decides to come after her."

"If he does come down, then he's going to be the one in trouble."

Leaning a hip against the countertop, Derrick crossed his arms over his chest. "You're going to have to talk to me about Leah, otherwise I'll be in the dark if something funky does jump off."

"You're going to have to promise me that you won't repeat what I'm going to tell you."

"Come on now, Kay. Haven't we always been able to keep each other's secrets?"

"You're right, Derrick."

He listened intently, his impassive expression concealing the rage that made it almost impossible for him to draw a normal breath as Kayana repeated what Leah had revealed about how her husband had beaten and thrown her down a flight of stairs in their home, then lied as to how she'd sustained the injuries that had placed her in a drug-induced coma.

"Shit!" he spat out between clenched teeth. "The SOB was trying to kill her."

"If it wasn't his intent to kill her, then it was to beat her into submission."

"It's a good thing she didn't hang around for him to finish

the job." Derrick knew guys from college who would slap their girlfriends to keep them, as they professed, in their place. And although his parents argued constantly, his father had never attempted to raise his hands to strike his mother.

"Leah told me she came here rather than to her family in Kentucky because she's afraid her father would do something to her husband."

"Does her husband know she's here?"

"Probably, because that's what they were arguing about. She said when she told him she was coming down here again this summer he went apeshit, because he wanted her to go away with him."

"I suppose he'll be going away by himself unless Leah changes her mind and decides to go back to Richmond."

"That's not going to happen, Derrick. She's planning on filing for divorce."

Derrick silently applauded Leah for ending her marriage to an abusive husband. "I don't want to interfere in what goes on between a man and his wife, but if she is serious about divorcing him, then I will get involved if he does show up. If he doesn't leave, then I'll call the sheriff and have him forcibly removed.

"He's a judge, Derrick."

Derrick's mouth was smiling when his eyes weren't. "I'm not impressed. There hasn't been scandal on Coates Island since Mr. Campbell discovered he was sterile and that his children were actually fathered by his next-door neighbor who had been was sleeping with his wife."

Kayana wagged her head side to side. "That was a hot mess because Mrs. Campbell packed her bags and moved next door and left her children with her devastated husband because they had his last name."

"It was beyond a hot mess, Kay. One of the Campbell boys was on the high school football team with me, and the kid was so full of rage that when he tackled someone on the opposing team he would body slam them and always get ejected for unnecessary roughness."

"Mr. Campbell should've put those kids in counseling to deal with their mother abandoning them to live with her lover who just happened to be their biological father. Those are very serious issues for teenagers to have to deal with."

Derrick's eyes crinkled in a smile. "Spoken like a therapist. Speaking of therapy, Kay, do you miss counseling clients?" he asked.

Kayana walked over to the sink with dirty dishes and filled it with hot water before adding a squirt of liquid soap. "No. Once I resigned from the hospital, split from James, and left Atlanta, I mentally erased every memory of my life up to that point. It wasn't until I came back to the island and began working here that I felt whole again. Between counseling patients and/or their families at the hospital, occasionally filling in to counsel clients at Mariah Hinton's private practice, and playing hostess for James whenever he invited his colleagues and family members to our home for some inane function, I was pulled in so many directions that I'd lose track of the days. One time I got up on Sunday to go into the hospital because I thought it was a workday. James's cheating gave me the excuse and strength I needed to get off the roller coaster and discover who I was and what I didn't want."

Derrick patted her back. "Been there, done that."

Kayana's Atlanta lifestyle mirrored his when he'd worked for a Wall Street investment firm. While hers was a merry-go-round of social engagements, his and Andrea's had revolved around the unpredictability of the stock market. Spending hours on the phone with their clients, buying and selling stock had begun to take its toll. Once they returned to their high-rise apartment with views of the Hudson River it wasn't to unwind and relax, but to eat a hastily prepared dinner, go to bed, only to wake early the following morning to repeat the prior day's activity.

"The difference between us, Derrick, is you didn't stay in New York when compared to the number of years I lived in Atlanta."

"Don't forget that we were expecting a baby, and Andrea didn't want to raise it in the city."

"True, but didn't you say you were looking to move to one of the suburbs."

"Yeah, but—"

"But once you made a decision to leave Manhattan you acted on it. You guys came back here, lived with Mama while your beach house was being built. You stepped in to help Mom and Grandma Cassie run this place, while Andrea took care of Deandra and managed the Café's finances. Meanwhile, I didn't have chick nor child and I still put up with a husband that had turned our home into a club because he needed folks in his face, otherwise he felt he wasn't having a good time."

"That's all behind you, Kay, because now you're married to a man who can be as reclusive as Howard Hughes."

Kayana narrowed her eyes at her brother as she slipped on a pair of rubber gloves and scraped the dishes before putting them into the commercial dishwasher. "You got jokes about my husband?"

He held up both hands. "No. I'm not maligning my brother-in-law. It's just that since you two have been married he rarely comes here anymore. And FYI, I happen to like him a lot better than I did your ex."

"FYI, so do I. The reason Graeme doesn't come in as often as he used to is because I've been giving him cooking lessons."

Derrick had made it a practice not to get involved with his sisters' personal lives once they married. When he'd teased Kayana about Graeme Ogden gawking at her like a lovesick teenage boy every time he came into the restaurant, she'd turned on him like an angry cat, stopping short of telling him to mind his own business. He did stay out of it, until he was forced to confront Kayana about her relationship with the New England schoolteacher when his sister appeared to retreat into herself, and he feared she was headed for an emotional breakdown. He managed to get her to agree to see Graeme again after she claimed he was hiding a secret and refused to tell her unless they were married.

She'd accepted the man's proposal, he revealed his secret, and they were married on Christmas Eve at Graeme's family's estate in Newburyport, Massachusetts, with the entire Johnson clan in attendance. Derrick had closed the Café for two weeks and gone back to Florida to spend time with his family, while Kayana and Graeme honeymooned in the United Arab Emirates.

Derrick knew he'd changed once he returned to Coates Island. The time he'd spent in Gainesville with his daughter forced him to see what he'd been denying for much too long. She was no longer a little girl but a young woman. Deandra had made the decision to live in Florida during her senior year, and being away from him had permitted her to mature more quickly than if she'd remained on the island. They'd had an in-depth father-daughter talk in which she accused him of smothering her. She said that he hadn't wanted her to grow up because one day she would leave him to start her own life, and he feared losing her as he did her mother. And he knew his daughter was right. It had taken an eighteen-year-old girl to tell her forty-eight-year-old father what he'd refused to acknowledge. It was time for him to stop mourning and living in the past. He was still young enough to fall in love and marry again like her aunt Kayana.

"Speaking of Graeme cooking," Kayana said, breaking into his musings, "we decided to cook out on Sunday, only if it doesn't rain. Why don't you come and join us."

"That sounds like a plan. What's on the menu?"

"Grandma Cassie's mac and cheese and a few other Johnson family secret dishes."

"You got me at the mac and cheese. I don't know how you do it, Kay, but you're able to duplicate our grandmother's recipe for mac and cheese every single time."

"That's because she had me make it over and over until I got it right."

"And that's why you make the sides while I concentrate on the meat."

"We all have our gifts."

"You're right about that."

"I also invited Leah to join us, so can you please pick her up and bring her with you?"

"That shouldn't be a problem. Be sure to let her know that I'll be picking her up."

"I'll send her a text," Kayana promised.

"Speaking of meat, what if I bring a few steaks. Some of them having been aging for nearly a month, and lately I haven't been getting many requests for steak."

"That's because many of the locals are older and don't eat a lot of red meat, Derrick. We sell more steak, brisket, pulled pork, and ribs in the summer than during the off-season."

"You're right about that. I'm going to take an inventory of the meat we have on hand, and then do an analysis of the bills we paid the butcher over the past two years. That should tell me if I'm ordering too much of each item for any given month."

Kayana waved her hand at the same time she shook her head. "Why do you have to be so analytical? Just stop ordering so much steak."

"We run this restaurant on analytics."

"This isn't a large company where everything has to be measured and accounted for, Derrick. We are running a family-style eating establishment where we raise prices between

eight and ten percent every other year to offset higher costs
for food and utilities. We know the dishes the locals like and
those the vacationers prefer and make them available. I'm
also aware that you make up projections every year, so how
did we do last year?"

"We did extremely well."

"There you go, brother love. Now if Leah has agreed to
make the baked goods, then your bottom line should be even
better because you won't have to pay Lena's Bakery. Personally, I think she's overpriced."

"She is a little overpriced, but she's the only bakery on the
mainland willing to deliver what we want."

"Between ordering the ingredients you'll need and paying
Leah, you should save a lot of money."

"Leah won't accept any money." He held up a hand when
Kayana opened her mouth. "Please let me finish. When I offered to pay her, she went for my throat. And I wasn't about
to get into an argument with her, because I witnessed enough
verbal back-and-forth with our parents to last me two lifetimes. She claims because we're not charging her rent—"

"I would never charge my friends rent," Kayana said, interrupting him. "No one is using the apartment, so why not
let her stay there."

"You misunderstand me, Kay. I don't have a problem with
Leah living upstairs. But what I don't want to do is take advantage of her working for free."

"It's called barter, Derrick. I'm certain you're familiar with
the term, Mr. Number Man."

"You don't have to be facetious, Kayana."

"I'm not being facetious."

Derrick didn't want to argue with his sister and remind her
whenever she attempted to best him she would refer to him
by the sobriquet. "Go home to your husband."

"You're pissed with me, aren't you?"

"No. I am not pissed with you. Stop what you're doing and go home. I can finish up here."

She took off the gloves. "I'll see you Sunday around two. You can bring steak if you want."

Derrick cursed under his breath as he watched his sister walk out the back door. He wasn't as upset with her as he was with himself. He wanted to tell Kayana that he envied her. After nearly twenty years of marriage she'd discovered her husband had not only cheated on her but had gotten another woman pregnant. She'd sworn off men, refusing to even acknowledge any who were remotely interested in her until a man who had vacationed on the island the year before purchased a home on Coates Island because he'd fallen in love with Kayana.

If he had been younger and cynical when it came to affairs of the heart, Derrick would have called the man crazy to buy a house just to be close to a woman who would not give him the time of day. But he had to give it to Graeme. He saw what he wanted and went after it. And in the end Kayana was given a second chance at love, while as her brother he found it impossible to move forward.

Andrea had been dead five years, yet he'd refused to let go of her memory. When she knew she was dying she made him promise not to grieve for her, that he should find someone to love him as much as she had. He'd promised her while knowing it was an empty promise.

Andrea was gone; however, a part of her lived on in their daughter. Not only was Deandra her mother's clone, but they also had similar personalities. That had been more apparent during their last reunion. She possessed the same streak of independence that had drawn him to Andrea. Deandra had become a leader among her peers and not a follower. She'd run for a position on the high school's student council and, despite being a new incoming senior, won. When he'd asked her what she wanted to study she said she hadn't figured that out yet. He'd teased her, saying she had inherited her mother's beauty and her intelligence. Andrea had graduated at the top of her class in high school and college.

It was Saturday, and Derrick did not have to concern himself with prepping for the next day. If need be, he'd come in very early Monday morning or Sunday night to get a jump on things. He heard three rapid knocks on the rear door. It was the driver's signal that he'd left bags of clean laundry.

Since he took over managing the restaurant after his grandmother passed away and his mother moved to Florida to look after her grandchildren, he'd made it a practice to hire college students for the summer. They were responsible for bagging garbage, sweeping and mopping the dining room and kitchen, loading and unloading the dishwasher, and maintaining the restrooms. This freed him to cook and keep track of the restaurant's inventory.

Andrea had brought every item in the restaurant online, including accounts payable, payroll, and taxes. Derrick knew with a single keystroke how many pounds of bacon or cartons of eggs were on hand. The task of computerizing the business had been monumental, but Andrea relished it, because she had complained constantly about several file cabinets filled with bills and receipts going back decades. Once she completed bringing everything up to date she shredded paper that, if audited, they didn't need.

It took Derrick ninety minutes to empty the laundry bags and stack aprons, towels, and tablecloths in the supply closet, clean off tables, sweep and mop the floors, and clean the restrooms. After bagging the garbage and placing it in the dumpster behind a partition in the corner of the parking lot, he returned to the restaurant and turned off lights, set the building alarm, and closed and locked the rear door.

He didn't want to think about the woman in the upstairs apartment who'd been savagely beaten by a man because she'd attempted to challenge him. Kayana said Leah had planned to file for divorce, and Derrick hoped it would end amicably. He slipped behind the wheel of his Toyota Highlander, tapped the button to start up the engine, and maneuvered out of the parking lot.

Three minutes later he pulled into his attached two-car garage and entered the house through a door leading directly into a mudroom. After leaving his shoes on a mat, he walked into the house with its open floor plan where he'd experienced the some of his most joyous times as a husband and father. However, the joy was short-lived when he'd kept a vigil at his wife's bedside as she hung onto life, and he'd prayed for her to let go so there would be no more pain. Andrea had loved the two-story, four-bedroom, three-bath house facing the beach and shaded by a copse of palm trees, but after she was diagnosed with cancer she'd spend most of her free time on the front porch or in the tiny cottage behind the main house reading or napping.

The garden shed had been originally used as an additional guest bedroom with inviting features such as French doors, painted shutters, and window boxes overflowing with colorful blooms. Andrea had also planned for Deandra to move into the cottage once she turned sixteen to allow her a sense of independence before leaving home to attend college. It had taken his daughter more than year before she ventured inside her mother's sanctuary, and it was only to do her homework or study for exams. Derrick rarely entered the cottage and instructed the cleaning service that came biweekly to clean his home to dust, vacuum, and open windows to let in fresh air.

He headed for the staircase and his bedroom. Normally he would've gone to the room he'd set up as a home gym to log five miles on the treadmill after several repetitions of lifting weights. At six-four and tipping the scales at two twenty-five, and rapidly approaching fifty, Derrick knew it was a race against time and hoped to slow down the loss of muscle tone.

He stripped off his clothes, leaving them in the hamper in

the second-story laundry room. Andrea had insisted on installing the room on the same floor as the bedrooms to avoid having to carry the bags or baskets of clothes up and down the staircase. Derrick brushed his teeth and showered in the en suite bathroom. Wearing only a pair of pajama pants, he sat on a leather recliner in an alcove off the master bedroom. It had taken him several months before he could sleep in the room once he'd become a widower, because too many pieces were a constant reminder of what he'd shared with his late wife.

When he'd disclosed this to Kayana, she recommended he solicit the services of an interior designer and decorate the bedroom to suit his taste. A California king bed with a leather headboard replaced the off-white hand-painted sleigh bed. Matching dressers and chest of drawers in mahogany gave off a more masculine appeal. It was the same with the reading corner that was converted to a space with a wall-mounted television, and a storage unit spanning the width of the wall contained shelves filled with books, magazines, and an extensive collection of movie and music discs. One door on the unit concealed a mini fridge and the other contained mementos from when he'd been a standout as a running back for the Alabama Crimson Tide football program. His dream of being drafted into the NFL ended when he injured his knee, tearing his ACL.

Although he'd erased every memory of Andrea sharing the suite with him, Derrick had not slept with another woman in the house. It would not have been possible when Deandra lived there, and even now with his daughter living in Florida he still couldn't bring himself to do it.

He had not taken on a monastic lifestyle; he did see one woman several times a month. The town was far enough away from Coates Island and the divorcée with three adult children who'd left home enjoyed his company as much as he did hers. However, both were content with their current marital status. She did not want to remarry, and Derrick did not regard it as something he would entertain at this time in his life.

He flipped through several channels until he found one showing highlights of a Carolina Panthers football game going back three years. Derrick would be the first one to admit that he was a sports junkie and made no apologies when he'd spend hours watching encores of baseball, basketball, football, and hockey games. He'd found himself glued to the television during the FIFA World Cup soccer competition and, every four years, the Olympics.

Sports had become his pleasure, for which he refused to apologize. The game ended with the Panthers winning with a touchdown with five seconds left on the clock. He found another channel with a basketball game on the west coast and settled back to watch that, too. He didn't have to get up early and open the Café, so it had become his time for watching late-night TV.

It was after one in the morning when Derrick finally turned off the television and got into bed. He fell asleep almost immediately, but it was a disturbing dream that kept him from a restful night's slumber. It was Leah's face, swollen, bruised, and bloodied that shook him awake. He sat up quickly, looking around the room. There was enough illumination coming from baseboard nightlights to tell him there was no one else in the bedroom with him.

It wasn't a dream but a nightmare. It took a lot longer for him to go back to sleep, and he wondered if he'd made a mistake telling Kayana that it was okay to put her friend up in the apartment. And maybe if he hadn't asked and she hadn't told him how Leah had sustained her injuries he would feel less uneasy about her taking up residence in his place of business.

But on the other hand, he'd given his word she could stay, and anyone living on Coates Island knew the Johnsons never went back on their word. And now that he was aware that her husband was a judge he hoped the man wouldn't attempt to use his judicial influence to intimidate him or his sister for harboring his wife. Hopefully, Leah had documented his assault as leverage for the deposition phase of her divorce.

Exhaustion finally won out, and when he went back to sleep there were no macabre images to disturb him.

Chapter 8

Leah noticed the gleaming black SUV pulling into the parking lot and smiled when she saw Derrick get out. Kayana had sent her a text earlier that morning letting her know that Derrick would come and get her at two thirty, and his smile matched hers as she approached him. She couldn't pull her gaze away from his muscular, powerful biceps on display in a blue golf shirt he had paired with relaxed jeans and low-heeled black boots. His declaration that he worked out every day was evident, because there appeared not to be an ounce of fat on his lean upper body. He hadn't worn a hat, and she was slightly taken aback when she stared at his cropped gray hair. The color shimmered against his smooth mahogany complexion like polished silver. She was grateful she'd worn sunglasses so he couldn't see that her eyes were figuratively eating him up.

He cupped her elbow and led her to the passenger side of the SUV. "You look very nice."

Leah's smile grew wider. "Thank you."

She wasn't certain whether he was referring to her casual

outfit or her hair, which she hadn't blown out, allowing soft waves to frame her face. She had also applied a light cover of foundation, followed by a layer of loose face powder. The makeup concealed some of the discoloration, and with the sunglasses anyone glancing quickly at her wouldn't be able to discern the imperfections.

She did not have time to react when Derrick released her elbow, bent slightly, and scooped her up in his arms and settled her on the leather seat, as her heart pumped a runaway rhythm against her ribs. She pretended interest in fastening her seat belt when he rounded the vehicle and slipped behind the wheel.

"Your vehicle smells new."

He smiled at her. "It is. My old pickup had seen its best days." Reaching up under the visor, Derrick took down a pair of sunglasses and put them on the bridge of his nose. "I hope you brought your appetite, because Kay and Graeme claimed they're cooking enough for a small army."

"Who else have they invited?"

"Just us. I don't know if Kay told you that she OD'd on hosting gatherings at her home when she lived in Atlanta."

"She did," Leah confirmed. "When we had our first meeting we gave each other an overview of our lives just to break the ice. I hold the honor of being the oldest and the only one with children."

"How old are your sons?"

"They are soon to be twenty-nine."

He gave her a quick glance. "I hope you don't mind my asking, but how old were you when you became a mother?"

"I don't mind, Derrick. I gave birth a month before my nineteenth birthday."

"You got married at eighteen?"

"Yup. And my loving husband was thirty-five."

"He was twice your age."

Leah smiled as she stared through the windshield. "He

missed it by one year. There were times when I felt more like his daughter than his wife." Noises came from her stomach, and she put a hand over her midsection. "Sorry about that. My stomach has been talking to me all day."

"What is it saying?"

"Feed me."

Derrick chuckled. "Well, your belly will get its wish. Graeme and Kay live down this street."

A gnawing hunger had forced her out of bed at dawn. Throwing on a short silk robe over her nightgown, she'd quickly brushed her teeth, splashed water on her face, and then made her way down the staircase to the kitchen. She'd peered inside to make certain Derrick hadn't come in, although she knew the restaurant didn't open on Sundays. The last thing she wanted was for him to see her in her bedclothes or the abrasions on her shins.

Confident that she was alone, she'd opened the refrigerator and found a container of sliced fruit and some leftover chicken. After brewing a cup of coffee, she'd microwaved the chicken and sat down to enjoy her unconventional breakfast. Satiated, she'd cleaned up and returned to the apartment to go through the closet to select something to wear for a backyard cookout.

Dresses and skirts were rejected because they exposed too much of her legs. It had taken a while before she decided on a white man-tailored shirt, royal blue cotton slacks, white tennis shoes, and a serviceable yellow straw hat she was able to roll into a cylinder and carry in her tote.

The morning had passed quickly as she made the bed and ironed all the wrinkled garments hanging in the closet. Leah hadn't taken the time to neatly fold the clothes she'd packed before leaving Richmond. She'd wanted to conclude all the items on her to-do list before encountering Alan. She still wondered what her sons had said for him to leave the house once she'd been discharged from the hospital. Even now, she was uncertain what she'd say or do if she happened to come face-to-face with him. Leah wanted to hate Alan with every fiber of her being, yet she couldn't. She kept telling herself he wasn't worth it, that losing her was punishment enough.

Leah closed her eyes and made a silent vow that it was to be the last time she would give Alan Kent any energy. He wasn't worth her time dwelling on him. And if she was truly honest then she would say *it* wasn't worth her spit.

Derrick got out and came around to help Leah out. And if she had adult sons, where were they while their mother was being assaulted? The revelation that she was a mother wasn't as shocking as the gap between her and her husband's ages. What, he mused, would possess an eighteen-year-old girl to marry a man old enough to be her father? And she'd admitted that he'd treated her like a daughter.

He could not fathom his eighteen-year-old daughter coming to him with the news that she was in love with a much older man. Derrick would first question whether the man was a pedophile who preyed on young girls. His answer to Deandra would be "*hell no*"; then he would make certain her so-called intended left town with a promise of pains leading to death if he remained.

The front door opened, and Kayana waved to them. "Go on in, Leah. I have to get something from the cargo area." He had packed an ice chest with an assortment of aged steaks—ribeye, porterhouse, and filet mignon—and several bottles of rosé, red, and white wines. He gave Graeme the chest when he came out of the house to meet him. "I hope you can use some of the things in there."

The retired high school math teacher smiled at him. "You know you didn't need to bring anything."

Derrick patted his shoulder. "You haven't lived in the south long enough to know that folks never go to someone's house empty-handed."

"Give me time to learn, because Kayana has been teaching

me a lot of southern sayings like full as a tick, till the cows come home, fixin' to do, and sweating more than a sinner in church."

"We do have a lot of them."

"Come on in the kitchen, Derrick. I figure we'd grill outside and eat in the screened-in porch."

Derrick liked the layout of the updated two-story, two-bedroom cottage. The first time he'd come to Graeme's house he'd been greeted excitedly by a sand-colored poodle puppy. "Where's Barley?"

Graeme set the chest on the kitchen floor. "He's probably outside with the ladies."

He studied his brother-in-law, who appeared to have put on some weight. His face was fuller, and the puffiness and dark circles under his large gray eyes he'd had before he'd married his sister were no longer evident. Although Graeme was five years older, he claimed less gray hair than Derrick.

"You look contented, Brother Ogden."

Lines fanned out around Graeme's eyes when he smiled and patted his belly over a faded Harvard sweatshirt. "I have your sister to thank for that, Brother Johnson. She is truly incredible. There are times when I'm forced to pinch myself to make certain I'm not hallucinating."

Derrick smiled. "It sounds as if you're living the dream."

"That I am." He hunkered down and opened the chest. "What the heck did you bring?"

"I gave you some steaks that have been aged for about thirty days and I know I won't sell in the next month or two. I shrink-wrapped them this morning. The only seasoning you'll need is salt and pepper before you put them on the grill."

"Kayana marinated some chicken and fish, but I suppose they can wait for another day, because these steaks have just become a priority. Thanks, Derrick."

"No problem."

"Kayana introduced Leah as her friend," Graeme said in a low voice, "but I remember her coming to the island last year as a vacationer. Is she now a local?"

"She is for now." Derrick was certain Kayana would fill her husband in on Leah's status, but doubted whether she would disclose anything else about her friend. Besides, she'd breached Leah's confidentiality when he coerced her to tell him how she'd sustained her injuries.

"Are you drinking wine, beer, or something a little stronger?" Graeme asked.

"I'm fine with beer. Do you need my help with anything?"

"No. I'm good here."

"I'm going outside see if Kayana needs something." Derrick had said Kayana when he meant Leah. He was trying to understand why her adult sons hadn't protected her from their father's fury. There was only one way to find out, and that was to get her to trust him enough to confide in him as she had in his sister.

The day was perfect for grilling outdoors. The early-spring afternoon temperatures peaked in the low-seventies with brilliant sunshine and a hint of a breeze. Graeme and Derrick took turns manning the grill while Leah and Kayana set the table in the screened-in porch with four place settings. Graeme had suggested eating indoors because the landscapers had disturbed a wasp's nest, and there were still some lingering around.

Leah hung on to every word as Kayana told her about her honeymoon in the United Arab Emirates. She claimed to have been overwhelmed by the wealth and the skyscrapers that appeared to rise from the desert floor and disappear into the clouds. She revealed that Graeme had left their Abu Dhabi hotel room early one morning and returned hours later with a surprise wedding gift of thirteen-millimeter South Seas drop pearl earrings capped in yellow diamonds. She'd thanked her new husband in the most intimate way possible, and after ordering room service they spent the entire day in their suite.

Hours later Leah reclined on a chaise and closed her eyes as her fingertips made tiny circles in the poodle's fur as he lay beside her. Barley had taken an instant liking to her, whining and going up on his hind legs for her to pick him up. She waited until she'd eaten much too much to oblige him.

"Are you all right, Leah?"

She opened her eyes and smiled at Derrick. Something about his face had nagged at her the first time Kayana had introduced her to him what now seemed so many months ago, but now that she'd had close contact with him it finally hit her. His dark complexion and dimpled smile called to mind the actor and former male model Richard Roundtree.

"I'm full as a tick." She'd eaten perfectly grilled medium-well ribeye, Kayana's incredibly delicious mac and cheese, deviled eggs, and grilled corn in the husks. Derrick and Graeme shared a smile with her statement.

"You're not the only one who ate too much," Kayana said, as she rested her head on her husband's shoulder.

Leah averted her eyes when she saw Graeme press his mouth to Kayana's hair. The gesture was so tender and intimate that she felt like a spy. It was obvious that not only were they in love, but they also loved each other, and what they'd shared during their brief marriage was something that had been missing in hers of long duration: passion.

She didn't want to dwell on what she'd been missing; otherwise she would drown in a maelstrom of self-pity from which she would never emerge. Her intent was to get out of her current situation and start over. Perhaps she would travel abroad during school holidays and spend her summers on Coates Island. Leah had even thought about buying property on the island to use as a retreat whenever she wanted to get away from Richmond. Barley moved, stretching out front paws before settling back into a more comfortable position against Leah's thigh.

Graeme pressed another kiss on Kayana's hair. "I've asked Kayana to teach me how to make her grandmother's mac and cheese, but she said it would take too long for me to get it right."

"Tell him, Derrick, how long it took for Grandma Cassie to give me her approval that I'd mastered her mac and cheese."

"Probably years. Our mother and grandmother were hard taskmasters. I really didn't want to learn how to cook, but I wasn't given a choice. Me, Kay, and Jocelyn were mandated to work in the Café's kitchen during our school recesses and holidays. I used to complain that I didn't want to learn to cook because I wanted to be a football player. My father would advocate for me, but there was no way he could stand up against two strong women tag-teaming him while claiming they had sacrificed everything to keep the doors open, so the next generation had better step up and learn the business."

"Leah, did you know that my brainiac brother nearly made it all the way to the NFL?" Kayana asked her.

She met Derrick's eyes, smiling. "No, I didn't." That explained his obsession with working out every day. Once a jock, always a jock.

"He attended the University of Alabama on full academic and athletic scholarships. He was an outstanding running back, and scouts from the NFL came to every game to watch him."

"What happened, Derrick?" Leah asked him.

"I tore my ACL in my senior year."

"Were you distraught that you didn't go pro?"

"Initially I was, but when I look back and see the number of players with brain injuries, I realize it was the best thing that happened to me."

"So, you went from football to running the Café."

"He took a detour and worked on Wall Street for years before finally finding his way home," Kayana interjected.

Derrick glared at his sister. "Leah doesn't want to know about that, Kay."

"But I do," Leah said quickly. She wanted to know everything she could about the man who enthralled her as no other in her life had. Even when she'd met Alan he hadn't had that effect on her.

"I'll tell you later." There was a finality to his promise.

The focus shifted to Leah when Graeme asked what she taught. "I was an English literature teacher for years before I was appointed as headmistress at an all-girls prep school."

"How do you compare teaching at a public school to running a private school?" he asked.

"I never taught at a public school. My first and only tenure has been at Richmond, Virginia's Calhoun Preparatory Academy for Girls. What about yourself, Graeme? Did you teach at a private school?"

"No, because I'd attended a Boston private school and saw how teachers gave kids grades they didn't deserve because their parents donated big bucks to keep them enrolled."

"How long did you teach?" she asked Kayana's husband.

"Twenty years. Initially I planned to put in thirty before retiring, but there were other things I wanted to do before I got too old."

Leah also wanted to do other things before she retired, but she hadn't created her Plan B. "I have at least another fifteen or sixteen years before I can consider retiring."

"Have you planned what you want to do once you retire?" Derrick asked her.

"Read, travel, and read some more."

Throwing back his head, Derrick laughed. "Now I know why you and my sister are besties."

"Don't knock reading, brother love," Kayana said, smiling. "If it hadn't been for books, Leah and I would've never become friends and book club buddies."

"What's the allure of women bonding over books?" Derrick questioned.

"It's a sisterhood thing," Leah explained.

"Yes, it is," Kayana confirmed. "Are you aware that black women read more than any other demographic group?"

Graeme gave his wife a skeptical glance. "You're kidding, aren't you?"

"No, she's not," Leah said. "There are hundreds of black book clubs all over the country that get together on average of once a month to discuss books. Some meet in libraries, restaurants, or alternate members' homes. Dudes bond over sports while we tend to bond over the printed word."

"Dudes do read," Derrick said defensively.

"Yes, they do," Kayana confirmed, "especially the *Sports Illustrated* swimsuit issue."

"That's not right."

"That's sexist."

Graeme and Derrick protested at the same time as Leah leaned forward to fist bump Kayana. The conversation shifted from books and education to national politics. Fortunately, everyone agreed when the name of a candidate was mentioned.

Leah could not help but compare this gathering to the ones she'd had whenever she and Alan met with other couples. The conversations were usually dominated by the men, while their significant others tended to nod in agreement like bobblehead dolls. She realized most were too intimidated or sought to downplay their intelligence to stay in their place.

She'd wanted to scream, shake them, and tell them there wasn't a need to be in lockstep with their husbands because they feared being traded in for a newer, more submissive model. The one time she'd disagreed with one of Alan's colleagues, all conversation ceased as the throbbing vein in her husband's forehead indicated his rage and disapproval. And once they returned to Kent House, all hell broke loose when he reprimanded her for challenging the judge. It was Leah's turn to lose her temper when she reminded him that she wasn't going to remain silent when someone, anyone, spouted bigoted rhetoric. And it was the first time that Alan called her white trash and said that the instant he realized she'd come from a trailer park he should've run in the opposite direction; her acerbic comeback was he hadn't run because he craved her trailer park pussy like a junkie craved crack. He'd stalked out of the house and stayed away for almost a week, and she knew he'd gone to the Bramble House to hook up with one of his whores.

"Now I know why you and my sister are friends."

Leah wanted to tell Derrick Kayana was her only friend, and other than her brother's wife, she was the closest she could get to claiming a sister.

Kayana blew her brother an air kiss. "It's because great minds think alike."

Leah spent the next two hours on the porch with her new friends ignoring the slight ache in her side. She hadn't taken a pill in twenty-four hours, and that meant her body was on the mend. Like quicksilver, the weather changed, the skies darkening and the wind increasing in velocity. It was spring and the season for above-average rainfall and tornados. Leah was more than ready to leave when Derrick suggested it was time to take her back to her apartment.

She gave Barley a belly rub, and then pressed her cheek to Kayana's and then Graeme's, thanking her hosts for their generous hospitality. Derrick took her hand, leading her to his vehicle. The short drive back to the Café was completed in silence, each lost in their private thoughts.

Derrick assisted her down after parking in the lot behind the restaurant. "I'm going to be in the kitchen for a while to get a jump on tomorrow's menu. Can I fix you something for a midnight snack?"

"No, thank you. I don't want to see another crumb of food for the rest of the day."

Derrick winked at her. "Just asking."

"I'll see you tomorrow." She waited for him to open the door and disarm the alarm, and then she climbed the staircase and unlocked the door to her apartment. She now thought of the charming space as her home, even if it was only temporary. Leah had never regarded Kent House as her home despite living there for more than half her life.

She changed out of her clothes and into a tank top and a pair of shorts. By the time she'd entered the reading room and turned on a floor lamp and tuned the audio component to a station featuring classical music, it had begun raining. The sounds of rhythmic tapping of rain against the windows and the Chopin piano concerto created a relaxing backdrop when she opened *The Alienist* to pick up where she'd left off. The only positive thing that had come from her relationship with Adele Kent was she'd introduced Leah to classical music. Before she married Alan's father, Adele had trained for a career as a classical pianist. She'd won several state competitions yet gave up her dream to become wife, mother, and social doyenne for the commonwealth's capital city.

After Leah fed and put her sons in their cribs for an afternoon nap, Adele would summon her to the solarium for tea, when she'd wanted to lie down and rest after breastfeeding two infants. Leah had been warned by her doctor that it wouldn't be easy breastfeeding twins, that she had to increase her caloric intake and take naps whenever she could. She had come to enjoy the music more than the tasteless cucumber sandwiches and the older woman's incessant chatter about her plans for a dinner party or fund-raiser. Once Adele moved out of the house and into the nursing facility, Leah no longer had high tea. But habits were hard to break; she'd hang out in the solarium to read and listen to music.

In the three weeks since Leah had come to Coates Island she had baked mini regular, buttery, and cheese biscuits, doughnuts, scones, and quick breads with a variety of butters and jams for Kayana and Derrick to sample and approve.

All her bruises had faded, and she felt comfortable going into the dining room when diners were present. She couldn't believe how quickly she'd become acclimated to getting up before dawn to go down to the kitchen to bake before Derrick or Kayana arrived. And her heart rate no longer kicked into a higher rate whenever she and Derrick shared the same space.

She finally finished *The Alienist*. It had taken days before she was able to rid her head of the atmospheric pager-turner with it's realistic descriptions of gruesome murders. She also had filled pages of her steno pad with notations she'd jotted down after finishing each chapter. After the first two nights, she chided herself for reading the book before retiring for bed because she tended to dream about the spine-chilling scenes.

Leah's bond with Kayana grew even stronger when it was her turn to prepare brunch. It allowed them more time and private moments together. "I've begun researching firms handling high-profile divorce cases," she confided to her friend.

Kayana wiped her hands on a towel. "Do you think they'll refuse to represent you once you tell them you're suing Judge Alan Kent for divorce?"

"I'll find out once I contact them. There has to be at least one firm that will not allow themselves to be intimidated. And I'm willing to spend every penny I have to rid myself of the bastard."

Kayana removed her bandana and bibbed apron. "Don't forget that you have a secret weapon."

Leah nodded. "You're right. I have the doctor's report, my sons if they're called to testify, and I also took pictures of my body with my cell phone. If you don't mind, I'd like to upload them to you as backup in case I lose my phone."

"Send them. I'll make certain Graeme doesn't get to see them or he may decide he likes redheads better than brunettes."

"Don't play yourself, Kay. Graeme is so in love with you that a woman could walk around naked in front of him and he wouldn't even glance her way."

Kayana scrunched up her nose. "I kinda like him, too."

"Kinda, Kayana? You're crazy about the man."

"Truth be known, I adore him, Leah. After I divorced James I was so turned off on men that I got pissed if one even smiled at me. But once I got to know Graeme I realized I wasn't being fair to him, because I tended to paint all men with the same broad brush. I want you to remember that once you divorce Alan. If you find someone willing to love and make you happy, then go for it."

Leah laughed. "I'm not even divorced and meanwhile you have me hooking up with someone else."

"I'm not saying you should remarry right away. Give yourself some time to reflect on what you want and need before you decide whether you want to make the relationship permanent."

Leah chewed her lip. "How long did it take you from the time you started dating Graeme to know you wanted to marry him?"

"It didn't take that long. We had our first date in June, and we married Christmas Eve."

"That's fast. In other words, you dated for about six months."

Kayana sighed. "I'll be fifty in three years, Graeme is going to turn fifty-three in a few days, and because we don't have children we didn't want a long engagement like younger couples."

"I can understand that." Leah thought about her own situation. She wasn't responsible for anyone but herself.

Kayana unbuttoned and took off the chef's jacket. "I've already locked the front door. I'm going to go to Shelby to pick up a birthday gift for Graeme. It's not easy shopping for a man who has everything he needs."

"Has he dropped any hints?"

"No."

"Didn't you say he's an aspiring author?" Leah asked.

"Yes."

"Why don't you buy him a designer pen and have his name engraved on it. He can use it to autograph books once he's published."

"You're a genius, Leah!"

"No, I'm not." And she wasn't. She had given Alan a similar gift for Christmas during a phase when they were able to be civil to each other.

Kayana hugged her. "Thanks so much. Once Derrick gets here, please let him know I had to leave to go shopping."

"Will do."

Leah waited until the door closed behind Kayana to take the broom out of the utility closet. She'd volunteered to help clean up after the restaurant closed for the day. Derrick and Kayana had set up no more than six tables for use during the off-season to minimize cleanup. Leah removed the tablecloths, left them in a pile in a corner, and wiped down the tabletops. She knew if Adele saw her cleaning off tables, sweeping and mopping floors, she would sternly remind Leah that she paid folks to do housekeeping. She heard Derrick come in as she pushed the long-handled broom over the floor.

"Where's Kay?"

She glanced at him over her shoulder. "She had to leave because she needed to do some shopping."

"How are you today?"

Leah smiled. "I'm good."

"When you finish with that I'd like you to come into the kitchen. I want to show you something."

"Okay, boss."

A frown flitted over his handsome features. "Please don't call me that."

Leah heard the censure in his voice, wondering who or what had set him off, because normally he was very cheerful whenever he came in early in the morning or later in the afternoon. "Sorry about that."

"It's okay."

Was it really, Derrick, she thought, as she continued sweeping. She'd returned to the kitchen to see what Derrick wanted to show her when the cell phone she'd left on a shelf rang. "Please let me take this call."

He nodded. "No problem."

Picking up the phone, she recognized the caller's name. It was Calhoun Academy's administrative assistant. "Hi, Erin."

"Leah, I'm calling you on my cell because I don't want to use the school's phone, because you know all the calls are recorded."

Her heart stopped and then started up again as Leah sank down to one of the stools at the preparation table. "What's up?"

"I just wanted to warn you that you're going to be fired."

"Fired!" She hadn't realized she'd shouted the word until Derrick turned to stare at her.

"There was an emergency board meeting last night, and there was a unanimous vote to let you go because you'd abandoned your position without authorization. The officers decided they couldn't afford to leave your position vacant, so they asked Merrill Livingston to take your place until she's officially appointed in the fall."

"But they can't fire me, Erin. They know I'm on medical leave."

"I know that, but someone on the board uncovered an arcane clause in the school's charter that states anyone on medical leave would have to submit medical verification every thirty days. They sent you a certified letter, return receipt, to your home two weeks ago asking that your doctor mail or fax a statement verifying your return date. They gave you five days to send in the documentation or you would be terminated. I checked your personnel file and you have enough accrued sick and vacation time for the next four months, which means they'll continue to direct deposit your salary, but it's your position that was in jeopardy."

Leah ran a hand over her face. "I left Richmond after I was discharged from the hospital to stay with friends while I recuperate."

"Didn't your husband tell you about the letter?"

She went completely still. "Why are you asking about him?"

"He signed that he'd received the letter."

Leah knew instinctively that Alan had read the letter and failed to call or email her about its contents. "I'm going to contact someone on the board asking them to delay sending out the termination letter until I get in touch with my doctor."

"It's too late, Leah. A messenger is scheduled to deliver it to your home tomorrow morning. Maybe when you come back to Richmond you can request to meet with the board and ask them to reinstate you."

She wanted to tell Erin she hadn't planned to return to Richmond until the third week in August. Her shoulders slumped in defeat as a feeling of helplessness washed over her. "Thanks, Erin, for the heads-up. And you don't have to worry about our conversation. My lips are sealed."

"Thanks, Leah. You know I really need my job."

Leah ended the call, struggling not to cry. She wanted to tell Erin she also needed her job, but for entirely different reasons. She needed to show employment when she went to the bank for a mortgage. Her head popped up, and she saw Derrick with an incredulous look on his face. It was obvious he'd overheard her conversation.

"I just lost my job." The tears filling her eyes overflowed, and she clapped a hand over her mouth to stifle the sobs building up in the back of her throat.

Chapter 9

Derrick approached Leah and eased her off the stool, wondering how many more hits she would have to deal with before she would be able to right the wrongs. First she had to recover from her husband's vicious attack and now it appeared as if she'd lost her job.

Wrapping his arms around her waist, he pulled her close. "It's going to be all right."

"No, it's not," she mumbled. "It's getting worse. I just lost my job, and I know for certain that my husband had something to do with it."

When Leah had first come to the island wearing a pair of oversize sunglasses covering the upper part of her face, Derrick had recognized an inner strength in her that communicated she was a fighter. That had been apparent when he offered to pay her for baking, and she'd threatened to pack up and leave.

"How can you be so certain?"

"He was responsible for me getting my first position as a teacher at the prep school after I'd graduated college. It was a little intimidating at eighteen to teach girls who were only a few years younger than myself. But once I discovered I was pregnant I resigned to become a stay-at-home mother and go back to college to earn a graduate degree. Then I reapplied years later and was rehired. I taught there for twelve years before the school board approved me to become head-mistress. None of that would've happened without Alan's influence."

"Are you saying he got you hired *and* fired?"

"Yes."

Derrick listened intently as Leah revealed the school's charter's arcane rule and her husband's receipt of the certified letter. "He's really that vindictive?"

"Most people don't know the man to whom I've been married for thirty years. Yes, he can be charming, generous almost to a fault for causes he believes in, but behind closed doors when he doesn't get what he wants he turns into a monster."

"What about your sons?"

"Alan could win Father of the Year every year. He adores his sons and they'd always worshipped him. Until now," she added.

"What changed?"

"I told you I fell down the stairs. But the truth is my husband pushed me down the staircase. We'd had a disagreement and he became so enraged that he beat me. We'd always had arguments, but that was the first time he'd laid a hand on me. When I woke in the hospital more than a week later I discovered Alan had called our sons to tell them I'd had an accident. When I told them what he'd done to me, they were ready to take him apart, but I begged them not to say or do anything to him because I didn't want them involved in something I planned to remedy on my own."

"Do they know you're planning to divorce their father?"

"Yes. And they are completely supportive."

Derrick released her waist and cradled her face. His heart

turned over when he saw the flood of tears in the bright blue eyes. Seeing a woman cry was his Achilles heel. He'd tried to put on a brave face during Andrea's illness but failed whenever he saw her cry. Leah wasn't his late wife, but somehow he was still able to feel her pain.

He did not want to believe that she'd lived more than half her life with a cruel, selfish man who manipulated not only her but also her career. However, the straw that broke the proverbial camel's back was his physical attack. And he wondered how she'd been able to successfully conceal her husband's cruelty from their sons.

"Is there anything else he can do to you?"

"I don't think so. I discovered Alan canceled all his credit cards on which I'm authorized to sign after I left Richmond. He probably thought I would max them out to get back at him. But it appears after being married to me for so many years he never took the time to know who I am."

"Narcissists never do, because it's always all about them."

She managed a tight smile. "I never thought of him as a narcissist, but a spoiled, indulgent man who's used his family's name and money to get whatever he wanted."

"And he wanted you." Derrick's question was a statement.

"I suppose he did."

Derrick dropped his hands as he stared over Leah's head. He did not want to believe she could be that naïve. It was obvious Alan Kent had pursued her because he wasn't able to accept rejection. "You suppose, Leah? Did you not marry the man and give him children?"

"Yes, but . . ."

"But what?"

"I wasn't his first choice as a wife."

Leah's revelation that Alan had no intention of marrying her spoke volumes, and it was obvious he'd spent years filled with resentment because he was in love with another woman. "He married you because you were pregnant."

Leah's spiked eyelids fluttered. "It was the only reason he married me, and there was never a time during our marriage that he let me forget that."

"Something is not adding up, Leah. You claim he loved his sons, yet he resented marrying you because of them."

"He loved his sons because they are Kents, while I was just someone that carried them to term so he could boast that he was responsible for fathering another generation of Kent men."

"That sounds crazy," Derrick spat out.

"It may sound crazy to people like you or me, but for a family with roots that go back to when the colonies were still under British rule, it means a lot to them. It's all about family name and honor. Kent men served with distinction in every war in this country beginning with the Seven Years War. The only exception was the Civil War, when they paid others to serve for them. And because no Kent man was an officer in the Confederate Army, their lands weren't confiscated. The mention of the Kent name will open doors closed to most others that aren't in their social circle. He comes from a long line of politicians, lawyers, and judges. He's a judge, as were his father and grandfather."

"Are you saying you stayed in a toxic marriage because of the privilege of being a judge's wife?"

Leah closed her eyes as she struggled not to lose her temper. Did Derrick actually believe she hadn't divorced Alan before now because she didn't want to give up her status as the wife of Judge Alan Kent?

"You know nothing about my marriage, so I resent your insinuation."

"You're right about that, Leah. I don't know anything about your marriage except what you've told me."

There were so many things she wanted to tell Derrick about her past, but she feared he would think of her as a social-climbing wanna-be who'd set her sights on a much older man and had deliberately gotten pregnant to trap him into a loveless union.

"I've told you enough."

"Does my sister know?"

"Yes. I've told Kayana everything, because I trust her, Derrick."

"Do you actually believe I would repeat what you've told me to other people?"

"I don't know."

He threw up a hand. "You're living on my property and you don't trust me?"

Leah's temper exploded. "What the hell do you want from me!"

"I want you to trust me, because I'll need to know how to react if your crazy-ass husband decides he wants to come here and start trouble. This is Coates Island and not Richmond, and it's here where my family's roots go back to when North Carolina was still a colony under the British crown. We may not hold the same political sway as the Kents, but let me warn you that if Alan Kent comes here making trouble, then he's going to get his ass handed to him."

Panic replaced her anger. "I don't want you involved in this."

"Too late, Leah. I am involved because you live here."

"What if I leave?"

"And just where are you moving to? The B and B may have a few vacancies, and there's always the boardinghouse."

Leah did not want to leave the space that had become her sanctuary, where once she closed the door she was able to relax and indulge in whatever she wanted without someone telling her what she could and could not do. Kent House had become a prison without bars where Adele sought to monitor and control everything she did from the time she woke until she retired for bed.

"I don't want to move," she admitted after a pregnant pause. She'd called the agent handling the island's vacation properties to inform her that she did not intend to rent the bungalow for the coming season once Kayana offered her the use of the Café's second story apartment.

A hint of a smile lifted the corners of Derrick's mouth. "And I don't want you to. You have a home here for as long as you want." He paused. "I don't know what it is, but a sixth sense is telling me your husband is not done with trying to make your life a living hell. Do your sons know that you're here?"

"Yes. I sent them a text letting them know where I am."

"Do you think they'll give that information to their father?"

"No," Leah said emphatically. "I told them I was going into an unofficial witness protection program and they weren't to tell anyone where to find me."

"What about your parents?"

"All they know is that I'm recuperating on the island where I vacationed last year. They never liked Alan, and if my father found out that he'd put his hands on me he would kill him."

"What he needs is a good old-fashioned ass whooping, so he'll know how it feels to hit a woman."

"There are other ways to best Alan. I've been compiling a list of firms I plan to call and ask if they will represent me. I told Kayana I didn't want alimony or a settlement, but that's changed now that I'm unemployed. I'm going to ask for a settlement with enough money to equal my salary for the next sixteen years."

"Do you think he'll agree to it?" Derrick asked.

"He'll have to, or I *will* subpoena the hospital to release my medical records when I told the doctor how I'd sustained my injuries. I've also photographed my body and sent the pictures to Kayana for safekeeping in case I lose my phone. Then there are my sons, who have agreed to testify to what I've told them in confidence."

Derrick smiled, bringing her eyes to linger on his straight white teeth. "It looks as if you've covered all of your bases."

"I did learn a little something about the law with a husband and two sons as lawyers."

"That sounds like an overload of jurisprudence."

Leah laughed for the first time since answering Erin's call. "That's all I heard whenever Caleb and Aron came home on school break. I have to admit the best thing to have come from my relationship with Alan are my sons."

"You're lucky, Leah, because they could've turned out like him."

"I'm more than lucky. I'm blessed. You said you wanted to show me something," she said, deftly steering the conversation away from her personal dilemma.

"Yes." Derrick reached for her hand. "Come with me."

She followed him to a corner in the kitchen and a workstation with a desktop, printer, landline phone, and fax machine. A trio of two-drawer file cabinets lined one wall. He picked up a sheet of legal paper and handed it to her.

"Let me know what you think."

It was a mockup of the menu with an effective date beginning the Memorial Day weekend. It was only during the summer months the Seaside Café offered their dinner guests sit-down service between the hours of five and eight p.m. She perused the items for starters, appetizers, salads, sides, entrées, and beverages. And then Leah saw it. Derrick had added desserts. She'd made an assortment of sample mini-cakes, breads, and cookies for him and Kayana, and they'd selected what they predicted would become customer favorites.

She clasped her hands in a prayerful gesture. "Thank you."

"No, thank *you*, Leah. I don't know if you realize it, but you missed your calling. You are a very gifted baker."

"I have my mother and grandmother to thank for that." Derrick angled his head as he smiled at her. It was a motion she'd come to recognize whenever he appeared to be thinking about something.

"I know we talked about this before, and you went off on

me. But now that you've joined the ranks of the unemployed, I'd like to offer you the position as baker for the Café for the summer season."

Leah wanted to tell him that although she'd lost her position at the school she wasn't destitute. She would be paid her accrued sick and vacation time. And she also wasn't willing to go down without a fight. She intended to challenge the school to convince them to reinstate her. When she'd informed the board members she was taking medical leave no one had informed her of the arcane rule about updating her leave every thirty days. She also needed to be employed when she went to secure a mortgage for property.

Leah managed a small, tentative smile. "I don't want to fight with you about money because I think of it as gauche, but I'm willing accept the mandated minimum wage for an hourly worker."

Attractive lines fanned out around Derrick's large near-black eyes when he smiled at her. "Now, that wasn't so difficult was it?"

"No."

He stared at the wall calendar attached to a corkboard. "We have a little more than ten weeks before the summer season starts; meanwhile I'm going to put you on the payroll because you've been helping out after hours. And once you begin baking full-time I'll give you a raise."

"Okay." Leah didn't want to debate with Derrick because she'd argued enough with Alan to last her several lifetimes.

"I just noticed that this coming Sunday is Easter Sunday. I'm going to invite Kayana and Graeme over to the house for dinner. Would you mind hosting it with me?"

Her smile was dazzling. Leah had forgotten that Easter came earlier than in past years. "I'd love to."

Derrick took a step, lowered his head, and kissed her cheek. "Thank you."

He'd kissed her cheek when it was her mouth Leah wanted

him to kiss. It had been much too long since she'd experienced even a modicum of tenderness with a man and even longer since she'd moved out the bedroom she shared with a man for eighteen years and into one at the opposite wing of the house. She didn't know or care if Adele knew she wasn't sharing her son's bed once Aron and Caleb moved to New York to attend college; it had become her first act of defiance to physically and psychologically divorce Alan, unaware that ten years later she would seek to make it legal.

"Hold on, let me call Kay to see if she and Graeme will be available." He tapped the speaker button, and then dialed Kayana's number. "Hey, sis," he said when Kayana's voice came through the speaker. "I'm calling to find out if you and Graeme have plans for Easter Sunday."

"Not really. We plan to—"

"Keep it clean, Kay," he said, cutting her off. "Leah's here and I have you on speaker."

"Leah and I have discussed things I know would make you blush, Derrick. Tell him, Lee."

"You've got that right!" Leah confirmed. She recalled one of their book club sessions when the topic of vibrators came up and she had admitted to Cherie and Kayana that she used them. After all, it had been ten years since she'd shared a bed with her husband, and even in her late forties her libido was still strong.

"What I was going to say before you got virtuous on me, brother, is that Sunday is Graeme's birthday and I've decided to make a special dinner for him."

"I'm willing to make Easter dinner, and I'd like you and hubby to come."

"What's on the menu?" Kayana asked Derrick.

"Rack of lamb with an herb crust."

"We're coming! Leah, my brother makes the most delicious lamb I've ever eaten. Once you eat his you'll never order it anywhere else. Derrick, do you want me to bring anything?"

"Mac and cheese," Leah said loudly before Derrick could answer his sister.

"I'll make mac and cheese if you make your mini Bundt sour cream pound cakes. You know how I am when it comes to dessert. They are truly my weakness."

Leah remembered Kayana telling her that she made certain to limit her intake of anything made with sugar or she would overindulge. When she'd baked samples for Kayana and Derrick, she'd made miniature batches of everything.

Derrick rested a hand at the small of her back, and Leah went still before relaxing and enjoying the light touch. "Mini it is," she said breathlessly.

"Maybe I should let you ladies decide on the menu."

Kayana's soft laugh came through the speaker. "I'm game if Leah is."

Derrick dropped his hand. "I'm out. Kay, you can talk to Leah."

She sat at the desk, lifted the receiver off the handset, and disengaged the speaker feature. "Where are you?"

"I'm at a shop looking at pens."

"Call me back on my cell when you finish shopping."

"Thanks. Later, Leah."

"Later."

Leah ended the call and saw Derrick staring at her. "What?"

"That was quick."

"She's busy, so she'll call me back later. Is your lamb as delicious as Kayana says it is?"

Leah remembered the first time Alan took her to the Bramble House, where he'd ordered lamb chops. She had to admit as a teenager she'd been slightly overwhelmed and impressed with the dapper, erudite lawyer who had made it known he was very interested in her, that he had been willing to stop seeing his girlfriend to date her. Now in hindsight Leah realized that should've been their first and last date, yet when he'd used his influence to secure a position for her at the prestigious Calhoun Academy she'd agreed to go out with him for a celebratory dinner. It would become a night to remember and would dramatically change her life.

Derrick crossed muscular arms over his chest. "That's something you'll have to let me know."

"Do you have to order the lamb?"

"No. I have a few racks in the freezer."

"Where do you buy your meat?" Leah asked him.

"I have a butcher on the mainland that knows exactly what I want. My grandmother ordered meat from his uncle years ago, and she was so impressed with the quality of their products that they've become our go-to butcher. During the summer the owner will call once a week to ask what we need because we serve three meals a day. I'll place the orders and he will dress the meat, package and date it, and have it ready when I come to pick it up. When I get racks of ribs I don't have to waste time removing the membrane because he'll do that for me."

"Why do you remove it at all?"

"If I cook the ribs on a grill or smoker with the membrane, it will prevent the ribs from fully absorbing the flavor, and they'll also have a tougher texture."

"How often do you order lamb?"

"It depends. I usually try to have several racks on hand during the spring because that's when it's most popular."

"Do you grill or smoke them?"

"I prefer to grill them if they're separated into chops."

Leah rarely came down to the dining room between the hours of ten and two, preferring instead to remain in the apartment reading, listening to music, or watching television. And now with the increase in daytime temperatures she'd put on a hat to protect her face from the rays of the sun. The heat from the sun on her exposed arms and legs was the balm she needed to feel revived. She had come to enjoy sitting on the sand and watching seagulls fighting over crabs and other sea life washed up on the beach with the incoming surf. It had become her time to clear her mind while her body continued to heal. All the bruises had faded while there were occasional twinges of discomfort in her ribs, which had taken the full impact of the fall.

"Although I like lamb, I rarely eat it," Leah admitted.

"Have you ever eaten shawarma?" Derrick asked her.

Her expression mirrored confusion. "I don't think so."

"Shawarma is a Middle Eastern dish made up of meat cut into thin slices and stacked in a cone-like shape and slow roasted on a vertical rotisserie or spit. When I lived in New York there were food trucks that offered shawarma, and you knew which was the most popular by the number of people on the sidewalk waiting to place their order."

"I've seen televised travel shows where the hosts eat shawarma. Is lamb always used for the dish?"

"Originally it was made with lamb or mutton, but today's shawarma ingredients can be lamb, chicken, beef, or turkey. Personally, I prefer one made solely with lamb."

"Would you consider making it for the Café?"

Derrick chuckled. "Surely you jest."

Leah detected a hint of censure in his tone. "No, I'm not joking," she snapped.

Derrick sobered quickly with her comeback. "Let me impress on you that the Café is a two-person operation, and during our busy season Kay gets up at dawn and she's in the kitchen by five to prepare a buffet breakfast when we open the doors at seven. We close at ten and reopen from noon to two for a buffet lunch. Then it is a sit-down dinner from five to eight, and most times I don't get out of the kitchen until ten or eleven at night. We do this six days a week. The only break we get is Sundays when we offer brunch ten to one. Grilling and smoking meats frees up time where Kay and I can concentrate on making sides."

"Have you thought about hiring another cook?"

"I did last summer when I brought in a retired short-order

cook for the dinner hours. I'm not certain whether he'll be available this year, because he was talking about moving to Georgia to help a cousin set up a roadside barbecue joint."

Leah knew what she was going to propose would either shock or anger Derrick. Even after interacting with each other for two months she still was unable to gauge his moods. Most times she kept her distance, which also allowed her feelings of lust to lessen. Other than his kissing her cheek or resting his hand at the small of her back, Derrick hadn't touched her in what she thought of as a gesture of affection. She was his sister's friend, and he related to her as a friend.

"My plans have changed now that I've been fired, and that means I have to wait for the school board to reconvene for the new school term before I can request a hearing. And that means I'll be here through Labor Day. I'm a quick study, so I wouldn't mind standing in as your sous chef."

Derrick struggled to understand his sister's friend. It was obvious she'd lived a privileged lifestyle as evidenced by the jewelry she'd worn last summer, and then there were her clothes. The garments she wore were what he considered chic. Blouses, slacks, sweaters, and jackets that were favored by a particular class of women. When she'd come down to the kitchen in a man-tailored shirt, jeans, and white deck shoes, her red hair held off her face with a navy and white headband, and with her bare freckled face, she reminded him of the Ralph Lauren models on the pages of glossy fashion magazines.

He had hesitated to ask Kayana about Leah, because he didn't want his sister to misconstrue his intent. He was attracted to her in a way a man was to a woman, yet he did not want to act on it. After all, she was still a married woman. And Derrick had an unwritten rule never to date married, engaged, or women casually dating other men. He'd witnessed altercations between couples that never ended well and were branded into his memory.

There was something about Leah Kent that was innocent

and sensual at the same time. Although slimmer than most women to whom he'd found himself attracted, she wasn't what he thought of as skinny. He liked that she didn't attempt to conceal her freckles with makeup, which afforded her a fresh-faced look. However, it was her eyes that he'd found mesmerizing. They were a startling light blue and would sometimes appear green whenever her moods changed. And although he didn't have what he thought of as a particular type when it came to race and ethnicity, he did briefly date one white girl in college. They went out several times but stopped short of sleeping together. Both decided it was better to remain friends than become lovers.

He had also come to resent Kayana's insistence that he begin dating again because it wasn't good for him to spend so much time alone now that his daughter had decided not to spend her senior year at home with him on Coates Island. Derrick knew she was right; however, it wouldn't be easy for him to have a relationship with a woman when he had to concentrate on making certain the Café remained viable. His hours were too erratic to commit to social events or making and keeping a date.

"While I will admit that you are an amazing baker, that doesn't mean you'll necessarily make a good cook. Kayana is a genius when it comes to duplicating my grandmother's mac and cheese and our mother's creole chicken with buttermilk waffles, yet it took her years to perfect those recipes. Allowing you to assist me during the summer isn't long enough to teach you what you'll need to know when it comes to certain dishes. All chicken, whether grilled, smoked, or fried, is brined for a minimum of twenty-four hours."

Leah rested both hands at her waist. "Do you really think I don't know what brining is, Derrick? Regardless of what you think of me, I did not grow up in a mansion with servants and someone to chauffer me to and from school. I lived in a trailer park the first nine years of my life, where I shared a bed with my grandmother. Then we moved to a rental apartment that was so small that my father had to put up partitions for makeshift bedrooms.

"My great-grandparents were sharecroppers, and there was a time when both grandparents worked in cotton mills, and I knew the only way to improve my lot in life was through education. I studied my ass off every chance I got, accelerated twice, and graduated high school at fifteen with a full academic scholarship to Vanderbilt. But how smart I was didn't matter to the girls whose parents could afford to pay their tuition without securing student loans because they still considered me trailer trash.

"Then I met and got involved with Alan Kent, who probably thought of me as a novelty, and the first time we slept together he didn't use protection and I ended up pregnant. He wanted me to have an abortion because he'd planned to propose to a woman whom he'd been dating for several years, and when I refused all hell broke loose. His girlfriend left him, while his mother was madder than a wet hen when told her precious son had impregnated some lowdown girl who was the first in her family to graduate college."

Derrick stared at Leah, complete surprise freezing his features. It was apparent he had misjudged her. His first impression was that she was a wealthy woman who'd tired of vacationing at exclusive foreign resorts and had come to Coates Island to mingle with common folks.

"How did your family react to you marrying him?"

"They were totally against it, because my parents felt that Alan had taken advantage of me, but Adele Stephens Kent, as she liked to announce herself, did not want any stray grandkids, so it was imperative that her son marry me. Once the twins were born I was given a reprieve, but only for a while. I was assigned a nanny to help with the boys, and once they began walking Adele felt it was time to turn me into what she referred to as a woman befitting my husband's status. I was forbidden to make my own bed or remove my dish from the table because that was why she'd employed help. When I told her I knew how to make a bed, cook, dust, and vacuum, and that it was a tradition in my family that we cleaned the house from top to bottom for the spring and fall, she screamed at me to forget whatever the Berkleys did because I was now a Kent. I was taught how to set a table for a formal dinner, how to address elected officials, and the proper etiquette for serving and hosting high tea. I'd attended so many garden parties, fund-raisers, and so-called society weddings and engagement parties that I'd occasionally feign not feeling well. Meanwhile, Alan and I presented as the perfect couple, while we were bitter enemies behind closed doors. It was during this time that I went back to university to get a graduate degree. And once my sons were enrolled in school I was rehired to teach at the Calhoun Academy."

"Had you planned to have more children?"

Leah looked at him as if he'd spoken a language she did not understand. "No. If I'd had a different husband, then yes. Two days after my sons left Richmond for college I moved out of the bedroom I'd shared with their father, and that was more than ten years ago."

Derrick could not imagine living in the same house as his wife and not sleeping in the same bed with her. "Was he upset?"

Leah grunted. "Not at all. Alan had what I call a love nest in a place about thirty miles outside of Richmond where he and his friends conducted their extramarital affairs, so he never lacked for female company. I told you before that he's very generous, and as long as he is willing to give them what they want, women will continue to see him. There was never a time when I felt like a wife to Alan, because I wasn't allowed to cook for him, and it was only after his mother was in a nursing home and he was away on business or a golfing outing that I would give the chef and housekeeper time off

and make some the dishes I'd remembered from my childhood."

"So, you really can cook."

An attractive flush suffused her face. "Ye-ah. And because
we didn't have a lot of money Mom would make big pots of
food to last for several meals. It would be collard greens or
cabbage with pieces of smoked meat. Then she would make
fricassee chicken with light, fluffy dumplings, lima beans,
pig's feet, beef ribs, meatloaf, and oxtail stew. My favorites
were fresh and smoked neck bones. Occasionally we would
have beef stew, only because my father always requested it. It
was always fried chicken on Sundays with macaroni and
cheese, potato salad or white rice, and giblet gravy. Everyone
liked sliced cucumber in white vinegar with salt and pepper,
corn on the cob, green beans, and lima beans. My brother is
sensitive to acid, so we never added tomatoes in his salad.
Then dessert was either gingerbread with applesauce, pound
or lemon cake, and sometimes Mom would put fruit cocktail
in the Jell-O mold. We had ham for Easter and turkey for
Thanksgiving, because the man that owned the used car dealership where Daddy worked as a mechanic always gave his
workers turkeys and hams for those two holidays, and an
extra week's pay for Christmas. We were poor, Derrick, but
we never went hungry."

Derrick felt as if she'd just chastised him. Smiling, he
walked over to Leah and pulled her close to his body. Resting
his chin on the top of her head, he could feel her trembling.
He wanted to ask Leah where her father was during her ordeal when she'd had to deal with a cruel and indifferent husband and domineering, interfering mother-in-law? Had her
parents known what she was going through or had she neglected to tell them?

Derrick could not have imagined his daughter marrying a
man and not noticing the signs that she was either being
emotionally or physically abused. Even if Deandra pleaded

with him not to interfere, he would ignore her and get involved. Not only was she his flesh and blood, but she was also the last link between him and the woman whom he'd loved unconditionally.

He felt Leah shaking, and he knew she was crying. Cupping her chin in one hand, he gently eased her head up. Moisture had turned her eyes a shimmering teal blue. She probably had believed marrying a wealthy man would improve her life, when it had become the reverse. It was apparent she was happier living in a trailer and an apartment than in a mansion with live-in staff. She had a husband who not only cheated on her but had also beat her when she got up the courage to defy him.

"It's over, Leah. You never have to go through that again." A wave of fresh tears flowed down her face, and Derrick lowered his head and kissed her parted lips. He hadn't planned to kiss Leah but offer her healing; but it turned into something more than he expected as healing changed to an unbridled hunger when he took her mouth, caressing it until she pressed her breasts against his chest in an attempt to get closer.

Derrick's hands slipped down her back and cradled her hips. He pulled her against his middle at the same time he felt his penis stir until he was fully erect. Leah tightened her hold around his neck, groaning as she pushed her hips against his groin, and Derrick knew he had to stop or he would be guilty for taking advantage of Leah's vulnerability, in a way her husband had done, and it took herculean strength for him to reach up and remove her arms from around his neck. Both were breathing heavily when he ended the kiss. Her response communicated that she was as physically attuned to him as he was to her.

Leah's face was flushed with high color, making it almost impossible to discern her freckles. "I'm sorry about that," Derrick apologized.

She smiled through her tears. "I'm not." Suddenly she sobered. "Thank you for reminding me that I can still feel like a woman."

Derrick reached out to touch her and then pulled his hand away. At that moment he didn't trust himself to kiss her again. "I don't want you to ever forget that you are a woman, Leah. In fact, you're a very sexy woman."

Wiping away her tears with her fingers, she bit her lip. "There are times when I don't feel very sexy."

"Don't you ever let anyone tell you that you're not."

She sniffled. "Thank you, Derrick. Do you know you're very good for a woman's ego?"

He wanted to tell her that he didn't want to stroke her ego, but for as long as she remained on Coates Island he wanted to right the wrongs she'd suffered even before she became Leah Kent. "I need to start on tomorrow's menu before it gets too late." Derrick averted his head, smiling. Although kissing Leah was something he hadn't planned, he had to admit that he'd thoroughly enjoyed it.

"And I need to mop the dining room and clean up the restrooms." She headed in the direction of the utility closet, then stopped and turned around. "You didn't answer my question, Derrick."

A slight frown furrowed his smooth forehead. "What was it?"

"Can I be your sous chef?"

He ran a hand over his face and shook his head. Leah was like a dog with a bone. She wasn't going to let it go. "Okay."

"Is that a yes or a no?"

He winked at her. "It's a yes." He wasn't prepared when she raced toward him and jumped up in his arms, her arms going around his neck and her legs around his waist.

She kissed his cheek. "You'll never regret it."

"I better not," he said in her ear.

He patted her backside and set her on her feet. At that moment he wondered who she actually was, the sexy woman who had had to grow up much too quickly when she'd become wife at eighteen and mother at nineteen, or the effervescent teenage girl that had lain dormant for so many years and was now teasing and playful.

Right now, it didn't matter to Derrick because he liked both the sexy *and* the playful Leah.

Chapter 10

L eah smiled as she turned into the driveway to Derrick's beach house to find the garage door open. When she'd called to tell him she was on her way, he told her he would leave it open for her to pull her car in. She maneuvered next to his Highlander, shut off the engine, and got out. She picked up the container with dessert off the seat and a bouquet of flowers in a colorful hand-painted vase from the floor behind the second row of seats, leaving a baking sheet covered with flour-rubbed dish towels over unbaked Parker House rolls on the passenger-side seat.

Earlier that morning she'd driven into town and purchased the flowers from a shop on Main Street. She hadn't had the ease of driving around on the island last summer because as a tourist she was given a vacationer permit to park in designated lots, allowing her to get around the island either on foot, bicycle, or jitney. There was an island-wide ordinance that vacationers were not permitted on local roads because it led to congestion and impacted the quality of life. She planned to talk to Kayana about getting her a resident sticker, because after all she would be living in the upstairs apartment through the tourist season.

The door leading from the garage opened, and she went still when Derrick came down the stairs to meet her. He'd covered his white shirt and dark slacks with a bibbed apron. Whenever she recalled the taste and feel of his mouth on hers every nerve in her body tingled; and when she remembered writhing against him she was unable stop the waves of shame attacking her when she least expected it. He had to know that he had aroused her as she had him. And once she'd felt his erection pushing against her thighs she'd wanted to beg him to make love to her. Her body had been on fire, and even after she'd finished cleaning up and retreated to the apartment, the need to assuage what had been years of sexual drought was stronger than ever.

Using a vibrator to relieve the buildup of sexual frustration had become a temporary reprieve as an alternate to sexual intercourse. Inasmuch as she'd told Derrick how long it had been since she'd had sexual relations, she did not want him to think she was using him replace what she should have had with her husband.

However, whenever she looked back on her relationship with Alan, Leah knew she hadn't been a prisoner, that she could have taken her children and left him. There was no doubt she would've been facing a long and costly legal battle to retain full custody of her sons, yet she would have been willing even to share custody with Alan if it meant being rid of him.

But fear and intimidation from her husband and mother-in-law had stripped her of any modicum of self-confidence as they manipulated her life from sunrise to sunset. The few times she'd picked up the phone to call her parents, she'd lost her nerve because she feared her father's reaction. Within minutes of her exchanging vows with Alan, Larry Berkley had whispered in her ear that anytime she wanted out he would come and get her.

And now, nearly thirty years later, she still hadn't called her father because at her age she was too old to run to Daddy as she had as a little girl. She was old enough to be a grand-mother, and it was time for her to stand up and face the real-ity that she was going to be in for a vicious fight for her freedom once Alan was served with a summons that his wife was divorcing him. It had taken several weeks, but she had narrowed down the list of law firms she planned to contact to ascertain if they would be willing to represent her. There was one in particular headed by a team of female attorneys well versed in matrimonial law who had won several high-profile cases for their clients. They were number one on her list of six. Hopefully she wouldn't have to exhaust the list be-fore starting over from scratch to research out-of-state firms with attorneys licensed to practice in the Commonwealth of Virginia.

She smiled when Derrick took the cake carrier and flowers from her. "Happy Easter."

He lowered his head and brushed a light kiss over her mouth. "Happy Easter to you, too."

Leah bit her lip to stop its trembling. She hadn't expected him to kiss her. It was his first display of affection since their passionate encounter in the Café's kitchen when she'd poured out her heart to him about her upbringing and marriage. She was certain Kayana never suspected anything had happened between her and Derrick when he came in the next day at closing to help his sister with the Saturday menu. He'd spent all his time in the kitchen while she had busied herself clean-ing the dining and restrooms. And by the time she'd returned the cleaning supplies to the utility closet, he was in the walk-in freezer and didn't see her when she closed the door to the kitchen and took the staircase to the second story.

He did call her later that night to let her know he planned to serve dinner at three and then gave her directions to his house. Her voice was shaded in neutral tones when she vol-unteered to come over early to set the table.

Leah had ended the call and debated whether to set the table for formal or informal dining; she decided on the latter, because there were only going to be two couples. In the past she had hosted gatherings in Kent House's formal dining room with upward of twenty guests seated around the table. The chef had a staff of assistants and servers for the required five- and six-courses meals. Prior to the arrival of their guests, Leah would inspect the table to make certain the fish and salad forks and plates were in the proper position at each place setting. Adele would come in and check behind her, if only to complain if there was a water spot on the crystal or a speck of tarnish on the silver, blaming her for not closely supervising the servants. That was when she most detested her mother-in-law, who looked for any reason to belittle or embarrass her, while constantly reminding her that if Alan had married Justine Hamilton she never would have to correct her. Justine had been raised knowing exactly what to do as a woman in her class. And that was also when Leah wanted to remind Adele that Justine had married a man who'd fathered two children with her maid, and when she'd discovered her husband's infidelity he divorced her, gave her the big house, a generous settlement, and moved to Miami's Little Havana with his new wife and children.

Leah forgot about Alan, Justine, and Adele as she carried the pan of rolls and followed Derrick up six stairs and into a mud/laundry room that opened into a pantry and then an enormous kitchen. The mouthwatering aroma of garlic and herbs tantalized her olfactory nerves. Derrick's beach house was designed with an open floor plan where the kitchen and breakfast nook flowed into the dining, family, and living rooms. The walls were painted a pale blue-gray, harmonizing with shades of blue, white, and gray upholstered chairs, love seats, and sofas.

"Your home is beautiful."

Derrick smiled. "Thank you. If you want I'll give you a tour before Kay and Graeme get here."

"Please." She sniffed the air. "Something smells delicious."
"It's the herb crust. I made it with fresh breadcrumbs, about a half dozen cloves of finely chopped garlic, fresh parsley, and thyme leaves, mixing them in softened butter to form a paste. I just put the lamb in the oven on a low temperature, estimating the cooking time should take about two hours."

The sound of an Isley Brothers' classic song flowed throughout the space from hidden speakers. She set the baking pan on the countertop as she sang along with the lyrics to "Don't Say Goodnight." Leah recognized the tune because her former college roommate had grown up with her parents playing music from the seventies. Cynthia had brought a turntable and collection of vinyl records with her, and Leah had come to appreciate what had been designated protest music as much as the artists on the Top 20 contemporary music list.

Derrick stared at Leah as he set the cake carrier on the kitchen island. "You know this song?"

"Yes. My college roommate grew up listening to her parents' music and she turned me on to soul and R and B when most kids our age were into rap and hip-hop."

"So, you like old-school jams?" he asked, smiling.

"Some of them. I've also grown quite fond of classical music, too."

"Did your roommate also turn you onto the three B's?"

Leah gave him a puzzled look. "What are the three B's?"

"Beethoven, Bach, and Brahms."

Throwing back her head, Leah laughed, baring her smooth throat. "What do you know about them?"

"Probably as much as you do or more. I have sister-in-law who happens to be a concert pianist. When I lived in New York I tried to attend all her concerts in the tri-state area. A couple of years ago she went to Africa. She met a Nigerian doctor, married him, and now teaches piano to kids that exhibit exceptional musical talent."

Leah sobered. "I don't want to give my mother-in-law credit, but she did introduce me to classical music." She told

Derrick how there was always a classical composition playing in the solarium whenever they had high tea.

"You're really full of surprises."

"Why would you say that?"

"Just when I believe I've figured you out, you shock me
with another revelation."

"Are you saying you misjudged me?"

"Absolutely," Derrick admitted.

Leah's pale eyebrows lifted. "What was there about me
that you found so confusing?"

"I must confess that when I first saw you I thought you'd
come to the wrong place to spend the summer. Coates Island
has always been known as a vacation spot for families. We
rarely get single folks, or even young couples like those on
Myrtle Beach. Our vacation rentals are somewhat expensive
for an island that is only two miles long with one eating establishment, because the locals don't want their properties to
become transient motels where folks stay a week or two, and
then move on."

"So, you're saying I didn't meet the profile of the folks that
summer on the island?"

"That's exactly what I'm saying. I figured you were married because you were wearing a wedding band, but it was
how you didn't interact with some of the other vacationers
whenever you were in the Café. Most of the time you had
your head in a book, which was a signal that you didn't want
to be disturbed. Then, when I discovered you were in a book
club with Kay, I figured perhaps you weren't that stuck up
after all."

Leah's mouth opened, but no words came out for several
seconds. "You thought I was stuck up?"

"Come on now, Leah. I'm no fashion expert, but I know
enough about women's clothes and especially shoes to know
yours didn't come off a department store rack. And even the
restaurant's waitstaff was whispering about your jewelry.
Fast-forward six months later and you return battered and

bruised with no rings on your fingers or diamonds in your ears. Then you reveal that you're married to a judge that beat the hell out of you because you said something that he didn't like. You claim you haven't shared a bed with your husband in more than ten years, although your adult sons were already out of the house. What I don't understand is why."

"Why what, Derrick?"

"Why did you stay?"

A momentary expression of discomfort crossed her face as she lowered her eyes. "You don't know how many times I've asked myself the same question, and each time I come up with the same answer. I don't know. Perhaps I kept telling myself it would get better, when I knew in my heart of hearts that it would never get better because Alan wasn't going to change. Some men cheat because they like it, and others because they can. But for Alan it was both. There were times when I told myself if I threatened to leave he would stop, then I heard his father did the same to his mother, so like father, like son." Her head popped up as she gave him a direct stare. "I did not stay with Alan because of his money or because he is a judge. I stayed because I'd learned to deal with the bullshit. Last summer was the first year we did not vacation together, and coming here was like being released from prison after serving a lengthy sentence. I think folks nowadays call it doing a bid. But my first act of rebellion was buying the Audi as a birthday present for myself. All before Alan would go with me to purchase or lease a new car."

Derrick bit back a smile when she'd mentioned "doing a bid." It was obvious she was more than familiar with street slang. "Your husband didn't know you were coming down here?"

"No." There was a trace of laughter in the single word. "I knew he was taking our sons away to celebrate their passing the bar. What had originally been scheduled as a monthlong stay was extended to two months when Alan added an African safari to their itinerary. I'd gone online to research vacation rentals and discovered there was an available bungalow here on Coates Island. It was far enough away from Richmond, and Adele was in the nursing home, so I could go anywhere and do whatever I wanted without having someone spying on me.

"Kayana and Cherie gave it to me straight no chaser after I'd shared details about my life that I'd never told anyone else up to that time. Unburdening myself to them was akin to spending hours on a therapist's couch. What I really appreciated is they never told me to leave Alan. That was a decision I had to make on my own. However, there was one thing I knew I didn't want to do was take another vacation with him, and that's when I contacted the rental agent to come back here this summer. Alan found the agreement and went ballistic when I told him he couldn't stop me. And you know the rest."

Derrick did know the rest, and what Leah endured before she'd been physically assaulted by her husband confirmed that she was an exceptional woman to have stayed in a dysfunctional marriage and not emerge completely broken. It was obvious her husband had recognized her strength when she'd refused to have an abortion and he had systematically tried to break her spirit, but despite the difference in their ages and with his mother as ally, he'd failed.

Rounding the island, he took her hands and pressed a kiss on the back of each one. A dreamy smile parted her lips, bringing his gaze to linger there. "I'd like to apologize for jumping to conclusions about you."

Leah took a step, bringing them closer. "There's nothing to apologize for, Derrick. A lot of people have misjudged me all my life, but what I refuse to do is change who I am or what I've become. I happen to like the new and improved Leah."

"And I like her, too," Derrick said truthfully.

He liked Leah, enjoyed spending time with her, yet Derrick knew their association would never go beyond friendship until she sued her husband for divorce. He did not want to become involved with a woman who could possibly change her mind and decide she wanted to work to save her thirty-year marriage. And she wouldn't be the first physically abused woman to reconcile with her abuser. After all, Leah had put up with constant ridicule from her husband and mother-in-law for more than half her life, and still she stayed. She'd admitted not sharing a bed with her husband for more than a decade, and she still did not leave him. And when she finally challenged her husband, the result was a savage beating that resulted in her being hospitalized. However, Derrick had to give her credit for revealing to her doctor and sons that her injuries weren't the result of an accident, but domestic abuse. Her medical report and her sons' willingness to testify against their father were the weapons that she could use or not use to legally free herself from a man who had controlled every aspect of her life until she'd had enough.

He'd wanted to do more than give her a chaste kiss in the garage. Everything about Leah shouted sophistication, with the royal blue dress in a stretchy fabric clinging to every curve of her slender body while exhibiting more skin than she had since coming to the island. The asymmetrical neckline bared her throat, the capped sleeves her arms, and the hem ending at her knees her legs. Derrick knew she'd spent time on the beach in the sun because her once-pale body had taken on the hue of a ripened peach. She'd brushed her hair off her face and pinned it in a twist at the nape of her neck.

"What are you thinking about?" Leah whispered.

"It's not what, but who. You look incredible." Derrick hadn't lied to Leah. She'd applied a light cover of makeup to accentuate her best features: eyes and mouth.

Leah demurely lowered her eyes. "I try."

"You don't have to try."

He wondered what her husband had said to Leah to make her doubt her looks. She was an extremely attractive woman, tall and slender with strawberry-blond hair, jewel-like blue eyes, pert nose, and lush mouth. And seeing her in the body-hugging dress and heels made her a head-turner.

Derrick thought of himself as a normal man who liked women; however, he'd always been very discriminating when becoming involved with a woman. Unlike some men he didn't have a type. It was personality and intelligence rather than race, ethnicity, and body type that topped his list of criteria. His sister and Leah had bonded over books, yet it went beyond their love of reading. He'd watched and overheard them talking and laughing together about the antics of some of Leah's students or Kayana's clients.

And he'd made a serious faux pas when judging her. Everything in her deportment indicated she'd lived a privileged life as a judge's wife. When Kayana had informed him Leah was married to Judge Alan Kent, Derrick had gone online to research the man whom he suspected had assaulted his wife as evidenced by the bruises around her throat.

Derrick knew Leah was going to be in the proverbial fight of her life when seeking to divorce a man who used his family's name and the power of the bench get his way. He wanted her, got her, and it was obvious he wasn't going to make it easy for her to be rid of him. Alan Kent had a plan, and that was to make her financially dependent on him. He'd used his influence to have her discharged from her position as headmistress at the prep school and had denied her the use of his credit cards. Derrick wasn't certain if Leah was financially solvent, but he had reassured her that she would always have a home at the Seaside Café.

"Are you ready for a tour of the house?"

She flashed a wide grin. "Yes."

Leah wondered if Derrick's wife had decorated the beach house or if they'd employed the services of a professional interior decorator. The monochromatic blues paired with white predominated every room. A sea of blue floral area rugs and

Wedgwood blue furnishings in Derrick's daughter's bedroom with a full-tester bed, high chest-on-chest, and a plump settee were sophisticated and inviting.

Leah stared at a collection of photographs on a round table near the window seat. She couldn't pull her gaze away from the incredibly beautiful woman with large light-brown eyes, delicate features, and a flawless nut-brown complexion. The resemblance between his late wife and their daughter was remarkable, and she knew Derrick would never forget the woman to whom he'd been married, because his daughter was her mother's clone.

The two guest bedrooms were mirror images of each other with slate blue walls. One had a queen-size bed and the other smaller one had white twin beds. The linens were the perfect contrast to the botanical designs in the quilts, framed prints, and upholstered armchairs with matching footstools. When Derrick stopped outside the master suite and Leah walked in, she went completely still. Gray and white had replaced the repeated blue-and-white palette in the other rooms in the house.

A California-king mahogany bed with a leather headboard, matching triple dresser, and chest of drawers allowed for a more masculine appeal. It was the same with the reading corner that was converted to a space with a wall-mounted television and a storage unit spanning the width of the wall; shelves were filled with books, magazines, and an extensive movie and music collection. Pale-gray, wall-to-wall drapes were opened to allow for unobstructed views of the beach.

"You're probably wondering why this room looks different from the others," Derrick said behind her.

Leah turned to find Derrick leaning against the doorframe. "I do, but I can figure that out. You didn't want to be reminded of your wife."

Derrick inclined his head. "Yes. There was a time when I

couldn't sleep here because everything reminded me of Andrea. I was sleeping in the larger guest room until Kayana suggested I hire a decorator to give it a complete makeover."

"Did you retain the services of a decorator for the rest of the house?"

"Andrea did. She grew up on Long Island, and her best friend's family had a summer home in the Hamptons, and she'd always talk about the blue-and-white rooms. So, when we bought this place, she insisted on decorating using the same colors. The only difference is the outbuilding, which I'll show you now."

Leah followed him down a narrow rear staircase. She peered into a space that was set up as a home gym. There was a treadmill, exercise bike, NordicTrack elliptical, dumbbells, and rowing machine. It was obvious Derrick did not have to leave the convenience of his home to get a full-body workout. He opened a door that led to the backyard. The sun had disappeared behind dark storm clouds.

Derrick tapped a keypad on a shingled garden shed and opened French doors to the structure that had been converted into a bedroom with painted cornflower-blue shutters matching the doorframe; window boxes and planters overflowing with colorful blooming flowers, a paved walkway, and a manicured lawn revealed particular attention had been paid to the interior and exterior to transform an outbuilding into comfortable living quarters.

The tiny cottage was filled with homey touches and garden accents, with a hutch displaying items usually found at flea markets or lawn sales. Two Depression glass vases were filled with green-and-white dried hydrangeas. Wrought-iron chairs, an antique desk, a twin bed with a pale-green wicker headboard, and framed prints of Audubon birds and flowers made it the perfect space to nap and while away the hours doing absolutely nothing.

Derrick moved over to stand next to her. "This was our go-to guest bedroom whenever Andrea had friends and family over. There is a commode, vanity, and shower stall behind that door in the corner next to the wardrobe. Andrea had planned for Deandra to move in here when she turned sixteen to give her a sense of independence."

"Did she?" Leah asked.

"No. Deandra was thirteen when Andrea passed away, and it has taken a while for her to adjust to losing her mother."

Leah could not imagine losing her mother. Even at sixty-eight, Madeline was still spry and full of life. "Did you put her in therapy?"

Derrick's icy-black eyebrows flickered. "Both of us were in therapy. I was prepared to lose Andrea, but it was my daughter that most concerned me. She'd come home from school and sit at a table at the Café to do her homework. And whenever I'd ask her if she was okay she would give me the pat answer that she was. It was when she'd become practically monosyllabic that I called Kayana for advice. That was when she said we both needed counseling. Once we had individual and family sessions, Deandra was able to verbalize her emotions. She was angry with her mother for getting sick and dying."

"Why would she blame her mother?"

"Andrea had complained about extreme fatigue and excruciating back pain for more than a year until I finally convinced her to go to the doctor. After a battery of tests she was diagnosed with stage-four pancreatic and bile duct cancer. There were times when Deandra overheard me pleading with her mother to undergo chemotherapy, but Andrea refused. She also did not want to go into hospice, and two months following the initial diagnosis, she passed away at home. I hired a live-in nurse to make certain she was comfortable until the end."

"Losing a parent at that age has to be traumatic for any child. How is she doing now?" Leah asked Derrick.

"Thankfully, a lot better. She spent last summer in Florida with her aunt, cousins, and grandmother, and then asked me if she could spend her senior year there because she was planning to attend a local college. I must admit I gave it a lot of thought before I finally told her she could stay once I realized she only had one more year before she left for college."

"How often do you get to see her?"

"Not often enough, but I try not to be the overprotective dad. The entire family flew up from Florida to attend Kayana and Graeme's wedding in Massachusetts, and I flew back with them and spent almost two weeks there. I'd made plans to see her during the Easter break, but she has other plans. It was a wakeup call for me that my little girl is growing up and doesn't need her daddy as much as she has in the past."

"Daughters always need their fathers, Derrick. I know if I'd called my father to let him know what I'd been going through, Alan would've never had the opportunity to put his hands on me."

"Why didn't you, Leah?"

She focused on the prints on the walls. "Because my father would be serving time as we speak. And knowing how protective my sons are of me, I pleaded with them not to do or say anything to their father, because I intend to blindside him if he decides to contest the divorce."

"Have you served him yet?"

Leah shook her head. "No. I just finished researching firms I intend to call this week to ask if they'll represent me. The Kent family roots run deep in Virginia, and there's always the possibility that many of the attorneys are not only familiar but may have some connection to Alan. Whenever I'd attend a social event with him, he would introduce me to someone with political or legal connections."

"Have you considered hiring an out-of-state firm?"

"Yes, but only if I exhaust my first list. Now that I've lost my job it's not necessary for me to live in Richmond." Derrick gave her a long, penetrating stare. "What's the matter?"

"You plan to live here?"

Leah had given her future a lot of thought since getting the call from Erin that she was losing her position at the prep school. She'd planned to return to Richmond and purchase a house or condominium because she wanted to live close to her place of work. But, on the other hand, if she did decide to purchase a condo on the island, then she would apply for a teaching position in one of the nearby school districts. Having to drive to work while living on Coates Island was not a drawback, because she wouldn't have to deal with rush-hour traffic.

"I've seriously been thinking about it. Maybe I can purchase one of the two-bedroom condos that went up several years ago, and hopefully get a teaching position either on the mainland or even in Shelby," she said, revealing her thoughts aloud.

"Living here year-round is going to be culture shock for someone who has lived all her life in a cosmopolitan city."

"Maybe for someone else, but not for me. I just can't imagine returning to that circus where I had to perform like a trained monkey to everyone's satisfaction. When I came down here last summer I knew I had to go back to Richmond, so I was mentally prepared and knew what to expect. But it's different now. If and when I go back it will be short-term."

"What if your divorce turns out to be long *and* contentious?"

Derrick was asking Leah a question she'd asked herself over and over, and the answer was always the same. "I hope that's not going to happen after I inform Alan that I have medical documentation of his assault and that his sons are willing to testify against him. Although Alan is semi-retired, I don't believe he would want to ruin his illustrious judicial career with a charge of spousal abuse. Enough talk about my soon-to-be ex, because I intend to make this Easter the first of many more where I can enjoy it with folks I want and like."

Derrick waited for her to leave the shed and then closed

the French doors. "What do you think about holding your book club meetings here?"

Leah stared at him, tongue-tied. "Are you really offering the she-shed for our meetings?" she asked, once she'd recovered her voice.

"She-shed?"

"Yes," she said, smiling. "You guys have your man caves, and this is what women would call a she-shed."

Derrick smiled. "Well, live and learn. And yes, you can have full use of the she-shed. And I'm willing to even give up my kitchen for you to prepare your refreshments."

"Where will you be during this time, because we don't want to put you out?"

"I'll be in my bedroom's mini man cave or the family room either watching a game or a movie."

"Does Kayana know about your generous offer?"

"Not yet. But I'm certain she'll go for it, because after spending seven days a week at the Café I'm certain she'll appreciate a change of scene."

Leah knew Derrick was probably right. When she'd volunteered to host one of the meetings, Kayana and Cherie had enjoyed coming to her bungalow where she'd prepared a Mexican-inspired buffet with spicy salsas; empanadas; hard and soft beef, chicken, and shrimp tacos; quesadillas; guacamole; and crispy tortilla chips. She knew she had impressed her friends with her cooking acumen because Kayana and Cherie were effusive with their compliments, while she was too ashamed to tell her new friends that she had never prepared a meal for her husband at any time during their marriage.

They returned to the house, where Derrick handed her an apron to protect her dress. Leah washed her hands and began the task of covering the dining table with a light-blue tablecloth, and then set out four place settings with china, silver, and crystal. She unwrapped the bouquet of flowers and arranged them in the vase for the table's centerpiece.

When Kayana and Graeme arrived, Derrick set out the platter with herb-crusted lamb chops, a large glass bowl filled with Greek salad, a cloth-covered basket of hot, golden-brown rolls, and bottles of red wine and chilled rosé. Kayana held a pan of macaroni and cheese with two oven gloves, placing it on a trivet. Graeme stood behind her cradling a carton of wine.

"You're good for my brother," she whispered in Leah's ear. "This is the first time he's hosted anything in more than five years."

Leah wanted to believe it didn't have anything to do with her but with his daughter's plan not to share the holiday with him. Although she was still attracted to Derrick, she did not want to delude herself into believing, kisses aside, he wanted more from her than friendship.

Perhaps it was better they not become involved with each other, because she needed to focus on ending her marriage. "He's a good guy, Kayana."

"I know that, Leah." She leaned in closer. "But it's about time he's come out of his shell to invite a woman into his home. And I'm glad it's you, because you deserve to have a man treat you with respect."

Chapter 11

Kayana's words about her being good for her brother stayed with Leah as she took a sip of Irish coffee Graeme made to accompany mini sour cream pound and red velvet Bundt cakes. Was she, Leah mused, good for her brother, or knowing her circumstances had he felt sorry for her? What Leah did not need was pity. She'd never felt sorry for herself despite what she'd put up with while married. There was never a time when she'd told herself that she couldn't leave, that she had to remain Mrs. Alan Kent. What she'd done was use her sons as an excuse because of their close bond with their father. And Leah knew if Alan had not been a good father, she would have filed for divorce years ago.

She exchanged a smile with Kayana over the rim of the mug. Her friend looked very chic in a red sheath dress with cap sleeves, and her hair styled in a mass of tiny curls framing her small, round face, while large South Seas drop pearl earrings capped in yellow diamonds dangled from her pierced lobes. Derrick's sister appeared blissfully happy as Graeme's wife. She knew what her friend had gone through with her first husband, who'd cheated on her with one of his colleagues. Unlike herself, who had remained in a dysfunctional marriage for three decades, Kayana had ended hers a year before she'd celebrated her twentieth wedding anniversary, while Leah had rationalized and used her sons as an excuse not to leave her husband.

Despite her never being hit by a man before, Alan's assault had given Leah the courage she needed to dramatically change her life. And it wasn't for the first time she'd wondered whether she would've stayed if he hadn't hit her, and the answer was she would. After all, she'd spent the past ten years not sharing a bed with Alan and probably would have continued for the rest of their natural lives.

"Leah, how do you like the Irish coffee?" Graeme questioned.

She smiled at the retired schoolteacher. "I like it, even though it's a little strong."

"The coffee or the whiskey?" he asked, smiling.

It was as if marriage also agreed with Graeme. Whenever she'd encountered him at the Café last summer, he appeared stoic and standoffish. There had been no warmth in his large gray eyes, and he'd rarely smiled. "The whiskey."

"I'll make the next one for you with less whiskey."

Leah put up a hand. "Please don't. If I have another one I definitely won't be able to get behind the wheel of my car."

"You can always come home with us," Kayana volunteered.

"Or she can stay here, Kay," Derrick offered, "because there's more room here than at your place."

Leah smiled at Derrick, and then his sister. "Thanks for the offer, but I'm good."

"We'd serve alcoholic libations during our book club meetings," Kayana said, "but there were a few occasions when we would get so lit up that it was hard to concentrate on the discussion."

Leah laughed softly. "It was Cherie that used to complain that the drinks were too strong."

Derrick touched the corners of his mouth with his napkin. "Speaking of your book club, I told Leah that you ladies are welcome to hold your meetings in the backyard shed."

Kayana's smile was dazzling. "I can't believe we'll now have a she-shed."

Derrick slowly shook his head. "Leah called it the same thing. Since when did a garden shed become a she-shed?"

Kayana make a sucking sound with her tongue and teeth. "You guys have man caves, so why can't ladies have their she-sheds?"

"That's what I told him, Kayana," Leah said.

"I don't have a man cave," Graeme grumbled under his breath.

"We have a family room, darling," Kayana drawled, "and that's the closest you're going to get to a man cave. If you want one, then you have to be willing to sell the house and build one with enough space to have a man cave."

Graeme shook his head. "No thanks. I happen to like our little house."

Leah knew most of the one- and two-bedroom bungalows on Coates Island were more than ninety years old, while Derrick's beachfront house and the condos were among the newer structures on the island.

Derrick met Leah's eyes. "Do you really talk about books at your meetings?

"Yes. Last year we read and discussed Octavia Butler's *Kindred*, Edith Wharton's *Ethan Frome*, and Jane Austen's *Pride and Prejudice*."

Derrick whistled softly. "Slavery, a cheating husband, and sisters on the prowl looking for husbands. I would've liked to have been a fly on the wall when you had your meetings."

"Maybe you should join us, Derrick," she said.

"That's what I said to Graeme once he recommended a number of Octavia Butler's titles," Kayana revealed.

Derrick waved a hand in dismissal. "Thanks, but no thanks. I'd rather spend my Sunday afternoons watching ball games, and because my brother-in-law is committed to join me, you ladies are on your own."

Graeme lifted his mug in Derrick's direction. "Now that I'm no longer teaching, it's baseball, hockey, and basketball before books. And, Derrick, you're more than welcome to spend Sunday afternoons at my house while our ladies take over your place for their meetings."

Leah lowered her eyes and stared at the residue of cake crumbs on the dessert plate. Graeme had referred to her and Kayana as his and Derrick's ladies. She wanted to tell him he was mistaken. She wasn't Derrick's lady in the literal sense; she was his employee.

Derrick lifted his mug, acknowledging Graeme's offer. "By the way, what titles have you ladies selected for this summer?"

A beat passed before Leah said, "We've scheduled *The Alienist*, *Love in the Time of Cholera*, and *Memoirs of a Geisha* for the first three weeks."

Graeme's eyebrows shot up in surprise. "Don't you think it's odd that you've selected period novels that have been made into movies?"

"No."

"Not at all."

Leah and Kayana had spoken at the same time. "Although we may have seen the movies or the miniseries, we'll still read the books and discuss them in depth," Leah said. "I just finished *The Alienist*, and there are scenes in the book that were left out in the miniseries."

"I'm still reading my host selection, *Love in the Time of Cholera*," Kayana admitted.

Leah continued to sip the whiskey-infused coffee with sugar and topped off with a froth of whipped cream as the topic of conversation segued to a growing scandal involving several elected state officials who had been caught up in a sting involving high-priced call girls.

Without warning, a wave of indescribable joy swept over her, filling her with an emotion she had long forgotten. The dinner was reminiscent of the ones she'd had with her family as a child. It hadn't mattered to Leah whether she lived in a trailer park, apartment, or the rental house, just being with family members during holidays had become an indelible memory stamped on her brain like a permanent tattoo.

After setting the table and arranging the flowers, Leah had assisted Derrick making the Greek salad, halving grape tomatoes and kalamata olives, thinly slicing red onions, and cutting cucumber into half-moons, while he made the dressing with fresh basil, oregano, garlic cloves, the juice of fresh lemons, Dijon mustard, sugar, olive oil, and red wine vinegar. She noticed he made the dressing even creamier by slowly adding the oil to the blender while running it on a high speed.

She compared working with Derrick in his kitchen to her childhood home that was filled with delicious aromas whenever her mother and grandmother baked pies and cakes, while she had been relegated to snapping the ends off green beans or peeling potatoes. She especially liked when her grandmother made cole slaw, because she'd use thinly cut strips of collards, cabbage, and carrots to give the slaw extra crunch and bite as she tossed it with her secret dressing. And once she was old enough, she was given the task of scoring and decorating the ham with cloves.

What she did not want to remember were the Easters at Kent House, where Adele compiled the guest list, conferred with the chef for the menu, and sat at the head of the table opposite Alan as she monitored when each dish was to be served. At first Leah resented being usurped, because after all as Alan's wife she was to be mistress of the house, but after a while she was glad to relinquish the position because it meant she could spend more time with her sons.

Leah sucked in a breath, holding it until she experienced constriction in her chest. She had to stop reliving her past, even if only in her head. She had turned a corner the instant she'd loaded the trunk of her car with enough clothes and personal items to last her through the spring and summer and drove from Virginia to North Carolina. However, her plan to return to Richmond to live changed with Erin's phone call telling her that she'd lost her position as head-mistress at the prep school.

A part of her wanted to sue the school board for what she thought was an unlawful dismissal, while as a realist Leah knew it wasn't worth her time or resources to challenge them when she knew she would be in the fight of her life once Alan was served with divorce papers. After all, she was an experi-enced teacher and could apply for a position at a public or private school.

"I think I ate too much," Kayana announced.

"I know I did," Leah confirmed. She'd taken one bite of the herb-crusted lamb and had to suppress a moan when the tender, deliciously seasoned meat literally melted on her tongue. She'd had seconds of everything: lamb, macaroni and cheese, Parker House rolls, and Greek salad, along with a glass and a half of rosé. It had taken herculean restraint not to have a second serving of cake. She had baked four sour cream pound, four pistachio pound, and four red velvet mini Bundt cakes.

Derrick pointed to the cake platter. "There are a few of those guys calling my name, and I know if I answer them I'll have to work out twice as long for the rest of the week."

Kayana reached with a pair of tongs and placed one of the cakes on her plate. "Damn you, Leah, for making these little babies so freaking good."

Leah smiled. "The babies have lower calories, and there-fore less guilt."

Derrick took a bite of his third cake. "Now you see why I hired Leah as the Café's baker."

"It's only going to be for the summer season," she said quickly.

A rumble of thunder shook the earth, following by an ear-shattering crack of lightning. Seconds later fat raindrops pelted the windows. Kayana pushed back her chair, Graeme rising with her.

"I'm going to help you clean up, then Graeme and I are leaving before it starts coming down too hard."

Derrick also stood. "You guys should head out, because they're predicting a lot of rain."

"Are you sure?" Kayana asked.

"Yes," Derrick replied. "I'll call you tomorrow before I come by and drop off some leftovers."

Kayana kissed her brother's cheek. "Thanks."

Graeme shook his hand. "Thank you for the invite."

Derrick smiled, flashing deep dimples. "Any time."

Leah hugged Kayana and then Graeme, waiting until Derrick walked them to the door before she began clearing the table.

"You don't have to do that."

She peered over her shoulder when Derrick walked into the kitchen. "Do what?"

"Clean up. You've done enough, Leah." He closed the distance between them and rested his hands on her shoulders. "Thank you for being an incredible hostess."

Leah smiled up at him, her eyes caressing the lean jaw and lingering on the strong, masculine mouth she wanted to feel against hers. "Thank you for asking, because I really enjoyed everything."

Derrick stared at her from under lowered lids. "I really don't want to put you out, but it's best you leave now before the roads flood. Unless . . ."

Last summer when it had rained steadily for three days, some roads had become impassable, forcing people to remain indoors. "Unless what?" she asked when his words trailed off.

"You're welcome to stay over if you want." He smiled. "Unlike Kayana and Graeme, I do have guest bedrooms."

Under another set of circumstances Leah would've taken Derrick up on his invitation, if he'd indicated he wanted more than friendship. Emotionally, she was starved for companionship; she needed a man to hold her close; kiss her with tenderness; touch her body until she trembled with ecstasy;

and she needed to feel his erection inside her while reminding her she was a woman who had come to recognize the strong passions within herself. But it wasn't all about sex. That she could temporarily assuage with a battery-operated device.

She wanted at forty-nine what she hadn't had at nineteen, twenty-nine, and thirty-nine. She wanted to date. Have a man call her up and ask her if she wanted to share ameal, a movie, or even a long drive where they'd feel free to talk about any and everything. And she wanted to know what love was. Not the love she had for her family, and not the unconditional love she felt for her sons, but a love where she felt fully alive and willing to see both sides in order to make the relationship work. It couldn't be all her way or no way. But, more important, there had to be respect. The lack of it would be the deal breaker.

Leaning in closer, she kissed his cheek. "Maybe another time."

"Is that a promise?"

"Yes, Derrick, it is a promise."

The rain was coming down in torrents by the time Leah backed out of the garage. A minute into the drive she regretted declining Derrick's invitation to spend the night. She turned the windshield wiper blades to the highest speed, decelerated to less than ten miles an hour, and maneuvered into the parking lot at the Café without encountering a single vehicle. It was obvious the locals knew to stay off the road during a storm.

Leah unlocked the door, tapped in the code to disarm the alarm, and then armed it again before she removed her shoes, left them on the mat at the foot of the stairs, and walked on bare feet up the staircase.

She opened the door and entered the apartment to warmth and soft light from the living room floor lamp. Her pet peeve was walking into a dark house, and Leah had made it a practice to leave a light on whenever she knew she was not coming home until nightfall. She retrieved her cell phone from the crossbody and saw that she had two text messages. Both were from her sons wishing her a happy Easter and asking her to call them.

Leah knew Aron and Caleb were concerned about her because they were calling and sending her messages at least once a week, and each time she responded, she'd reassure them she was doing well. And she was. She lived in a charming apartment above a restaurant where she would become the resident baker for the summer season. She decided to take a shower and change into something less dressy before calling them, but first she had to charge her phone, because whenever she talked to either Aron or Caleb they tended to have lengthy conversations, while Leah would always tease them saying they'd chosen the right profession, because as lawyers they were definitely long-winded.

Thirty minutes later, Leah crawled into bed in a pair of strawberry dotted cotton pajamas and red fluffy socks, with her face slathered with a rich moisturizer. Reaching for the fully charged phone, she tapped Caleb's number. He answered after the third ring.

"Happy Easter, Mom."

Leah smiled. "Happy Easter to you, too. It sounds as if you're having a good time." She could hear music and laughing in the background.

"I am. I'm taking a little time off while the judge is on vacation. Right now I'm unwinding in Costa Rica."

"What made you decide to go to Costa Rica?" Caleb normally vacationed on St. Thomas or the Dominican Republic.

"I decided it was time to see another country. I wanted you to call me because I want to give you some good news. I proposed to Marisa, and she accepted. We came here to celebrate and for her to get some rest and unwind before she has to take finals. Right now she's asleep, and I don't want to wake her so you can talk to her."

Her mouth dropped, and she was unable to speak for several minutes. "Oh my gosh! I can't believe it!"

"Should I assume you're happy?"

"I'm deliriously happy. When's the wedding?"

"That's not going to be for a while, Mom. We want to wait until she completes her residency."

"But that may not be for another three to seven years."

"I know. We've talked about it and both agree it's better if we wait. And if it were up to me I'd marry her tomorrow, but it's her parents that are adamant that we wait. Both are doctors and Marisa is their only child, so it comes down to three against one."

"You're both young, and I don't mind waiting to become a grandmother."

A beat passed. "You want grandchildren?"

"Of course I want grandchildren." Leah sobered. "Are you saying you haven't talked about starting a family?"

"We're thinking of adoption. Why bring more children into the world when there are tons of kids languishing in foster care waiting for a family to call their own."

A swell of pride eddied through Leah with Caleb's pronouncement that he and his fiancée were planning to adopt. "It doesn't matter how many you adopt; they will still be my grandbabies."

"So, you approve of us adopting?"

"I don't understand you, Caleb. Why are you always surprised when I go along with whatever decision you make? I raised you and Aron to not only be independent of each other but to also think for yourselves. If you'd decided you wanted to become a teacher, veterinarian, social worker, or even an artist I would've supported you. And if you'd fallen in love with a man rather than a woman, you still would've had my support *and* approval. All I've ever wanted for you and your brother is for you to be happy, because there may come a time when you may be faced with something over which you have no control, so try and make the most of what you do have and can control."

There was a pregnant pause before Caleb said, "You know

you didn't have to stay with our father as long as you did if you were unhappy, Mom."

"I know that now. But that's the past, and I don't intend to dwell on it."

"Have you filed for divorce?"

"Not yet." She told him how she'd taken time to compile a list of firms and planned to begin contacting them the following day. "I'm not certain how they'll react once they realize I'm suing Judge Alan Kent."

"Maybe I can help you out on this end, Mom."

"How?"

"I know an attorney well versed in matrimonial law who is licensed to practice in Virginia. She's earned a reputation as a rottweiler going directly for the throat on behalf of her clients. Most of her clients are women who were married to wealthy or powerful men, so there's no doubt she would relish representing you. All you have to do is tell her what you want, and she'll make it happen."

"I'm not looking to embarrass or destroy your father, Caleb. I just want my freedom and enough money to cover my salary for the next sixteen years."

"What's up with your salary?"

Although they were adults, Leah loathed involving her sons in her marital discord with their father. She told Caleb about Alan's interference and failure to notify her of the letter addressed to her from the school board.

"Why didn't he call and tell you about the letter?" Caleb asked.

"Because he knew I would tell him to open it, read it to me, and that would've given me enough time to have Dr. Brady fax the medical update to the school."

"He's a fool, Mom. Doesn't he realize you being unemployed means he will have to pay you more alimony?"

"It's apparent he's fixated on being vindictive, and much to his detriment, because I intend to go through with the divorce and see it to the end."

"Whatever you decide or do, just remember, Mom, that Aron and I have your back."

"I hope what I'm going through with your father won't force you to take sides."

"He did that when he decided to use your face for a punching bag. Aron didn't want me to tell you, because you'd asked us not to do or say anything to Dad, but Aron did warn him not to go after you once he figured out where you were going."

A wave of apprehension swept through Leah, gnawing away at her confidence. "How did he find out?"

"He claimed he found the rental agreement for the vacation house in North Carolina and then called the agent who gave him the information he needed to figure out where you may be staying."

Leah closed her eyes. She wanted to tell Caleb that his father was a liar. He didn't find the rental agreement but had come into her bedroom suite and read it while she'd been asleep. She opened her eyes and stared at the colorful crocheted afghan on the foot of the bed. Luckily for her, she hadn't signed the agreement to rent the vacant bungalow where she'd stayed last summer but had found refuge at the Seaside Café. Once she'd confirmed with Derrick and Kayana that she did not have to move from the apartment, she'd sent her sons the address where she could be reached in an emergency.

"Just make certain Alan doesn't goad you into telling him exactly where I'm staying, because if he starts trouble I will have him arrested and locked up."

"Let's hope it won't come to that."

"I'm going to let you go so you can finish celebrating with your fiancée. Let her know I can't wait to meet her because I've always wanted a daughter."

"I will. As soon as I get back to the States I'll send you the contact information for Sabina Gagnon, because I don't have her number on my personal phone."

"Thanks, Caleb. Love you."

"Love you back, Mom."

Leah ended the call, smiling. She had been able to hear the excitement in her son's voice when he'd talked about the woman with whom he'd fallen in love and who had accepted his marriage proposal. And she admired his willingness to wait for his fiancée to establish her career as a doctor, which would also give them time to get to know each other, unlike it had been with her and his father.

Leah hadn't been married a year when she'd discovered the Bramble House was where Alan conducted his adulterous affairs. She never knew the names of the women who'd slept with her husband and did not want to know. Derrick had asked her if she'd wanted more children and she was forthcoming when she said yes, but only if she'd been married to a different man.

She tapped Aron's number, and he answered after the first ring. "Happy Easter, Mom."

"Happy Easter, sweetie."

"How is North Carolina?"

"Wonderful. How's it going with you?"

"I'll start my new position at the Kings County DA's office in a couple of weeks. It took a while to hear back from them until one of my law professors put in a good word for me. I've always heard it's not what you know but who you know."

At least he didn't have to rely on his father's influence, Leah mused. She was proud of her sons, who'd decided not to trade on the Kent name to advance their careers. Alan had been visibly upset after Aron and Caleb announced they were applying to law schools other than Georgetown Law, where generations of Kent men were alumni; however, his disappointment was lessened because they'd chosen his same career.

"Congratulations, Aron. I am so proud of you."

"Thanks. Have you spoken to Caleb?"

"Yes. He told me about his engagement."

"I shouldn't say this, but I am jealous of my brother. Marisa is incredible. She's smart and beautiful."

"I can't wait to meet her. What about you, Aron?"

"What about me, Mom?"

"Are you seeing anyone?"

Aron chuckled. "Do you know this is the first time you've ever asked me if I was seeing someone?"

"I never asked because I didn't want my children to think I was a busybody."

"It's Dad who's the meddler, because he's always trying to set us up with some of his colleagues' daughters or grand-daughters. I keep telling him I don't need help finding my own woman, but it just doesn't seem to register with him."

"It's been that way for generations of Kents. Many of the marriages were arranged."

"Well, that archaic tradition is going to end with me and Caleb."

Leah wanted to tell him it had ended with her. Unwittingly she'd been snared in a trap that had befallen so many vulnerable young women when they'd found themselves impressed *and* involved with older men. "Good for you."

"And to answer your question about me seeing someone, I was."

"Was it serious?"

"No. She played too many head games for me. She'd flirt with other men because she wanted to make me jealous. And then when I didn't react she'd throw a hissy fit."

"She sounds very immature, Aron."

"I realize that now that I've stopped seeing her."

"When did you break up with her?" Leah asked.

"A couple of weeks ago."

"The only advice I'm going to give you is to take some time for yourself before you begin dating again."

"I'm going to take a lot of time, Mom. I don't need any distractions now that I'm starting a new job. Hold on, Mom. I have another call, and I need to take it."

"That's okay, sweetie. We'll talk again at another time."

"Love you, Mom."

"Love you, too."

Leah ended the call, lowered the ringer, and set the phone on the bedside table. It wasn't often that she spoke to both her sons on the same day. Caleb now had a fiancée, while Aron was scheduled to begin a new career as a prosecutor.

She would also wait for Caleb to send her the contact information on the lawyer he'd recommended to take on her case. The sooner Alan was notified of her intent to dissolve their marriage, the sooner she would be able to plan her future.

Chapter 12

Derrick felt a restlessness akin to an itch he was unable to scratch, and he knew it had everything to do with Leah. It had been more than two months since she'd come to Coates Island, battered, bruised. That was then, and this was now. The bruises had vanished, and he got to see another side of a woman who had remained in a toxic marriage for more than half her life. She reminded him of a withering plant that had been neglected far too long but with food, sun, and water, she had revived to flourish as a vivacious woman who made him laugh and look forward to their next encounter.

Seeing her every day was a constant reminder what had been missing in his life: female companionship. His wife was gone, his daughter had elected to live in another state, and each time he opened the door to the beach house and encountered silence, he recalled Kayana teasing him about waiting to become a grandfather to begin dating again. He now looked forward to the beginning of the summer season if only to keep busy, and after he ended his shift for the night, he'd go home, shower, and go directly to bed.

His present schedule of preparing brunch on a two-week-on, two-week-off rotating schedule left him with too many hours to fill up with manufactured activities. There was just so much exercising and television watching he could cope with before leaving the house to sit on the porch and watch the seagulls swoop down and fight over remnants left on the sand from the incoming surf.

Leah coming to Coates Island and moving into the upstairs apartment had turned his life upside down. Touching and kissing her was a constant reminder of Kayana's insistence that he should be dating. And despite his protests, Derrick knew his sister was right. He went from the beach house to the restaurant and back again. Even sleeping with the divorcée had lost its appeal. It had been six weeks since their last encounter, and when he'd called to tell her he would no longer see her, he'd discovered she had blocked his number.

"Earth to Derrick."

Kayana calling his name shattered his reverie. "What's up?"

"You, Derrick. I've been talking to you, and it's apparent you'd zoned out."

It was Sunday, the restaurant was closed, and his sister had come in to pick up a few items she needed to restock her fridge. "I'm sorry, Kay. My mind was somewhere else."

Leaning against the countertop, Kayana folded her arms under her breasts. "Somewhere or someone?"

Slipping on the bibbed apron, Derrick looped the ties around his waist. "What are you trying to say?"

"Leah Kent."

"What about her, Kay?"

"You like her, don't you?"

He gave his sister a direct glance. He and Kayana had always been open and honest with each other, and with her training as a psychiatric social worker he always valued her advice. She had encouraged him to get his daughter into counseling following Andrea's passing, and it had taken several months, but he was able to see the changes in Deandra indicating she was healing emotionally.

"Yes, I like her."

"What are you going to do about it?"

"Nothing."

Kayana lowered her arms. "Nothing," she repeated. "I'm going to say the same thing to you that you told me about Graeme. You can't keep your eyes off her."

Derrick smiled. "That's because she's cute."

"Babies are cute. Little kids are cute. Puppies are cute, Derrick. Forty-something women are beautiful, lovely, attractive, stunning—"

"I get it, Kay," he said, laughing. "Leah is all that and more."

"Do you care to elaborate on the more?"

Derrick lowered his eyes. "She is rather sexy."

"Aww, sookie, sookie," Kayana drawled with a wide grin. "Brother love is physically attracted to my friend."

His expression changed, becoming a mask of stone. "Whether I'm physically attracted to her doesn't mean spit because I don't get involved with married women."

"Soon to be unmarried."

Derrick froze. Nothing moved, not even his eyes. "Say what?"

"Didn't she tell you?" Kayana asked.

"No. We don't discuss her marriage."

"What do you talk about whenever you're together?"

"Definitely not her abusive husband anymore," he said. "A couple of days after she came here I did ask her to be open with me about her accident because I'd suspected her husband was responsible for her injuries, and I needed to know how to respond if he decided to come after her."

Kayana rested her hands at her waist. "Things have changed for Leah, because she told me the other day that her husband has been served with a summons that she was divorcing him. He called her cell phone for the first time since she left him, and she let me listen to his voice mail message. He called her names I'd never repeat to anyone. Leah said she's going to save it as further evidence of his vindictiveness."

"It sounds as if she's in for a fight."

"I agree with you, Derrick. That's why she's going to need our support. Even though she has her sons to back up her claim that her husband assaulted her, don't forget he's still their father, and it's not going to be easy for them to forget all the good times they've shared with him."

"Let's hope he doesn't contest it, or he'll lose not only his wife, perhaps even his sons, but also his reputation and so-called good name."

"As they say, the ball is in his court, Derrick. He can either throw in the towel, or have his dirty linen aired publicly."

He smiled, nodding. "The judge should think of his current situation as a game show contestant facing the possibility of winning a big prize. And behind the three doors is an uncontested divorce, a white towel, and a pile of dirty linen. If he's smart, then he should choose the first or second door and get on with his life. If not, then his legacy will be as a domestic abuser."

"From what Leah has told me about him, I believe he's going to contest the divorce."

"Then it's his ass," Derrick predicted.

"I'm going to get what I need and then get out of your way."

He waited for Kayana to leave and was concentrating on cutting six chickens into quarters when Leah walked into the kitchen wearing an oversize white shirt, light-blue leggings, and matching ballet flats. With her bare face and hair styled in a ponytail she looked much younger than a woman approaching fifty.

Derrick smiled at her. "Good morning."

She returned his smile. "Good morning. I didn't expect to see you this early."

He glanced at the wall clock. It was 7:20. "I didn't plan to come in this early but since I was up I figured I'd get a jump on prepping meat for tomorrow." Derrick didn't tell Leah that he'd slept fitfully, got out of bed at five, worked out for an hour, and then came to the restaurant in an attempt to keep busy. "By the way, you just missed Kayana. She came in to pick up a few things."

"Are you a workaholic?"

"Why would you ask me that?" Derrick answered her question with one of his own.

"Because it's your day off, and you still come in to work."

"The tourist season will begin in another month, and I have to get into the mind set when we'll open at seven, close for a couple of hours between breakfast and lunch, and then lunch and dinner, and finally lock the doors sometime before ten at night." Derrick had told Leah a half lie. But there was no way he wanted to tell her she was the reason for his rest-lessness.

Leah sat on a stool. "That means I'll probably do most of my baking prep after you close for the night. Kayana told me she usually begins preparing for breakfast at five, so I'll come down at four to bake and finish up before she gets here."

"Just make certain you get enough sleep, because working in a restaurant can run you into the ground."

Resting her elbow on the table, Leah cradled her chin on her cupped hand. "The upside is I don't have to commute to work. And anytime I need a break I'll just go upstairs and take a power nap."

Derrick winked at her. "Showoff. As soon as I brine the chicken I'm going to make breakfast. What would you like?"

"Shrimp and grits."

"Hot damn! You must have read my mind."

Her pale eyebrows lifted. "Really?"

"Look in the refrigerator and you'll find a bowl of shrimp. Do you like old Charleston style shrimp and grits?"

"What makes it different from other recipes?"

"It's shrimp and grits on steroids, with bacon, andouille

sausage, green, red, and yellow bell pepper, chopped onion, minced garlic, half-and-half, Worcestershire sauce, shredded sharp cheese, and a pinch of cayenne pepper."

"That sounds delicious. Do you mind if I watch you make it?"

"What if you help me make it?"

"You've got yourself an assistant." Leah slipped off the stool and walked over to the shelf with aprons, tablecloths, and napkins. She put on an apron, covered her hair with a bandana, and washed her hands in one of the three industrial sinks.

It was her enthusiasm and willingness to help out in the kitchen that Derrick admired about Leah. He really did not need her assistance, but having her close by was a reminder of what he and Andrea had shared when dating. He knew it wasn't fair to compare Leah to his late wife in the same way he wouldn't want her to compare him to her soon-to-be ex-husband, yet it was the camaraderie of cooking together that he'd missed most from when he was married.

When he first met Andrea she'd told him up front that she was totally deficient as a cook. She could boil an egg, make instant coffee, toast, and heat up microwave meals. They'd dated for a year and were married for fifteen years when his wife turned her deficiency into proficiency in the kitchen.

Leah picked up a large colander and retrieved the ingredients needed for the shrimp and grits. "What's for dinner?"

Derrick smiled at her over his shoulder. "We haven't eaten breakfast and you're already asking about dinner."

"Sunday dinner was always a big deal at the Berkley house. We'd have a light breakfast before going to church. We always went to the early service and then returned home to begin cooking. Mama would always buy extra chicken liver, gizzard, necks, and backs because I would only eat them and not the legs or breasts."

Derrick threw back his head and laughed. "We have something in common. I like liver, gizzards, and wings."

"Do you know how to make dirty rice?" Leah asked.

"No. In fact I've never eaten it."

"It's like jambalaya, but with fewer ingredients. I haven't made it in a long time."

"Check the fridge, freezer, and pantry to see what we have on hand if you feel like making it. I know there are containers of chicken liver and gizzards in the freezer, along with several bags of frozen wings. Speaking of dinner, would you mind if we have breakfast here and dinner at my place?"

Leah executed a graceful curtsey. "Of course not."

If Leah thought of the apartment above the Café as her sanctuary, then Derrick's beach house was home. His arm had circled her waist as she sautéed ground pork for the dirty rice. She'd told herself that she was immune to Kayana's brother's sensual masculinity, but whenever he touched or kissed her she knew she had been in denial.

Her childhood dream of having a career was realized, while the dream of falling in love with that special man had been deferred—until now. Derrick had lost his wife, and she was in the process of ending her marriage to a monster. However, she was no eighteen-year-old with stars in her eyes because an older, wealthy man had expressed an interest in her, and she was not only older but hopefully much wiser when it came to her involvement with the next man.

Leah wasn't looking for marriage; she wanted a relationship where she felt comfortable enough with a man not to have to censor herself. She also needed the option and flexibility to come and go without needing his permission. And, more important, she needed him to respect her—something that was totally missing in her marriage.

Within minutes of picking up the phone to talk to Sabina Gagnon, Leah knew she'd hit the jackpot. The woman's rapid-fire, staccato style of questioning had initially unnerved her until Leah told her all she wanted was two million dollars to cover sixteen years of prorated salary and the legal use of her maiden name. She knew she had shocked Sabina when she rejected a bigger settlement for pain and suffering, but as the client she had established the terms.

Sabina was still awaiting a response from Alan's attorney, but just knowing he had been served was enough for Leah to finally exhale. She had endured three decades of bondage, and now that she knew emancipation was a possibility, she had resigned herself to wait for as long as it would take.

Derrick pressed his mouth to her hair. "I noticed you used the liver and gizzards, but not the hearts."

"I usually leave them out because even when chopped in the food processor they're still tough." She'd instructed him to finely chop the giblets, onion, bell pepper, and celery in a food processor, while she cooked the pork until there were no traces of pink. "I'm going to need a heavy saucepan." Derrick let go of her waist, and she immediately missed his protective warmth.

"One saucepan coming up."

"I need you to melt two tablespoons of butter and then add the giblet-vegetable mixture and sauté it until the onion is transparent. After that you can add the Creole seasoning, two tablespoons of salt, one teaspoon of Worcestershire sauce, a little crushed red pepper, and marjoram."

He added the ingredients she'd set on the countertop. "How much pepper and marjoram, babe?"

"Eyeball it, Derrick."

"One eyeball coming up," he teased.

Leah couldn't help laughing. "After you combine everything, you need to lower the heat to a simmer and cover the pot."

He inhaled the steam coming from the pot. "It smells wonderful."

"I'm going to let you make the rice because I still haven't perfected it like you and Kayana have."

"That's because we were graded whenever we attempted to make it. My mother would put our names on a chalkboard, and each time we made a pot she would give us a grade. Kay ruined so many pots that Mom threatened to ban her from the kitchen. The first time I got an A I couldn't stop teasing her, but I was never able to best her when it came to Grandma Cassie's mac and cheese or Mom's creole fried chicken."

Leah rested her head against his shoulder. "The Café's creole chicken is incredible. I don't intend to blow my own horn, but I can make awesome double-crunch fried chicken."

"I'll make the rice if you fry the chicken."

She smiled up at him. "That's a deal."

Leah did not have time to react when Derrick lowered his head and brushed his lips against hers in a kiss that was as light and gentle as a caress. Parting her lips, she went on tiptoe, moaning softly when his tongue dueled with hers. She managed to pull away because she knew if he continued to kiss her, she would shamelessly beg him to make love to her.

Her face was on fire, her body was on fire, and Leah knew if she did not put some distance between herself and Derrick, he would think she was a neglected, sex-starved woman who hadn't slept with her husband in more than ten years and wanted to use him to assuage her sexual drought.

She bit her lip and pretended to be interested in the skillet. The first time she saw Derrick she couldn't stop staring at him. Not only did he have a gorgeous face, but also the perfect body. And the contrast of his prematurely gray hair against his mahogany complexion was shockingly mesmerizing. Cherie had chided her for gawking at him because she was married, yet that hadn't mattered, because what Leah was going home to fell far short in comparison to what she was looking at.

She'd studied the photographs on the living room's fireplace mantelpiece and noticed Derrick was a more masculine version of his beautiful mother. There was a photo of him at his college graduation and another with him holding his infant daughter, and more with him, Kayana, and their sister as young children.

"Are you certain you want me to use chicken stock instead of water to cook the rice?"

Leah shivered as she felt Derrick's breath on the nape of her neck when he stood behind her. "Yes. It adds more flavor, because you're not going to drain it. Once the rice is fluffy you can add it to the pan with the chicken-vegetable mixture, and then the ground pork. Preheat the oven to three hundred degrees and put everything into a casserole dish for five minutes to absorb any remaining moisture."

"Is there anything else you want me to do?"

He was standing so close. Much too close for her to be able to draw normal breath. "Do you have anything for a salad?"

"I have enough romaine in the fridge to make a Caesar salad. Would you like me to make one?"

"Yes. But please don't put too many anchovies in the dressing."

"Whatever you wish, babe."

And it wasn't until he walked over to the refrigerator to get the chicken stock that she felt in control of her emotions. It had been more than three weeks since he'd kissed her in the garage, and that was the last time he'd demonstrated a modicum of affection. What had changed? And why now? Leah drained the excess fat from the skillet and set it aside.

Leah felt Derrick watching her as she dipped pieces of chicken sprinkled with garlic salt and pepper into a seasoned egg mixture and flour and then back into the egg mixture before she carefully dropped them into the deep fryer filled with peanut oil. "Double dipping will result in crispier chicken."

"Yes, ma'am."

She fried and drained the chicken and spooned the giblets into the middle of a platter and then surrounded them with crispy wings. Derrick had set the table in the breakfast nook with two place settings with wine and water glasses, the bowl of salad, and a tureen with the dirty rice. He took the platter from her and made room for it on the table.

"Red, white, or rosé? You're not driving, and Graeme brought over enough wine on Easter to last us for months," Derrick said when she hesitated.

Leah noticed he'd said "us," and wondered how many more times they would share dinner at the beach house. "White." And he was right about her not driving. She had left her car in the restaurant's lot once Derrick promised to drive her back.

He rested a hand at the small of her back. "Come sit and relax. You've done enough cooking today."

Leah slid onto the cushioned bench seat. "I enjoy cooking."

"I know you do, but I don't want you burned out before we even begin preparing for the influx of tourists. You really have no idea how hectic it can be."

"But everything appears to run so smoothly."

Derrick opened a wine cellar under the island and removed a bottle of white zinfandel. "The front runs smoothly while there is organized chaos in the kitchen. I can be a hard taskmaster whenever one of the waitstaff gives me the wrong order, so they've learned to check and double-check with the patrons as to what they want before placing their order."

Leah watched as he expertly uncorked the bottle. "Are you saying you're going to yell at me?"

"I don't yell, Leah. If my mother and father didn't yell and scream at each other, the sun wouldn't rise the next morning. And we know like clockwork that the sun always rises every day, rain or shine. The day my father packed his bags and left the house was the day I swore an oath that I would never raise my voice to anyone."

"You don't yell, so you must threaten."

Derrick returned to the table and met her eyes. "I don't threaten. I give verbal warnings. Three warnings in any one week and they're fired."

"How many have you fired?"

He smiled, flashing deep dimples in his clean-shaven jaw. "Only one since I took over managing the restaurant."

"How long has that been?"

"It will be four years in October."

There were so many more questions Leah wanted to ask Derrick, yet she did not want him to think she was interrogating him. Picking up the pitcher with ice-cold water, he filled her glass and his, and then repeated the action with the wine before sitting opposite her.

Derrick picked up his wineglass and stared directly at Leah. "To beauty and talent. A most winning combination." He bit back a smile when she demurely lowered her eyes.

Leah picked up her glass and took a sip. "Thank you."

"Did I embarrass you?" he asked when an attractive flush swept over her delicate features.

"No. It's just that I'm not . . ."

"It's just that you're not used to men complimenting you," Derrick said, completing her statement.

Leah's head popped up. "You're right."

Reaching for a pair of tongs, Derrick filled a plate with salad and handed it to Leah. "Your husband must have really done a number on you to make you believe men wouldn't be attracted to you."

Leah stared at her plate. "I was never aware if they were or weren't. Whenever we attended or hosted a social event I would morph into whatever Alan or his mother wanted me to be. Having my children is what saved me."

"Would you have stayed in the marriage if you didn't have children?"

"If I didn't have children, I never would've married Alan."

Derrick leaned forward. "You married him because you were pregnant."

"No, Derrick. Alan married me because I refused to have an abortion."

"Should I assume he blamed you for getting pregnant?"

Leah smiled. "You assume right," she said, filling her plate with rice and chicken. "I'm going to tell you how an eighteen-year-old college senior was beguiled by a thirty-five-year-old man and what ensued, and after I'm finished I don't want to talk about it again."

Derrick held up his hand. "You don't have to tell me."

"Yes, I do, Derrick. I want you to know what I've gone through to become the woman you see now. And I don't want you to pity me or say you feel sorry for me, because I'm not a victim."

He nodded. "Okay."

Derrick listened intently while eating dinner, his expression mirroring calmness as he successfully concealed his shock and awe when Leah revealed everything from the moment she bumped into Alan Kent and dropped her mother's Christmas gift to his vicious assault when she refused to agree to vacation with him. He noticed she'd refilled her wineglass three times while she hadn't touched the water glass. It was as if she needed the wine as a calming agent. And she was right. She wasn't a victim but a superwoman to have withstood verbal abuse from not only her husband but also her mother-in-law.

Reaching across the table, he held onto her left hand. "It's over, Leah. And you're safe. And if by some miracle he discovers you're living here, I don't want you to worry about anything."

"I'll tell you the same thing I told my sons. I don't want you involved in something that concerns me and Alan. I have a barracuda for an attorney, and I'm confident she'll get Alan to go along with my demands. We never had a prenup, so I could ask for a sizeable settlement. But I don't want alimony because I want a clean break. All I'm requesting is two million dollars to cover lost wages and two hundred thousand for legal fees."

"Your attorney's charging you almost a quarter million in legal fees?"

"No way. I factored in a generous bonus if she can get me what I want."

Derrick wanted to ask Leah if she also had barracuda tendencies. "Do you think he'll agree to your demands?"

Leah smiled. "We'll have to wait and see. Alan is hardly a pauper. He set up trust funds for our sons once they celebrated their tenth birthdays, and when his mother passes away he's her sole heir and beneficiary and stands to inherit millions. Alan won't blink an eye if he has to write a check to me and my attorney. He'll just have a little less to spend on his whores."

"I can't believe he's still whoring at his age."

"Once a dog, always a dog, Derrick. He doesn't think I know it, but he has to take a pill before he can achieve an erection. And coupled with his age, high blood pressure, and irregular heartbeat, that's a dangerous combination."

"What's he trying to do? Hasten his expiration date?"

Leah touched the napkin to the corners of her mouth. "I don't know. I think it's all about ego. It was the same with his father. They considered it a badge of honor to cheat on their wives and get away with it. What Alan failed to realize was that I didn't care who he slept with as long as he didn't touch me."

Derrick still was conflicted as he tried to understand why a woman would stay with a man whom she knew was cheating on her. The instant Kayana discovered her husband was having an affair she'd called him. His first impulse was to drive to Atlanta and confront his brother-in-law, but Kayana reassured him that she had everything under control. However, it was different with his youngest sister. He had appointed himself her protector, and once she told him her husband was filing for divorce Derrick did confront him. Errol was apologetic and said he didn't want to remain in a marriage where he and his wife argued constantly about how to raise their children, and he had to agree with his brother-in-law. He'd grown up in a chaotic household, and he didn't want a repeat for his niece and nephews.

Derrick thought about the divorces in his family: his parents and sisters. He was thirteen when he'd come home to find his mother singing, "O Happy Day," at the top of her lungs, and when he'd asked her why was she so happy, she showed him the court papers finalizing the dissolution of her marriage to a very unhappy man who had fathered her three children. Jocelyn's husband waited until he'd fathered three children to have a problem with her when it came to child rearing, while Kayana's husband had cheated on her with his colleague.

He stared at the clock on the microwave. "As of five-forty today, I suggest we end our Alan Kent book club discussion."

Leah scrunched up her nose. "I agree." She blew out a breath. "I think I drank too much wine."

Derrick patted his belly. "And I ate too much of everything." Leah continued to surprise with her cooking skills. The rice was delicious with just the right amount of heat to tantalize the palate. "I'd like for you to write down the recipe. I'm going to make up a few samples until I perfect it enough to add to the menu for a daily special."

"You really like it?"

"For a rice-eating Carolinian I love it."

"That's really a compliment coming from you."

"Although I rarely fry chicken, I did see how you make it, and I'm going to use your method. Perhaps we can have a wing night special. It's funny that you and Kay have come up with new recipes while I've continued with the traditional dishes that are customer favorites."

"What was Kayana's contribution?"

"Korean barbecue. During a trip to New York City, she told me that she'd visited several Korean restaurants and found herself instantly addicted to several of their dishes. Once back in Atlanta, she'd experimented with Korean barbecue, and after a few attempts was able to duplicate some of her favorites."

"The first time I ordered it for dinner I was hooked. Your waitress gave me the side-eye when I said I wanted two orders to go. She must have thought I was a glutton, because she knew I always dined alone."

Throwing back his head, Derrick let out a belly laugh. "How long did it last you?"

Pinpoints of color dotted Leah's cheeks. "Almost four days."

He sobered. "That long?"

"Yes. I wanted it to last because I was too embarrassed to come in after a couple of days and order it again."

"Well, you don't have to be embarrassed anymore, because I'm going to grill some for you."

"What do you use for the marinade?"

"Onion, garlic cloves, brown sugar, black pepper, soy sauce, sesame oil, pear, mirin, and ginger. Do you want short ribs or ribeye steak?"

"I don't have a preference. Why do you include a pear?"

"Most Korean barbecue recipes call for a pear, and I assume it's because they have a naturally high sugar content."

Leah closed her eyes and rested her head against the back of the bench. "I think I'm under the influence."

Derrick recalled her admitting she'd drunk too much champagne and ended up in bed with a man who had taken advantage of her naïveté, and that resulted in her becoming pregnant. He'd plied her with alcohol despite her informing him she didn't drink, because she had not yet reached the legal age.

"Why don't you go upstairs and lie down for a while."

She opened her eyes. "I'll be all right. I'm just going to sit here."

Derrick stood, rounded the table, and scooped Leah off the bench seat at the same time she let out a little shriek. "You'll be a lot more comfortable in a bed."

Leah pushed against his chest. "I'm okay."

Just like you were okay when you were too intoxicated to realize you'd had unprotected sex, he thought. "I'm still taking you upstairs." He shifted her body when he felt her breast against his chest.

"No-o-o!"

Derrick registered the panic in her voice and felt her trembling, while wondering if Leah was reliving the scene and the act that had changed her life forever. "It's all right, babe. I'm not going to hurt you." In fact, he wasn't going to do anything to her she did not want him to do.

He took the stairs two at a time, walked into the guest bedroom, and placed her on the bed. Sitting on the side of the mattress, he removed her shoes, and then reached over for the throw at the foot of the bed and covered her body. Dipping his head, he kissed her forehead.

"I'll be back later to check on you."

Leah caught his wrist. "Derrick."

"What is it?"

"I really like you."

He smiled. She was slurring her words. "And I really like you, too."

Derrick moved off the bed and left the room. He hadn't lied to Leah. He did really like her enough to invite her into his home. Even though his sister had nagged him about inviting a woman over for dinner to the point where he wanted to yell at her to mind her own damn business, he was glad he'd waited.

He liked Leah's bubbly laugh, her upbeat disposition, and their compatibility extended to cooking and old-school music. He'd tuned the radio in the kitchen to a station playing classic hits from the sixties and seventies while they'd prepared breakfast, and she knew the words to every Earth, Wind, and Fire and Roberta Flack song.

She liked reading, and he was into sports, and come summer she would resume her book club meetings while he
would get together with Graeme to watch baseball and the
NBA and NHL playoffs.

Derrick planned to clean the kitchen and then watch a
New York Mets game he had set to DVR. And when Leah
woke he would drive her back to the Café.

Chapter 13

L eah woke up with a dry mouth. "Never again," she whispered.

She remembered drinking more than two glasses of wine when one should have been her limit. Rolling over, she pressed her face into the pillow and reversed her position quickly and sat up. Bright sunlight came through the partially drawn drapes, and it dawned on her she was not only not in the bed in her apartment, but she had also overslept.

Sweeping back the sheet and lightweight blanket, Leah stared at the T-shirt with a fading logo. It was apparent Derrick had undressed her. She remembered him carrying her up the stairs and putting her on the bed, but nothing beyond.

I wasn't just under the influence, she thought. *I was drunk.*

Combing her fingers through her hair, she fell back to the pillows cradling her shoulders. It was as if history was repeating itself. Decades ago, she'd shared dinner with a man, drunk too much, and had unprotected sex. Fast-forward thirty years, and again she had too much to drink and found herself in a man's house—but not in his bed.

Her parents, expressly her father, had lectured her relent-
lessly before she left for college not to indulge in underage
drinking. Larry Berkley warned her about attending frat parties where boys deliberately got girls drunk and she might become a victim of gang rape. He compounded her fear when
he told her about girls going to bars and someone putting
something in their drink and never being seen again. Leah
had heeded their warnings, and during her three years at college she never attended an on- or off-campus party but made
it a practice to attend the Vanderbilt Commodores football,
basketball, and baseball games.

However, she'd let down her guard when agreeing to drink
champagne with Alan. Not only was it her first time drinking
with him, but after a few sips she'd immediately felt the effects when she'd shed her inhibitions. Leah had blamed Alan
for taking advantage of her while under the influence; however, she'd realized she also had to share blame, because he
did not force her to drink three glasses when in the past she
had barely finished one.

A dreamy smile parted her lips. Kayana was right about
her brother. He was a good guy. He had undressed her while
allowing her a modicum of modesty when he hadn't removed
her underwear. She felt pressure on her bladder and got out
of bed before she embarrassed herself. Leah walked into the
en suite bath and saw a sheet of paper taped to the vanity
mirror.

**Went to work. Did not want to wake you. I didn't set the
house alarm. Call me at the Café.—Derrick**

She planned to call him, but only after she brushed her
teeth and took a shower. Leah opened a closet in the second
floor bathroom and discovered shelves with terrycloth bath-
robes in various sizes, a supply of toothbrushes, combs, shampoo, conditioners, roll-on and spray deodorants, and facial

and body lotions; it was everything she needed to complete her morning ablutions.

Twenty minutes later, wrapped in a terrycloth robe, she reentered the bedroom and retrieved her cell phone from the tote Derrick had left on the chair with her blouse and leggings. After shampooing her hair and washing her body with a thick, rich bath gel, she felt revived.

After she tapped the number for the Seaside Café, Leah counted off three rings before Derrick's deep voice came through the speaker. "Good morning, sunshine."

"Good morning, Derrick."

"How are you feeling?"

"Wonderful now. Why didn't you wake me?"

"I figured you needed the sleep. I can't come and get you now because it's only minutes from opening. Do you want me to go upstairs to your place and bring you a change of clothes?"

Leah knew Derrick had an extra set of keys to the apartment. "Okay."

"What do you want me to bring?"

"A pair of jeans, socks, tennis shoes, and a T-shirt. And please bring my brush from the bathroom."

"What about underwear, Leah? Or do you plan to go commando for me?"

Her breath quickened as her cheeks warmed, and Leah was angry with herself for being embarrassed. After all, she was a mature woman with adult sons, yet Derrick's suggestion she go without her panties when they were together had her fantasizing about making love with him.

"I've never gone commando," she whispered. Derrick's chuckle caressed her ear.

"I embarrassed you, didn't I?"

"No, you didn't," she countered quickly.

"Yes, I did, Leah, because you're breathing heavily. And I definitely wouldn't mind if you decided not to put on panties."

Leah was barely able to control her gasp of surprise at his suggestion. It was obvious she wasn't the only one entertaining licentious thoughts. "I'm not going *out* without panties, Derrick."

"You can stay *in* without them."

"Please bring underwear when you come," she said, because she had no comeback to his hint.

"Will do, babe. I'll see you later."

Leah ended the call. Exchanging flirty repartee with a man was something she should've experienced in her teens or twenties, not when she was rapidly approaching the big five-oh.

She put on the ballet flats and went downstairs to the kitchen and opened the refrigerator. It was stocked with the ingredients she needed to make an omelet with smoked ham, mushrooms, red and green pepper, and yellow onion. Derrick had put the leftovers from last night's dinner in clear plastic containers.

Leah made the omelet, brewed a cup of coffee, and retreated to the breakfast nook to enjoy her breakfast. The first time Derrick had asked her to stay over she'd declined the invitation but did promise she would at another time. She smiled. Last night had become that time. She lingered long enough to brew a second cup of coffee from the single-serve coffeemaker, and as the clock inched closer to eleven she got up, cleaned the kitchen, and went upstairs to wash her clothes.

The hamper was half filled with Derrick's clothes and bath towels. She separated them by color and put up several loads. The bungalow she'd rented last summer had a washer and dryer, and she'd had to read the manual to learn how to operate the digital model. It was then she had experienced twin emotions of accomplishment and ineptness. In all the years she'd lived at Kent House she never had to do her own laundry. Adele reminded her, and not for the first time, that she'd hired people to cook, clean, and do laundry, while it was beneath Alan's wife to be seen doing manual or menial chores around the house.

After a while, Leah felt Adele had relegated her to a specific lifestyle in order to make her reliant on Alan. It was only after she'd begun teaching and earning her own salary that she was able to feel a sense of independence. And when she went to visit her parents before their scheduled move to Kentucky, she confided to her mother that the money she earned was hers to keep, and unlike her, she did not have to contribute to the household.

Madeline gave her the same advice she had been given by her mother: always keep a rainy-day account for herself. Madeline had said *rainy day* while Leah's grandmother had called it *fuck you* money, because a woman never knew when her husband would decide to leave and not come back, and meanwhile the wife had depended on him to keep a roof over her head and food on the table for their children. That was when Leah began depositing ninety percent of her take-home pay in a retirement account that wasn't contingent on the fluctuating stock market.

Although having enough money was never her concern, she was still inexperienced when it came to things other women her age had encountered. She'd gone from her father's house to her husband's house when she should've been teaching and traveling with friends and coworkers who were the epitome of sexually independent women. Then she would've been given the option of dating, sleeping with, and marrying whomever she chose.

However, whenever she found herself sinking deeper into the abyss of self-pity, Leah had to remind herself if her life had taken another path she never would've had her sons. They were the light of her life and her pride and joy. And she still could not understand how they had turned out so unlike their father when he had played such a pivotal role in their upbringing. She had admitted to Kayana that Alan was a much better father than a husband.

Although Aron and Caleb weren't perfect, they were well mannered and ethical. Even as teenage boys they were very discriminating when it came to dating, although they were popular with a few girls who flirted shamelessly with them. Whenever she'd asked either one whether they liked a girl, Caleb would complain she was too aggressive, or Aron's comeback was he did not want to hook up with anyone because it would interfere with his schoolwork. Once they left to attend college, she stopped asking them about the women with whom they were involved.

She smiled. Caleb's revelation that he had proposed to his girlfriend had not just taken her by surprise; she now knew for certain her sons would not bear any resemblance to former generations of Kent men.

Derrick parked the Highlander in the garage, then reached for the quilted weekender with the clothes Leah had asked him to bring and a shopping bag with a container of marinating ribeye steak. After hanging up with Leah he'd chided himself for teasing her about not wearing panties. He thought she was going to tell him that he'd gone too far, because he didn't know her like that, but when she didn't, he hoped she wouldn't hold it against him.

Perhaps he'd become rusty in the romance department. Andrea had died five years ago, and Leah was the first woman, other than his female relatives, to sleep under his roof. And he should have taken Kayana's advice to begin dating again, because he was mourning for someone that wasn't coming back.

But Derrick knew that hadn't been possible as long his teenage daughter lived with him. He did not want to introduce her to a strange woman when she was still grieving the loss of her mother. However, when Deandra went to Florida to spend the summer with her aunt, grandmother, and cousins and decided to stay rather than return to Coates Island, the situation, though unplanned, told him he should have stopped sleeping with the divorcée and have an open relationship with someone not based on sex.

He opened the door to the mudroom, leaving his shoes on the mat. It was a habit he'd developed when he returned from New York to help his mother manage the Café. Work shoes were never worn in the house, and he never came home wearing his chef's jacket and pants. They were deposited in bags to be picked up by the laundry service.

Derrick walked into the kitchen and stopped short. Leah stood at the sink in her leggings, ballet flats, and one of his University of Alabama T-shirts. Wavy strawberry blond hair covered the nape of her long neck. He set her bag on a stool at the island.

"Who is this strange woman, and how did she come to be in my kitchen?"

He knew he'd surprised her when she spun around and stared at him as if he'd grown an eye in the middle of his forehead. Derrick couldn't pull his gaze away when she covered her heaving breast with both hands.

"What are you doing sneaking up on me? You almost gave me a heart attack."

Derrick approached Leah and brushed a kiss over her mouth. "Never." He peered over her shoulder. "What are you making?"

"Dinner."

"What's for dinner?"

"Stuffed mushrooms, asparagus with Romano cheese, and spaghetti with garlic and oil. When I looked in the refrigerator's vegetable drawer I noticed the mushrooms and asparagus were going soft. I hate throwing away food, so I used my phone to search for recipes for stuffed mushrooms. And instead of boiling the asparagus I'm going grill them under the broiler."

Derrick winked at her. "You're going to spoil me if you keep this up."

Leah's blue eyes crinkled in a smile. "You do enough cooking, so it's time you let someone else cook for you. By the way, why do you have so much food in your fridge if you cook at the restaurant?"

"September to May I keep it stocked because I'm home every night. Remember, Kay and I rotate working two weeks on and two weeks off. I come in after the Café closes to help clean up while she preps for the next day, and she does the same when I'm working."

"That's what I call an equitable division of labor."

"It works for us, babe." He walked to the refrigerator and put the container with the steak on a shelf. "I marinated some ribeye for Korean barbecue, but we can have it for tomorrow's dinner along with fried rice."

"We're on a roll, Derrick. Southern last night, Italian tonight, and Asian tomorrow."

"Will you come up with a menu for the rest of the week?"

Leah shook her head. "No. I'm going to leave that up to you, because you're the one who lived in New York where there are thousands of restaurants with different dishes from all over the world."

Derrick knew she was right. He could dine at a different restaurant every day for a year and not visit the same one twice. He'd eaten in French, Chinese, Greek, Mexican, Cuban, soul food, Korean, Indian, and Thai restaurants.

"I'm going upstairs to shower and change, then I'll be back to help you."

"Take your time. I'm good here."

Derrick walked out of the kitchen and took the staircase to the second story. If Leah was good, then he was even better. Walking into the house to find her in the kitchen made him aware of what he had missed. It wasn't about sex. It was having someone to talk to and laugh with.

But he had to be very careful with Leah. She was his sister's friend, and Kayana would bring holy hell down on him if she suspected he was taking advantage of Leah. However, Leah wasn't as emotionally fragile as she appeared. She'd lived with a man who tried to break her spirit, but doing so made her even stronger. She wasn't a victim or a survivor. And she was a mother who'd raised her sons not to mirror their father's behavior.

Derrick entered his bedroom and saw the stack of folded clothes and towels on the leather bench at the foot of the bed. It was apparent Leah had kept busy doing laundry and cooking, no doubt to make up for when she was mandated to follow the dictates of her mother-in-law.

He knew when Kayana and Leah discussed books they also confided in each other about their marriages. His sister had resented her husband using their home like a nightclub where he'd entertained his friends and colleagues several times a month. She had put up with it until she discovered he'd cheated on her, and their twenty-year marriage came to a screeching stop. And Leah had put up with a cheating, dictatorial, verbally abusive husband until he hit her. The single act had galvanized her to leave and file for divorce after thirty years.

Both had married wealthy, prominent men who sought to conceal their clandestine affairs in order to preserve their status within their social circle. Derrick smiled when he recalled his grandmother's sage warning: "You may get by, but you'll never get away." His brother-in-law got his comeuppance because he married Kayana without a prenup, and it was apparent karma was breathing down Judge Alan Kent's neck, because Leah had threatened to expose him as a batterer if he contested the divorce.

Stripping off his clothes, Derrick walked into the master suite's bathroom and stepped into the freestanding shower with an oversize showerhead. Despite changing out of street clothes and into a chef uniform and cap, the smell of food permeated the fabric to cling on his skin and hair. His normal routine was shaving before showering, but tonight was different. He wanted to spend as much time with Leah as possible. He shampooed his hair and then soaped his body. After rinsing off, he stepped out and picked up a towel from a stack on a low bench and dried off. Dressed in a pair of walking shorts and T-shirt, he descended the staircase and made his way into the kitchen.

Leah hummed along with a classic Stevie Wonder song as she concentrated on cutting cloves of garlic into thin slices. She had admitted to Derrick that she loved cooking because it was a reminder of the normalcy she'd experienced when growing up. There was never a day in the week when she could not be found in the kitchen. She would come home after classes were dismissed, change out of her school clothes, and then make her way into the kitchen to do her homework while her mother would begin making dinner. Madeline always timed the meal to coincide with her husband coming home and taking a shower before the family sat down at the table. Leah had the responsibility of setting the table, while her brother cleared the table. After her grandmother passed away and her mother went to work in the dress factory, Leah assumed some of the responsibility to help Madeline prepare meals.

Leah saw movement out the side of her eye and smiled at Derrick as he joined her in the kitchen. She sucked in a breath when staring at his muscular legs in a pair of shorts. He admitted to working out every day, and it was evident.

"It looks as if you have everything under control."

He rested a hand at the small of her back and then gently massaged her shoulder blades. His warmth and the lingering scent of his body wash sent chills up and down her body as Leah pointed to the pan with four mushrooms stuffed with spicy sausage meat and topped with panko breadcrumbs.

"I just finished mixing the stuffing for the mushrooms. I had to use dry parsley when I would've preferred fresh."

"I normally don't keep fresh herbs in the house. If I know I'm going to make a dish that calls for them, I'll bring some from the restaurant."

"Why don't you grow some here and use them when needed?"

"I am not a farmer, Leah."

She smiled at him over her shoulder. "You don't have to be a farmer to have an herb garden. You can buy them already potted and replant them near the she-shed or line up small pots on the window ledge in the breakfast nook."

Derrick kissed her ear. "You can buy them and put them wherever you like, and I'll reimburse you."

"You don't have to reimburse me, Derrick. Buying a few herbs will definitely not bankrupt me. I'll probably buy them online rather than drive to a mainland nursery."

"If you order them online, then charge it to the restaurant's account."

Leah didn't want to argue with Derrick about money. "Okay."

He smiled. "What do you plan to buy?"

"Parsley, basil, mint, rosemary, thyme, sage, cilantro, oregano, dill, and lemongrass."

"Impressive."

She elbowed him softly in the ribs. "You're going to have to let me go so I can work here." As much as Leah enjoyed the press of his body against hers, she found it much too distracting.

Derrick took a backward step. "Is there anything I can help with?"

"You can put up a pot of water for the spaghetti."

He executed a snappy salute. "Yes, chef."

Leah wanted to remind him she was not a chef. There were only two places where she felt completely secure: the classroom and the kitchen. She'd encouraged her students to debate an author's motivation for writing a novel; and when the discussions became spirited Leah knew they were totally involved in the required readings.

Then there was the kitchen. If it was the heart of the house, then cooking was its life's blood. And Leah equated it to family. It was where people gathered for their meals, shared stories of what had occurred in their lives that day, and where recipes were passed down through countless generations. And for her, it had become the most inviting and comfortable room in the house.

"What are we drinking tonight?"

Leah slowly shook her head. "Definitely not wine."

Reaching into an overhead cabinet, Derrick took down plates and glasses. "Kayana said you guys were lit up during your book club meetings. What were you drinking?"

"We had martinis, margaritas, and one time it was a champagne punch. But there wasn't so much champagne that I wound up with a headache."

"So, you ladies went for the hard stuff?"

"Not every meeting. There was one where we served mocktails."

Leah had enjoyed the weekly get-togethers. She had bonded quickly with Kayana because they were closer in age and both had been married, while she and Cherie would figuratively bump heads when the younger woman would attack her without provocation. It was Kayana who came to her defense, and Leah viewed her as an ally and now as an unofficial sister.

She could have gone to Kentucky after the assault to stay with her immediate family and wait for her bruised body to heal, but instead had driven to North Carolina and the Seaside Café and her friend because she knew Kayana would not be judgmental. Even when she'd told her about her dysfunctional marriage, not once had her friend suggested she leave Alan. As a professional social worker, Kayana knew once Leah tired of the abuse she would leave. And she was right.

She had left Richmond in late January, and it was now the last week in April, and in that span of time Leah had come to know and like who she had become. She was free to go to bed and wake up whenever she wanted. And she did not have to concern herself whether she had to wear makeup or dress a certain way in case Alan brought someone to their home for dinner. The rigid, suffocating lifestyle she had endured for more than half her life was dead and never to be resurrected.

The month was also significant because of her sons' birthday. She'd gifted Aron with a Waterford crystal hockey puck paperweight and Caleb with a Waterford globe paperweight. It had become more difficult for her to come up with appropriate gifts for them. Alan had bought them new cars for their sixteenth birthdays, vehicles they'd left in Richmond once they left for college. They would drive them when they came back in between semesters, but when they announced their intention to live in New York Leah convinced Alan to donate the vehicles to two local charities.

Next year she would turn fifty, and if she lived to be eighty-one, then she would be able to celebrate thirty-one years of freedom compared to the thirty she had spent in emotional bondage.

"Sweet tea or lemonade?" Derrick asked Leah.

"Lemonade."

"I usually make it with club soda and grenadine so it's pink and fizzy."

"Show off."

Derrick blew her an air kiss. "Anything to impress my lady."

She sobered with his reference to her being his lady. Did she want to be his lady? Yes, she did. Leah wanted to be Derrick's lady, girlfriend, and lover. He was the first man who made her want all of him. And as much as she tried to deny it, she knew she was falling in love with Kayana's brother. He possessed every good thing she looked for in a man. He was kind, gentle, friendly, generous, and it was obvious he loved and supported his daughter and sister.

"Am I really your lady, Derrick?" The question came out before she could censor herself.

He met her eyes. "You could be, but only if you want."

Her lip trembled, and she bit so hard she could feel it pulsing. She was standing in the middle of the kitchen of a man who had enthralled her from the first time she saw him. Leah wasn't certain whether it was about his masculine beauty, but there was something about the man Kayana had introduced as her brother that communicated he was everything her husband wasn't and couldn't be.

At first she thought the attraction was solely physical until she witnessed the interaction between him and Kayana. His voice would change, softening in tone, whenever he tried to convince her to come around to his way of thinking. Kayana told her that even though she and Derrick were equal co-owners, it was her brother who had purchased the restaurant from their mother once she decided to retire.

"I do," she whispered. Those were the same two words she had uttered when asked if she would take Alan Stephens Kent to become her lawfully wedded husband. But Derrick wasn't Alan, and the two words now meant something entirely different.

Derrick blinked. "Do you know what this means, Leah? Once we begin, there will be no turning back. Let me know whether you're all in, because it won't upset me if you don't—"

"I'm all in, Derrick Johnson," she said, cutting him off.

Leah wiped her hands on a dish towel and approached him. Curving her arms under his shoulders, she pressed her breasts against his muscled chest and breathed a kiss on his throat. She wanted to kiss his mouth but knew that would prove disastrous because then she would beg him to make love to her over and over like an addict craving a drug. Light from overhead pendants glinted off his gray hair, turning it a shimmering silver.

Cradling her face in his hands, Derrick smiled. "I was hoping you would say that."

Her pale eyebrows flickered. "Really?"

"Yes really. That's why I packed several changes of clothes for you."

Her jaw dropped. "You were so certain that I would spend another night here?"

"Not certain, but hoping and praying," he admitted. "I put you in the guest bedroom last night when I really wanted you in my bed. And given your condition, I would not have taken advantage of you, but it has been so long since I've had a woman in this house, in my bed, that I've had erotic dreams about you."

Leah laughed. "Erotic enough that you wake up with an erection?" She knew she'd shocked him when she felt him go stiff. "Did I shock you?"

He smiled. "Yes. But I like that you feel comfortable speaking your mind."

"Then be prepared, because there are things that come out of my mouth that even shock me."

Derrick sobered. "We're not kids, Leah, so we should be free to say whatever we want."

Going on tiptoe, she pressed a kiss over one eye and then the other. He smelled so good that Leah wanted to taste him from head to toe. "I agree, as long as it's not mean and hurtful. How often do you want me to sleep over?" She had to know if he wanted her to stay a few nights a week or longer.

"Every night."

Easing back, she stared up at him. "Are you asking me to move in with you?"

"Yes. I want to wake up and go to sleep knowing you're in the house. And whenever I'm off I want to take you to someplace where you've never been. We can have movie night here or at the theater in Shelby. I want to do all the things with you that you missed during your marriage and what I've missed since becoming a widower."

A half smile parted her lips. "In other words you want us to date?"

"Yes."

"What about your daughter, Derrick? How will she react when she finds out you're living with a woman?"

"Let's get one thing straight, Leah. I love my daughter unconditionally, but I will not allow her to dictate what goes on in my life. I wanted her to live with me until she went off to college, but she opted to spend her senior year in Florida. I was upset because I wasn't ready to let her go, yet I didn't want to demand she come back home because that would've destroyed our relationship. She's eighteen and no longer a child. She can vote, enlist in the military, and marry without my permission. What she needs is my financial and emotional support. And that's what I give her. Once she enrolls in college in the fall she'll probably meet some boy who will become the center of her universe and I'll have to accept that Daddy is no longer the only man in her life. And to answer your question, however Deandra reacts will not affect our living arrangements. I want you here, and you're welcome to stay as long as you want."

"Thank you for clearing that up." What Leah did not want to do was come between Derrick and his daughter because of a belief she was trying to supplant her mother. "Do you expect me to sleep with you?" She had to ask because he'd said, "I want to wake up and go to sleep knowing you're in the house."

"I don't expect you to do anything you don't want to do. You should know I do want to make love with you, but only on your terms. And remember, you're always free to leave whenever you want."

Leah was momentarily stunned. Derrick was giving her a choice—something she'd never had with Alan. It had been his way or no way.

She wanted and needed to be made love to in the worst way, yet knowing she and Derrick would sleep under the same roof made that inevitable.

She struggled not to break down and cry happy tears. "Thank you."

The Beach House   221

Derrick kissed her forehead. "No, babe. Thank *you*. You're the best thing to come into my life in a long time."

Going on tiptoe, Leah pressed her mouth to his ear. "You don't have worry about getting me pregnant, because I had my tubes tied."

"And I'm too old to think about fathering more children. Kay's been teasing me about becoming a grandfather, and I keep telling her that I'm not ready for that. Maybe I'll be ready in another ten years."

"How old are you?" Leah asked.

"I'll be forty-nine in November."

"I'm six months older than you. I'll turn forty-nine next month."

"That's okay. I happen to like older women."

Leah landed a soft punch on his shoulder. "I'm not that old."

"You're not. When I first saw you, I thought you were in your late thirties."

"So you were looking at me?"

"Hell, yeah. I was checking you out. But when I saw your wedding band I knew you were unavailable."

"The ring was all for show, Derrick. I was always a mother but never a wife."

"Do you want to get married again?"

Leah shook her head. "No. Once is enough. I'd be content to spend the next thirty years of my life unencumbered. What about you? Do you want to remarry?"

Derrick angled his head. "I really don't think about it."

"Well, it looks as if we're both on the same page when it comes to marriage." She untangled her arms. "I have to finish cooking before my stomach starts growling."

"What did you eat today?" Derrick asked.

"I had an omelet this morning and nothing else."

"You need to eat more often, because I like a woman with a little junk in her trunk."

"Is trunk the same as booty?"

Derrick laughed. "Yes. Why?"

"Kayana told me that her brother happens to like women with some booty."

"She's right." He cupped her hips, squeezing her buttocks through the leggings. "You're getting there."

"So you're an ass man?"

"I like what's above the neck rather than what's below it. If I can't have an intelligent conversation with a woman, then it doesn't matter what she looks like. You just happen to be an H to T."

"What's that?"

"Head to toe, babe." He made a sweeping motion over his body. "All of it."

Leah stared at Derrick with a longing she was unable to disguise. When she'd revealed she had zero chance of becoming pregnant it had become an open invitation for him to make love to her. "I'd better get back to cooking or neither of us will eat tonight."

Chapter 14

Derrick experienced a gentle peace for the first time since becoming a widower. He wasn't one to believe he needed a woman to complete him, yet when he'd met Andrea she unknowingly had become the missing piece in his life. She'd left him, and his world would have shattered completely if it hadn't been for their daughter.

Now, five years later, he sat across the table from a woman who was physically the opposite of the woman whom he'd married and who had charmed him where he'd opened his heart to possibly fall in love again. There were so many things he had come to like about Leah: her wit, optimism, her low, sultry voice, and her confidence to say exactly what she felt.

Leah was so completely different from any other woman he'd met and known, and that left him slightly off-balance and guarded—something he'd never been before. Sleeping with the divorcée was something both wanted. It was sex with the promise of not asking more from each other. And a few times Derrick suspected he wasn't the only man in her life.

"Tell me about your wife, Derrick."

His head popped up, and he stared at Leah, wondering if she'd read his mind. The meal she had prepared was nothing short of perfection. The spicy sage-stuffed, breadcrumb-topped mushrooms, drizzled with garlicky-lemon liquid, were comparable to those he'd eaten at his favorite New York City Italian restaurant. The grilled asparagus dusted with garlic powder and Romano cheese were tender, and Leah had browned the garlic in an ovenproof skillet under the broiler and then cooked it on the stovetop with red pepper flakes, parsley, and chicken broth before adding the al dente spaghetti. She added grated Parmigiano-Reggiano, coated the pasta with the sauce before taking the skillet off the heat and adding virgin olive oil, salt, and pepper and tossing thoroughly. Derrick congratulated her again for concocting an incredibly delicious dish.

"What do you want to know?"

"How did you meet?"

Derrick rested his head against the seat back and closed his eyes. "I met Andrea at a social mixer in a restaurant where a lot of people that worked on or near Wall Street hung out after hours. She was sitting at a table with another woman crying inconsolably. Once she was alone I went over to her to ask if she was okay."

Leah leaned over the table. "What did she say?"

He opened his eyes. "Her fiancé had broken up with her because he'd met someone else. And that someone else was one of her coworkers."

"Pig!" Leah spat out.

"I remember Andrea calling him a low dog. I managed to convince her to leave and go for a walk to clear her head. We walked from Trinity Place to Kips Bay, where she shared an apartment with a friend from college."

"I know nothing about New York City. How far did you have to walk?"

"About three miles."

"Where did you live?"

"I had a studio apartment in the West Village. That's almost two miles from Kips Bay. Folks in Manhattan do a lot of walking, so it would take me about forty minutes to walk from my place to hers. She was a native New Yorker, having grown up on Long Island, and had graduated from Pace University with degrees in finance and taxation. She laughed when I told her I'd graduated from the University of Alabama with a double major in accounting and finance, and said it was a good sign that we both had majored in finance. She had a position as a money manager for a Wall Street company, while I worked for an investment firm. I gave her my business card and told her to call me when she was feeling better."

"How long did it take for her to call you?"

Derrick smiled when he saw excitement light up Leah's eyes. "Three months. When I finally met her again, she told me she had changed jobs, and she was seeing a psychiatrist who had prescribed medication for her depression. We dated for a year, then decided to get married. Andrea claimed she never learn to cook, so I prepared all the meals. We bought a condo in a high-rise overlooking the Hudson River, but only got to enjoy the water views on the weekends. Most nights we were too exhausted to do anything more than wolf down takeout and go to bed. Although we earned six-figure salaries and generous bonuses, both of us were close to burnout.

"Once Andrea told me she was pregnant, I convinced her to quit her job and stay home. That's when she talked about moving out of the city to one of the suburbs. We came down here on vacation, and when Andrea discovered a developer was building new beachfront homes she said we should buy one. I jumped at her suggestion because I was tired of the rat race. We sold the condo and all the furnishings before the baby was born and moved in with my mother until our house was finished. Meanwhile Andrea learned to make more than boiled eggs, instant coffee, toast, and heat up microwave meals. I helped Mom at the Café while Andrea managed the restaurant's finances.

"Deandra was six months old when we finally moved into this house, because Andrea went through a few interior decorators until she found one she liked. I would notice her grimacing every once in a while, and she complained about pulling a muscle in her back. No matter how often I would tell her to see a doctor she'd take a couple of ibuprofens and claim the pain was gone. But the pain would come and go over the years, and then one morning she was in so much discomfort that she couldn't get out of bed. I took her to the hospital, and after they ran a battery of tests, the result was stage-four pancreatic and bile duct cancer that had metastasized. She refused chemo and begged me not to send her to hospice."

"Why did she not want treatment that could possibly prolong her life?"

"She was tired, Leah. She had been in pain so long that she just wanted it to go away. I hired a live-in private-duty nurse to make certain she was comfortable, and when I'd come home after work the nurse told me Andrea would spend most of the day in the garden shed reading and napping. When she was too weak to walk, she'd sit in a wheelchair on the porch and stare at the ocean. She knew she was dying, and she made me promise not to grieve for her, that I should find someone to love me as much as she had. She lapsed into a coma and passed away a week later." Derrick closed his eyes for several seconds and exhaled a breath. "The hardest thing I'd ever had to do in my life was tell my daughter that her mother was gone and not coming back. I got into it with my in-laws because they wanted Andrea buried in the family plot on Long Island, while Andrea had put it in writing that she wanted to be cremated and her ashes scattered in the ocean. Her parents, brother, sister, and several cousins came down for the service, and left as soon as it was over."

"Why couldn't they understand it was Andrea's wish, not yours, that she wanted to be cremated?"

Derrick noticed Leah's eyes had filled with tears. He hadn't told her about Andrea to make her cry. "I don't know, babe. You can pick your friends but not your family."

Reaching for her napkin, Leah touched it to the corners of her eyes. I'm so sorry, Derrick. For you and your daughter."

He stood, came around the table, and eased Leah up. His arms circled her waist and pulled her close. "Please don't cry. Andrea cried so much that I cannot remember when she used to smile."

Leah sniffled as she buried her face against his shoulder. "I can't imagine waking up every day wondering if this is the day I'm going to lose the person I love."

"It was hard in the beginning, and I knew I had to stay strong not for myself but for Deandra."

"You are strong, Derrick."

"So are you, Leah. A lot of women would have shattered under what you had to go through. I can recall someone telling me very emphatically she was not a victim."

Leah lifted her chin, smiling. She scrunched up her nose. "I do recall hearing that, too."

Derrick massaged the nape of her neck. "Are you going in with me tomorrow, or you plan to stay here?"

"I'm going in with you. I have to put up several loads of wash and clean the apartment. And I also want to pick up my car in case I decide to drive into town." Leah paused. "I just remembered something, Derrick. If I'm going to live on the island then I'll need a resident sticker."

"I'll get a sticker for you. I also don't want you cleaning this house because I've contracted with a maintenance company to come in every other week to clean every room from top to bottom."

"Okay."

Derrick smothered a sigh of relief. He thought perhaps Leah would resent him telling her what not to do because of what she'd gone through with her mother-in-law. He dropped a kiss in her hair. "Thank you again for dinner. It was delicious."

"I'm practicing so when it comes time for you to interview for a sous chef I will be in the running."

"Are you still sure you want to work with me in the kitchen?" Derrick asked Leah.

"Of course I'm sure."

"What I don't want is for our working relationship to clash with our personal life."

"That's not going to happen, because I know when to separate the two. Remember, darling," she drawled, smiling, "I've had a lot of practice with compartmentalization."

"I'll try not to forget, *darling*." Derrick kissed Leah again, this time on the mouth, capturing her breath as her lips parted. He was no novice when it came to women, yet Leah was so very different from the others he'd dated. She did not hesitate when it came to speaking her mind, and he wondered if she'd always been that way or had been forced to do so as a defense mechanism. He ended the kiss, and both were breathing heavily. "Go relax, babe, while I clean the kitchen."

"It will . . ." Leah's words trailed off when her cell phone rang. "Excuse me, but I should get that call."

Leah retrieved the phone and walked into the family room. "Yes, Kayana."

"Did I disturb you?"

She folded her body down into an armchair. "No. Why?"

"Your voice just sounded different. I'm calling to let you know Cherie quit her job to go back to college in the fall. She said she's renting the same bungalow where you stayed last summer."

"When is she coming down?"

"Next week."

Leah smiled. "It sounds as if we're getting the book club back together sooner than later."

"You've got that right. She sounds really upbeat."

"Maybe she's finally gotten over the man that had her in a funk last summer, because she has a lot to offer a man that's worthy of her youth, beauty, and intelligence."

When first sharing a table with Cherie Thompson at the Seaside Café, Leah and the young woman had gotten off on the wrong foot, when Cherie accused Leah of being anorexic because there hadn't been a lot of food on her plate. She did come back and apologize.

Leah had invited her to join the book club with her and Kayana. She'd used the discussion of Octavia Butler's *Kindred* as an excuse to accuse her of having ancestors who owned slaves, and she even held it against her that she lived in the city that had been the capital of the Confederacy. They would occasionally verbally spar with each other, and Leah finally realized her relationship with Cherie would never evolve into one she had with Kayana.

"What about you, Leah?"

"What about me, Kayana?"

"Are you enjoying my brother's company?"

What did her friend expect her to do, lie? If she'd been forthcoming about the intimate details of her marriage, then she owed it to her to be honest about her relationship with Derrick. "Yes, I am," she whispered, not wanting Derrick to overhear her conversation. "In fact, I've decided to move in with him." She held the phone away from her ear when Kayana let out a high-decibel, piercing shriek.

"Nothing's wrong, darling. Graeme just came downstairs

to find out if I'm all right. Hold on. I'm going outside to talk because my husband has ears like a bat," Kayana whispered.

"Well, you did scream loud enough to be heard on the mainland."

"Sorry about that, Leah. Are you whispering because Derrick's within earshot?"

"Yes. And I don't want to go upstairs or outside because he'll know that I'm talking about him," she continued sotto voce.

"Point taken. Look, girlfriend, I've watched you and Derrick dance around each other for weeks, and you don't know how long I wanted to tell you guys to get on with it. I know you were attracted to my brother last year, and I know he won't admit it, but he also was checking out my redheaded book club friend."

Leah wanted to tell Kayana she was right because he had admitted to checking her out. However, there were some things she wanted to stay between her and Derrick. "And you're right about your brother, Kayana. He is a good guy," she said instead.

"I'm happy that both of you have been given a second chance at love."

"I think you're getting a little ahead of yourself. We're not at the stage where we can talk about being in love."

"That's next, Leah."

"When did you know you were in love with Graeme?"

A beat passed. "I really can't pinpoint when; I knew I liked him a lot even before we slept together. We went to the movies on our first date, and that escalated to going to his house to give him cooking lessons. That's when I realized that I really enjoyed his company. Then he got sick and I played Florence Nightingale, staying over at night to check on him and Barley. It was sometime later after he'd recovered that he asked me to move in with him."

"Did you?"

"No. It was only after we'd begun sleeping together that I

knew I was in love with him. I'd told myself over and over that I never wanted to get married again, but when the heart rules the head there's nothing you can do but listen to it."

"Aren't you glad you listened?"

Kayana laughed. "The day I told Graeme I was willing to marry him I knew I'd changed—and for the better, because I'd let go of the anger where I'd blamed every man for what I'd allowed James to do to me. I bit my tongue and put up with a lot of shit for the sake of my marriage, and what did it get me?"

"A reason to get rid of the snake so you could find some one that loves and respects you."

"Preach, sister. But it all wasn't wine and roses once I discovered Graeme wasn't who he said he was, and I broke up with him. But if it hadn't been for Derrick, I know I wouldn't have married him. But that's something I will tell you about when we see each other again."

"You're kidding!"

"No, I'm not. That's when I had to ask myself if I wanted to lose him or accept what he was offering me. And that is someone I could love and more importantly trust. You must get tired of me saying it, Leah, but you're good for Derrick and he's good for you. So, please don't blow it."

Leah smiled. "I must be listening to my heart, because when Derrick asked me to move in I knew he was shocked when I said yes. I'm too old to play games, and I've been unhappy for so long that it's time for me to know what love is."

"I love that song, Lee."

"Which one are you talking about?"

" 'I Want to Know What Love Is' by Foreigner."

"I like it, too."

"I'm not going to hold you because now that you're cohabitating we'll have to save the girl talk for our meetings."

"Are we going to wait until the start of the summer season to start our book club or begin when Cherie gets here?"

"I don't know, Lee. I just finished *Love in the Time of*

Cholera, and I plan to start *The Alienist* in a couple of days. I didn't realize that puppy was so long."

"It is a long read," Leah agreed, "but I have to admit Cherie suggested a winner. And you, being a therapist, will probably identify with it."

"I'm glad I didn't see the miniseries. I'm going to let you go so you can spend some time with your honey."

"Later, Kayana."

"Nite-nite."

Derrick had just closed the door to the dishwasher when Leah returned to the kitchen. "Our book club is reconvening earlier than planned."

Derrick stood straight and stared at Leah. "What happened?"

"Cherie is coming down next week."

He smiled. "So the book club is getting back together."

"Yup."

"Just let me know when you're going to have your first meeting so I can vacate the premises."

Leah moved closer to Derrick and reached for his hand. "You don't have to leave. We'll be in the she-shed."

Derrick stared at Leah from under lowered lids. He still was trying to process her willingness to live with him. He knew he was asking a lot from a woman who'd spent almost three quarters of her life with an abusive husband; a man who'd systematically sought to bend her to his will and failed.

"I've already promised Graeme that I would hang out with him. I'm going to take the gas grill out of the mudroom and set it up in the back. I'll have to go into town and pick up a few tanks of propane. So if y'all want to grill just let me know if you want steak, burgers, or links."

Leah's arms went around his waist as she pressed her chest to his. "What am I going to do with you?" she whispered.

"Keep me, babe."

She buried her face between his chin and shoulder and

breathed a kiss under his ear. "You don't have to worry about that, because I'm in this for the duration."

Derrick's right hand slid down Leah's back and cradled her hip. He'd wanted her for so long that he could not remember when he didn't. Whenever they were in the kitchen together it was all he could do to keep his hands off her. And knowing she was married and hadn't yet filed for divorce—for him that made her taboo. Kayana had told him about some of her clients in abusive marriages who talked about leaving their husbands, and some would. But then they returned, and the cycle of abuse would continue. Unfortunately their decision sometimes resulted in their deaths.

However, he knew it would be different with Leah because of her husband's status. As a judge for the Commonwealth of Virginia, his wife suing him for divorce after thirty years of marriage was certain to start tongues wagging and reporters scrambling over one another for interviews. And now that Leah had put the divorce train on the track and started it up, there would be no stopping it.

Derrick hadn't planned to ask her to live with him, but coming home and finding her in the kitchen preparing dinner conjured up memories of what he'd shared with Andrea. He knew it was unfair to compare Leah to his late wife because they were two different women. But the scene of domesticity was so powerful that it was something he wanted to relive every day over and over.

He'd asked and was totally shocked when Leah agreed to move in with him. However, he'd given her an out. He would not place any demands on her, and she had the option of staying or leaving at any time.

Derrick did not think he could love another woman after Andrea, but Leah had proven him wrong. When seeing her battered and bruised, his first instinct was to protect her. It was his father's insecurities that his wife earned more money, therefore becoming the family's proverbial breadwinner, that made him find something with which to argue with her, but it was Kenneth Johnson's advice to him that Derrick never forgot: *Never raise your hand to a woman.*

This is not to say his marriage was conflict- or drama-free. He and Andrea were able to resolve their disagreements without shouting and screaming at each other. However, there had been one incident. The house was built and ready for them to move in, but Andrea did not want to occupy a home without it being completely furnished. Derrick had tried to make her understand they'd imposed far too long on his mother's generosity living with her until they could occupy their new home, and she did not need the cries of a colicky baby interrupting her sleep. His wife stubbornly refused, and it was the first and only time Derrick raised his voice, stunning not only Andrea but also himself. He apologized immediately for losing his temper, but the outburst caused a schism in his marriage that had remained until it ended with Andrea's passing, because he'd revealed early on when they were dating about his parents' ongoing disagreements and promised her he would never raise his voice to her. It had been a promise he'd been able to keep until that time.

"I noticed you didn't put a nightgown or a pair of pajamas in my overnight bag," Leah said softly.

Leah's low, dulcet voice with a drawl that identified her as growing up in the South caressed his ear. He smiled. "It never crossed my mind."

"First you want me go to commando, and now you expect me to romp around naked as a jaybird."

Derrick kissed her ear. "I'm certain that's a sight I will truly enjoy."

"You won't think so when you see my stretch marks and the scar from my Caesarean."

"A woman's stretch marks are a medal of honor equivalent of a soldier being awarded the Purple Heart. She has to go through a living hell to bring a child into the world. And, in your case, it was two at the same time."

"My babies were eating good inside me, because both weighed over seven pounds at birth, and after more than sixteen hours in labor my doctor realized I wasn't going to deliver them vaginally."

"Seven pounds isn't a small baby."

"They still aren't small. Aron and Caleb are six-three and weigh close to two-thirty."

Derrick whistled. "That's definitely not small."

"That's the reason I pleaded with them not to jack up their father. They're like you and work out every day. Caleb kickboxes and Aron has a black belt in tae kwon do."

"Damn! I'm sure they can wreck a joint in less than two minutes."

"You're right about that. One time when I met them in New York and saw them coming down the street I noticed folks staring at them, not because they were identical, but they looked like football linebackers."

Based on their physical conditioning and self-defense proficiencies, Derrick knew Leah had a valid reason to ask her sons not to retaliate against their father. "I think I can remedy your nightgown dilemma by giving you a few of my T-shirts."

"Thank you, darling."

He smiled. "You're welcome, darling."

"What time do you plan to leave the house tomorrow morning?"

"Six."

"If that's the case, then I'm going upstairs to shower and turn in. You can leave the T-shirt on the bed."

Derrick wanted to ask which bed, his or the one in the guest room. "I'll be up a little later."

Chapter 15

Leah had no idea how long she'd been asleep when she felt the warm body next to hers. She'd brushed her teeth, rinsed her mouth with a peppermint mouthwash, and lingered under the warm spray of the shower longer than necessary as she tried to waste time waiting for Derrick to come upstairs. When she left the bathroom she'd discovered he had left the T-shirt on the bed in the guest room. That's when she realized he was true to his word. He was allowing her to choose where she wanted to spend the night: in his bed or in the one where she'd slept the night before. Last night she hadn't had a choice, but tonight she did, and it was not to sleep alone.

"What took you so long?"

Derrick draped an arm over her waist as he nuzzled the back of her neck. "Once I realized you were in my bed, I decided to wait until you were sleeping soundly before getting in."

"What time is it?"

"It's after ten. Go back to sleep, babe, because we have to get up early."

"Derrick."

"What is it?"

"You can't touch and kiss me and expect me not to beg you to make love to me."

"Baby, we don't have to do anything tonight. I'll give you all the time you need to get used to sleeping with me."

Leah turned to face him. There wasn't enough illumination from the baseboard nightlights to make out his expression. "I don't need any more time."

Derrick recalled Leah telling him she hadn't shared her husband's bed in more than ten years. And she was right about not needing more time. She was more than past due having someone love her the way she deserved.

He kissed her hair and inhaled the scent of coconut clinging to the silken strands. "Are you sure?" He felt her trembling.

"Yes, I'm very, very sure."

Waiting until her trembling subsided, Derrick swept back the sheet and removed the T-shirt. Supporting his weight on his forearms, he began at her hairline, trailing kisses over her forehead, the end of her nose, mouth, jawline, throat, breasts, belly, thighs, legs, and feet before reversing a path over the expanse of her velvety, fragrant skin. One hand moved up between her legs as a gush of moisture bathed his fingers. He knew she was aroused and ready for him to penetrate her, but Derrick wanted to prolong giving her the pleasure she'd missed for too many years.

Sliding down lower, he pressed his mouth against her mound and suckled her. His teeth gently nipped her clitoris, and she screamed, the sound raising hair on the back of his neck. Derrick continued tasting and licking Leah as she writhed against his mouth, as the moans and groans escalated into muffled screams.

"Pull-ese, Derrick."

Her plea had come out in two syllables, and he knew Leah was close to climaxing. Holding his erection in one hand, he parted her knees with the other and eased his penis into her vagina. Then he froze; he was only in halfway. He took a deep breath, and with a sure push of his hips he found himself fully sheathed inside Leah.

He moved slowly, tentatively testing how much he could thrust into her dormant body without hurting her. His hands traced a sensual path down her ribs and hips, and her body writhed an age-old rhythm that needed no tutoring regardless of how long she hadn't been made love to. Passion and lust pounded the blood through his head, heart, and loins.

Leah gloried in the smell of Derrick's freshly showered body, the feel of his skin against hers, his touch that sent tingles up and down her body, and the hardness sliding in and out of her body, setting her afire. He was much larger than she could have possibly imagined, stretching the walls of her vagina to capacity.

He quickened his thrusts, Leah following his pace as heat shot through her like an electric current; she felt the beginning of an orgasm and was unable to stop it from coming. Throwing back her head, she screamed, not a high-pitched sound but a low growl that subsided to long, surrendering moans as orgasms overlapped one another. A deep feeling of peace entered her as Derrick collapsed heavily on her sated body.

Smiling, Leah closed her eyes. A man with whom she'd fallen in love had offered her his heat, and passion had awakened the sexuality that had lain dormant for almost all her life. This single act of lovemaking had confirmed what she hadn't known the first time she saw Derrick Johnson. He would be the one to change her life.

It was Sunday, a day of rest, and Derrick promised they wouldn't do anything more strenuous than lifting a fork to eat. She had gotten up early to complete her morning ablution, when he joined her in the shower. They'd splashed each other like little kids before the kids' play turned into foreplay and then passionate lovemaking that left both struggling to breathe. The water had cooled along with their passions as they rushed to finish showering before they were chilled.

After a brunch with eggs Benedict, sliced melon, and coffee, she curled up on the bed in the she-shed to pick up where she'd left off in *Love in the Time of Cholera*, while Derrick settled into the club chair in the family room to watch a basketball game.

She lost track of time as she turned the pages of *Love in the Time of Cholera*, until a rumble of thunder jolted her into awareness. By the time she'd straightened the bed, fluffed up the pillows, turned off the lamps, and opened the French doors, the rain was coming down in torrents. She gasped, seeing Derrick standing outside with an oversize umbrella.

"You don't need to get drenched twice in one day," he teased with a wide grin.

Looping her arm through his, Leah lowered her eyes as heat suffused her face.

"Thanks for the umbrella."

"Any time, gorgeous."

She walked into the family room to discover Derrick had turned on the fireplace. The house had been built with gas fireplaces in every room. Cradling the book to her chest, she sat on the navy-blue leather club chair.

"Hey, I was sitting there."

Leah patted a space beside her thigh. "There's enough room for the two of us."

Derrick folded his hands at his waist. "There's no way both of us can fit on that chair, Leah."

"Come now, darling. Why don't you try it?" The last word was barely off her tongue when she felt herself lifted effortlessly off the chair. "Please put me down."

Derrick sat and settled Leah between his outstretched legs. "Now we can fit."

She leaned against his chest at the same time he rested his hands over her belly. Leah never tired of feeling the crush of his body molded to hers. "I can go upstairs and read while you watch your game."

"Stay here with me for a while. Please."

"Yes, I will stay." Leah didn't tell Derrick she'd agreed because he'd asked and not demanded.

"Do you like basketball?"

"I'm familiar with the game. I attended most of Vanderbilt's basketball, football, and baseball home games."

"What about frat parties?"

"No, because my father warned me about them."

"So, you were a good girl."

"I was a very good girl, Derrick. Remember I was only fifteen when I first went to college."

"Why do I keep forgetting that? In other words you were jailbait."

Leah glanced up at him over her shoulder. "That's something I made known as soon as guys tried to come on to me. It didn't take long for the news that Red Berks was taboo."

Derrick laughed. "Is that what they called you?"

"Yup. There were a few other red-haired girls, and we all had nicknames. Rebecca Fletcher was Red Fletch and Bonnie Scott was Red Scotty. Did you pledge a fraternity?"

"Nah. Between playing ball and having to maintain a B average to keep my scholarship I didn't have time to pledge. But I did attend a couple of off-campus frat parties."

"Did you enjoy them?"

"Not really. There was a lot of drinking, drugs, and hooking up."

"Are you saying you were a good boy?"

There came a pregnant pause before Derrick said, "Just say I was careful. I'd have a couple of drinks, but I didn't mess with drugs because I didn't know when I'd be tested."

"What about hooking up?"

"No comment."

"Did you have a girlfriend?"

"No comment, babe."

"I had a boyfriend in college," Leah admitted.

"I'm still not going to tell you about the girls I dated in college."

"Should I assume you don't kiss and tell?"

"You assume right, Leah."

Derrick's tone had a hard edge that Leah recognized immediately. "I'm sorry for prying."

His hands moved up under her breasts. "There's no need to apologize. I prefer the past remain in the past."

Leah wanted to tell him that was a lot easier for him than for her. Once she resumed her maiden name as Leah Berkley, then she would be able to let go of her past. "Please let me up. I want to go upstairs to get in some more reading before my eyes get too tired."

"Do you ever get tired reading?"

"Never." She slid off the chair. "I'll see you later."

Leah climbed the staircase to the second story. They had decided to forgo cooking Sunday dinner when Derrick brought home a pan of lasagna from the restaurant. The dish had become one of her personal favorites because he used thinly sliced Italian sausage instead of ground beef. He also included green peas in the recipe, which added natural sweetness.

She had gone online to order the herbs and spied the Aero-Garden Harvest, and decided to buy three, with six pods each for gourmet herbs, cascading petunias, and red heirloom cherry tomatoes. Leah planned to keep the herbs and cherry tomatoes in the kitchen and the petunias in the she-shed. She thought it ingenious to grow plants in water using an LED light in a device with automatic reminders for water and plant food.

She opened the book to where she'd left off when the rain began and lay on the recliner in Derrick's man cave. She had to admit it was a comfortable, inviting space that reflected the personality of the man with whom she had fallen in love.

Leah did not understand why he'd questioned her about reading when he had two shelves packed tightly with books. Many were nonfiction with a focus on finance, business, and economics, along with mysteries, true crime, military history, and a few biographies and legal thrillers. She'd teased him, saying he only read the *Sports Illustrated* swimsuit issue, but it was apparent she had misjudged him.

Leah had read less than ten pages when she found her eyes drooping. It had to be the weather. Rainy weather always made her sleepy. Setting the book on a side table, she slipped off her tennis shoes and jeans and got into bed. Leah buried her face in the pillow and whispered a prayer of thanks. It had been three days since Derrick made love to her for the first time, and she still could not believe the overwhelming joy she had come to feel—in and out of bed.

Leah's joy vanished like a drop of water on a red-hot skillet when she answered a familiar ringtone early the following morning. "Yes, Aron?"

"I just got a call from Dad that Grandma passed away."

She closed her eyes. Adele had always said she wanted to live to ninety, but apparently her wish hadn't been granted. "What happened?"

"The doctor said she had a stroke."

"Where are you?"

"I'm still in New York. As soon as I hang up I'm going to try to get a nonstop flight."

"Does Caleb know?"

"Yes. When I get my ticket I'll buy his, too, so we can come in together. Are you coming up, Mom?"

Leah wanted to say no, but knew she had to be there for her sons. After all, Adele was their grandmother. "Yes. How's your father holding up?"

"He's not good. When he called me he couldn't stop crying."

"There's no doubt he'd be upset. They were very close.

Call or text me once you know your flight. I'll be at the airport to pick you up."

"Okay. I'll talk to you later."

"I love you, Aron."

"Love you, too, Mom."

Leah was still clutching the phone when Derrick came out
of the bathroom. "What's the matter?"

Her eyelids fluttered wildly. "My son just called to let me
know my mother-in-law just passed away."

Derrick sat on the side of the bed. "When are you leaving?
You are leaving, aren't you?" he asked when she hesitated.

Leah nodded. "I have to. She *was* their grandmother."

"It's okay, babe. I understand you have to be there for
your sons."

She rested her head against his shoulder, feeding off his
strength. It was Derrick's week off, and he had gotten up
early to work out. "I'm going to leave now because I want to
get to Richmond before their arrival. I told Aron I would
meet their flight."

"Do you know when they're due to arrive?"

"Not yet. If I get there early, then I'll check into a hotel
near the airport and wait."

"Please call me once you get to Richmond, so I'll know
you arrived safely."

"I promise."

Derrick held her close until Leah told him she had to dress
and return to the apartment to pack a bag. She could feel his
eyes following her as she got off the bed and walked into the
en suite bath. Suddenly she felt like the Michael Corleone
character in *The Godfather*. Just when she thought she was
out, the Kents pulled her back in. She knew she would have
to face Alan during the deposition phase of their divorce and
prayed that would be the last time—if he chose not to contest
it. But knowing him as she did, Leah doubted he would give
up quietly.

And now there was Adele. She was still messing with her in death as she had in life.

Leah did not intend to be a hypocrite and shed tears for a woman whose sole reason for getting up every morning was to make her life a living hell. She wasn't going back to Richmond to mourn the passing of her mother-in-law. She was going back to support her sons who'd lost their grandmother.

Leah saw Caleb and Aron as they entered baggage claim. She'd parked her car in the airport lot and ordered lunch in one of the terminal restaurants.

Both had carry-on bags and were deeply tanned, which indicated they were spending time outdoors. She smiled when noticing women of all ages staring at the matched pair. They were close, as most twins were, but never competitive.

Leah had known early on they'd wanted to become lawyers when Alan would talk about some of the cases he was handling during dinner. They would ask endless questions until he would open one of his law books and show them the ruling on which he planned his defense for his client. All of the legalese bored Leah, and she would have preferred different dinner table conversation. Adele, on the other hand, appeared thrilled her grandsons showed an interest in the law and would become the next generation in a long line of Kent men to become lawyers and judges.

Leah hugged Aron, and then Caleb. "I'm parked outside."

Caleb draped an arm around her shoulders. "Have you been waiting long?"

She stared up into a pair of large hazel eyes at the same time a shiver eddied its way down her back. His eyes were so much like Alan's, and in that instant she felt she was looking at the man who'd blamed her, as he put it, for "fucking up" his life. Yeah, right. She'd fucked up his life giving him two healthy, intelligent sons. She'd continued to fuck up his life presenting herself as the perfect wife at social events. And she continued to fuck up his life when she looked the other way while he continually disrespected her by sleeping with other women during their marriage.

"No. I got in a couple of hours ago and decided to have lunch."

"We managed to grab something to eat while we waited to board."

"How's Marisa?"

"She's good. I wanted her to come, but she just completed her final exams and she's wiped out."

"Why don't you guys take a weekend off and come down to Coates Island and just hang out on the beach."

"Am I also invited?" Aron asked, walking several paces behind.

"Of course." They left the terminal and waited for traffic to stop so they could cross the roadway to the parking lot. "There's something I feel you should know." Aron and Caleb stared at her as if anticipating more bad news. "I'm involved with someone, and I've moved into his house." The seconds ticked as they continued to look at her.

Caleb smiled. "Good for you, Mom."

"Congratulations," Aron said. "When are we going to meet him?"

Leah hadn't realized she was holding her breath. At her age she did not have to answer to anyone as to how she wanted to live her life, but she felt she owed it to her sons to apprise them of her living arrangement if they did decide to take her up on her invitation to come to North Carolina.

"Is he good to you?" Aron asked.

Nodding, she smiled. "He's good to and for me."

"We know you don't need our approval, but Cal and I want you to know that you have our support. I hope he's not an attorney."

Leah laughed. "No. He was a stockbroker in his former life, but he's now one of the cooks at his family-owned restaurant on Coates Island."

"I told Marisa about how Dad would dominate the dinner

table conversation talking about his cases, and she made me promise never to talk shop at our table. Chitchat about clients and patients are verboten."

"Good for her, Caleb. It sounds as if you're going to marry a very smart woman."

Aron held out his hand. "Give me your fob. I'll drive."

Leah was grateful not to get behind the wheel again after driving nearly six hours to get to Richmond before their flight touched down. She slipped into the rear seat and exhaled. "You can drop me off at the Marriott Residence Inn or the Downtown Hilton. You guys can text me when the arrangements are finalized, and I'll meet you there."

Caleb, sitting in the passenger seat, turned to look at her. "No way, Mom. You're not going to stay in a hotel when you have a suite at the house."

"I *had* a suite, Caleb. Remember, I left Kent House."

"That doesn't matter," Aron said as he started the car. "You're coming home with us, and Dad will have nothing to say about it."

"I don't want trouble with your father, Aron."

"There's not going to be any trouble, Mom. Cal and I will make certain of that."

I hope there won't be, she thought. The last time she and Alan were face-to-face he'd tried to choke her to death. But that was then, when they were the only two people in the house; now she had the protection of her sons.

Leah gasped when she saw Alan standing in the great room holding a glass of amber-colored liquid. It had been almost five months since their last encounter, and it was as if he'd aged more than ten years since that time. His face was puffy, his complexion blotchy, and his bloated stomach hung over his belt.

"What's that bitch doing here?"

Aron walked over to Alan and took the glass out of his hand. "Watch your mouth, Dad," he warned softly.

Caleb glared at his father. "We asked Mom to come, and while she's here you *will* respect her."

"Do you realize she's divorcing me?"

"Yes, we do," Aron said, "and we don't want to get in the middle of it."

"I've been nothing but good to her, and meanwhile the bitch is fucking with me."

Aron grabbed the front of Alan's shirt with his free hand. "Didn't I warn you to watch your mouth."

"Aron, don't!" Leah screamed. "Let him go."

He did, wiping his hand on the front of his shirt as if he feared becoming contaminated. "One more ugly word about our mother and Cal and I are leaving."

Alan's eyes grew wild. "You can't leave me at a time like this."

"Yes we can, if you mess with our mother," Aron threatened. "Mom, go up to your room and we'll bring up your bags."

Leah curbed the urge to stick her tongue out at Alan like a mischievous child. She met his eyes. *Take that, you cowardly bastard.* He had no qualms when it came to hitting a woman, but he was too frightened to physically challenge his adult sons.

Leah walked up the staircase she'd been thrown down what now seemed a lifetime ago. She recalled falling, but once her head hit the floor her whole world had gone dark. If Alan sought to kill her, he hadn't succeeded. Not only had she survived but she also remembered what he'd done to her. It wasn't until she was seated on the chair where she'd slept before Alan attacked her that Leah thought of her promise to call Derrick.

"Hey, babe. How's it going?"

She smiled. "I'm here."

"Where are you staying?"

Her smile vanished. "I'm at Kent House. I had planned to

check into a hotel, but my sons overruled me. Right now they are running interference between me and Alan."

"Are you sure you're going to be all right?"

"The question should be, will Alan be all right." Leah didn't want to give Derrick the details of her sons' interaction with their father. She did not want to burden him with her marital disharmony when she and Derrick were so happy together. "I don't believe he wants to do anything that will alienate him from them."

"I'm glad they're there with you."

"Me, too." She paused. "I don't know whether Alan has begun making funeral arrangements, so I don't know when I'll be back."

"Don't stress yourself, Leah. I'll try and hold it down until you get back."

She laughed. "Are you saying the Café's going to fall apart without me?"

"I was talking about the beach house. It's not going to be the same with you away."

"I give you permission to sleep on my side of the bed." His deep chuckle caressed her ear.

"Thank you very much," he drawled in a spot-on Elvis Presley imitation.

A wave of exhaustion washed over her, and Leah knew it was more from tension than fatigue. She needed to lie down and take a nap, if only for an hour, and then get up and find out what Alan had planned for his mother's funeral. "Derrick, I'm going to hang up now. I'll call you tomorrow with updates."

"Don't bother, Leah. Just take care of whatever has to be done and only call me when you're on your way back."

"Thank you."

"No problem. Later."

She ended the call, and seconds later someone knocked lightly on the door. "Come in."

It opened, and Leah stared at the resident chef. Adele had

hired Noah Frazier within months of his graduating from culinary school, and he'd celebrated his thirtieth birthday a month before she married Alan.

"Welcome back, Mrs. Kent. I'm glad you're feeling better."

Leah wanted to tell the talented chef with soulful dark-brown eyes and a graying ponytail she was back, but not to stay. And she was feeling and looking a lot better than she did when she'd come home from the hospital. She'd watched him and the housekeeper recoil when they caught a glimpse of her battered face.

"Thank you."

"Mr. Kent wants to hold the repast here after the funeral services. I need to know how many guests you anticipate will attend."

"How many did you prepare for when Mr. Kent's father died?"

"It was well over two hundred. But then he was a judge, and a lot of folk came from out of state for his service. And given Madame Kent's age and that most of her friends have passed away, I think there will be a much smaller gathering."

"You're right, Noah. Make enough for seventy-five and whatever is left over please donate to a food kitchen."

"Okay. Again, it's a pleasure to have you back."

Leah did not respond and waited for him to close the door. She was more than aware that the employees that worked for Adele merely tolerated her dictatorial manner because they were paid well and had their own suite of rooms in the designated servants' quarters. Noah hadn't married, but she suspected he had an ongoing relationship with a woman he always hired for every catered event held at Kent House.

Leah knew he would always have a position at Kent House and wondered if he'd planned for his future once Alan passed away. And it had only taken one glance at the present owner to ascertain that he was in poor health and probably would not live to reach his mother's age of eighty-seven.

Alan's health was no longer her concern or her responsibility. She had relinquished both when he'd assaulted her. In other words, he was on his own.

Leah smiled and thanked people for turning out to cele-brate Adele's passing while applauding herself on an impec-cable performance. If the dead woman hadn't been Aron and Caleb's grandmother, whom they adored, she wouldn't have volunteered to pretend all was well between herself and their father.

They'd buried Adele in the family plot at a nearby ceme-tery the day before. Alan had followed his mother's wish that she not have a funeral but a memorial service, followed by a gathering at Kent House. Leah couldn't wait to take off the somber black dress, stockings, and shoes and get into some-thing more colorful.

Leah managed to hide her distaste when she noticed a woman hanging onto Alan's arm as he stood at the portable bar waiting for the bartender. She could not believe he would invite one of his whores to his mother's memorial. And it was obvious his penchant for younger women hadn't waned. The woman was young enough to be his daughter.

"What the hell is wrong with Dad? He knows you're here, yet he has some woman rub up on him like a cat in heat."

Leah looked up to find Caleb standing next to her. "Let it go."

"Don't you care?"

She stared straight ahead. "I stopped caring years ago, Caleb. Your father has always been a whoremaster, and why should he stop now?"

"You knew he was stepping out on you?"

Leah realized she and Alan had to have been incredible ac-tors to make their children believe they were a loving couple. "Yes, and I don't want to talk about it."

Caleb smothered a curse under his breath and then walked over to the bar. He whispered something in Alan's ear, and then took the woman's arm and escorted her out of the room.

Alan turned, glared at Leah, and mouthed what she knew were curses. She smiled and reached for a prawn off the tray of a passing waiter. She wanted to tell him his words no longer hurt her, and if he wanted a fight, then she was prepared for a knock-down, drag-out fight. And since he was going to keep messing with her, then she was going to ask for not two million dollars, but upwards of ten.

Chapter 16

Leah left Aron and Caleb in Richmond four days after the memorial service. She had only delayed her departure because it had been a while since she had spent some time with her sons, while they had decided to stay until the reading of Adele's will before flying back to New York. Kayana had sent her a text message that Cherie was on Coates Island, had settled into her bungalow, and couldn't wait for the three of them to be together again.

She was only ten miles from the island when she called Kayana to tell Cherie to meet her at the Café. The anticipation of seeing her missing book club friend was what she needed to shed the pretense of having to be gracious, when she wanted nothing more than to be away from what she thought of as make-believe. Everyone had only glowing sentiments for Adele, but Leah knew she could be cutthroat and manipulative. However, she did not want to speak or think badly of the dead because they could not defend themselves. She was on her way home to her friends and the man she had grown to love. She had heard women speak of the men in their lives as their rocks, and Derrick Johnson had become her rock.

Leah maneuvered into the parking lot behind the Seaside Café and cut the engine. The restaurant was closed for the day, and the white van with the restaurant's name and logo on the side was missing, which meant Derrick had gone to pick up some supplies. She parked next to Kayana's SUV and tapped the code to access the rear door.

Leah walked through the kitchen and into the dining room and saw Cherie sitting at a table with Kayana. Cherie had let her hair grow out, and her natural hair framed her face like black, wispy clouds.

Cherie noticed her and stood up, arms extended. "You look incredible!"

Leah hugged the younger woman and kissed her cheek. "So do you."

Cherie held her at arm's length, her light-brown eyes narrowing. "What happened to your bling?"

Leah met Kayana's eyes. "Kayana didn't tell you."

Retaking her seat, Cherie patted the one next to her. "No. Sit down and give me the deets."

Leah knew she was talking about details. "I'm divorcing my husband."

"Well, damn, Red. You said he's a lot older than you, so why don't just wait for him to kick the bucket?"

"I can't wait that long."

Cherie leaned back in her chair. "I go away for a year and come back to find Kayana married and you getting divorced. What made you decide that you'd had enough after all this time?"

"He hit me."

Cherie twisted her mouth as she slowly shook her head. "Did you cut him low?"

Leah couldn't help but laugh. "I would have if I'd had a

knife. But I did manage to knee him in the balls, and that's when he pushed me down the staircase."

"Shit!" Cherie spat out. "What did your sons say or do?"

"I'll tell you everything after Kayana whips up a few drinks. Because you're going to need one once I finish."

It was as if they'd never parted when Kayana made the sour apple martinis she'd served for their first meeting, as Leah told Cherie everything that had happened to her that rainy day in January and why she'd left Richmond for Coates Island. "I just went back for a few days because my mother-in-law died, and I wanted to be there for my sons."

"You're a better woman than me, because I would've let my boys jack up their father if he'd hit me."

Leah took a sip of the deliciously frothy cocktail. "I got something better for his ass. When I got to the house and he called me a bitch, I had to stop Aron from hitting him, because he's not worth them losing everything they've worked for. And because he continued to disrespect me by inviting one of his whores to the memorial service, I called my lawyer and told her I'm no longer willing to settle for two million but to get as much as she can from him. Now that he's inherited his mama's share of the estate, I want it all."

Kayana gave her a fist bump. "That will learn him about disrespecting the mama of his kids."

"What if he doesn't want to give up the ducats?" Cherie asked.

"He'll give them up or lose his so-called good name when I let the Commonwealth know that Judge Alan Stephens Kent beat the hell out of his wife."

With wide eyes, Cherie stared at her. "You would really do that?"

"Yes, I would. Alan just can't let well enough alone. Calling me a bitch in front of my kids and flaunting his whore at their grandmother's memorial service took the rag off the bush. Now I'm going for the jugular."

"He must have taken a page out of my ex's book," Kayana

said. "He'd invite his whore to our home every chance he got. It would've continued if the dumb shit had wrapped up his meat and didn't get her pregnant. He waits until he's eligible to join AARP to be saddled with a little baby. It serves his stupid ass right because he couldn't leave well enough alone."

Cherie raised her empty glass. "That calls for another round."

Leah stood up with Kayana. "I'm going to need something to eat or I'll be on my face."

Derrick walked into the dining room, and Leah felt her pulse quicken. Not seeing him for a week, now he made her heart dance with happiness, and she knew her feelings for him went beyond what they'd shared physically. He came closer and leaned down to kiss her.

"Welcome home."

"It's good to be home."

Derrick stood straight. "You ladies are drinking without eating?"

"I was just going to get something from the kitchen," Kayana told her brother.

"Sit, Kay. I'll bring it."

Kayana looped her arm through Derrick's. "I also need to make another round of martinis."

"Whoa! You ladies are about to get lit up!"

"Not to worry, brother love. You can be our designated driver."

Cherie waited while Kayana and Derrick went into the kitchen before she turned to Leah. "I knew it, I knew it, I knew," she intoned. "When I saw you staring at Kayana's brother with your tongue hanging out, I knew you had the hots for him."

"Well, nothing was going to happen because I was still living with Alan, and he claimed he never got involved with women that were in relationships with other men."

"I don't know why, but I never figured you would go for dark meat."

"And I'd never figured you would go for white meat." She knew she had struck a nerve when Cherie averted her face. Leah had hoped Cherie would stop goading her, but it was obvious the younger woman was still angry about her ex, who just happened to have been white.

"I'm sorry, Leah. That was uncalled for."

"If you knew it was wrong, then why did you say it? You're how old? Thirty-three—"

"Thirty-four," Cherie corrected.

"You're thirty-four and you still act like a spiteful teenager. How many times are you going to apologize for saying something better left unsaid?"

Cherie closed her eyes. "I've been working on myself. When I met you last year I thought you were so lucky because you were married, and that's something I always wanted for myself."

Leah dropped an arm over Cherie's shoulder. "Remember me telling you I hadn't slept with my husband in ten years and that he cheated on me throughout our marriage. That's not something I want for any woman. I envied Kayana when she told us she'd left her husband once she knew he'd cheated on her. Meanwhile I didn't get the nerve to leave mine until he tried to kill me. I told you before that you have the looks and the smarts to get any man you want. Just don't settle for one that tells you what he believes you want to hear."

Cherie nodded. "How is it with Kayana's brother?"

"In three words, a-may-zing."

Cherie laughed. "Good for you. Are you going to marry him?"

"No. We're content to live together."

"Damn, Red. You do move fast."

"Once you get to our age you don't have time to play games."

"That's what Kayana said about her and her new husband."

"Derrick has offered us his she-shed for our meetings."

"He has a she-shed?"

"He calls it a garden shed, while I call it a she-shed. It's really charming and perfect for our meetings."

"When are we going to hold our first meeting?"

"We have to ask Kayana if she's finished reading *The Alienist*. And if she has, then maybe we can meet this Sunday."

"Did you enjoy it?" Cherie questioned.

"It's masterpiece of fiction writing. But I must admit some of the murder scenes were so graphic that I found myself closing the book and not wanting to pick it up. But I knew I had to finish it to find out who was doing the killings."

"I told you it was dark."

Kayana returned with a chilled pitcher of martinis. "Derrick's bringing an antipasti platter."

"Did you finish reading *The Alienist*?" Leah asked her.

She set down the pitcher. "Yes. And I loved it. Thanks, Cherie, for recommending it."

Cherie inclined her head. "Does this mean we can begin our first meeting this Sunday?"

"I don't see why not," Kayana confirmed. "Did Leah tell you we have a new venue?"

"Yes. She mentioned a she-shed."

"It's much better than meeting on the patio, and my brother has offered his kitchen."

Cherie refilled her glass. "I hope we're not going to put him out."

Kayana rolled her eyes upward. "Girl, please. He and Graeme have already made plans to hang out at my house and watch ball games until their eyes bug out."

"I heard that, Kay," Derrick said, when he reentered the dining room carrying a large serving tray with a platter of cold appetizers, forks, small plates, and cocktail napkins.

"If I didn't want you to hear it I would've whispered," she retorted.

Derrick set the tray on the table, turned on his heel, and walked away. "Is your brother upset?" Cherie asked Kayana.

"Nah. Derrick rarely gets upset. Right, Leah?"

She smiled. "Right." Leah wanted to hang out with her friends, but she also needed to reunite with her man. Spending the week at the Kent House, despite its immense size, was suffocating, and she prayed it would be the last time she would have to walk through its doors.

Derrick heard the garage door go up and knew Leah was home. He was waiting for her when she walked into the kitchen. "How did it feel to get the gang back together?"

Smiling, Leah approached him and hugged his waist. "Wonderful. And thank you for the antipasti or I would've had to call you to drive me back."

Derrick cradled her to his chest. "What did you do last summer when you had to go home?"

"Kayana would drive us or we'd take the jitney. I'm going upstairs to shower and change into something a lot more comfortable. Please wait for me to come down."

He wanted to know how she'd fared in Richmond, but if she didn't mention it, then he wouldn't. Rather than put pressure on her, he would wait for her to open up to him.

Derrick did not have long to wait before Leah returned with damp hair and wearing an oversize T-shirt, shorts, and socks. "Would you like a cup of coffee?" he asked when she settled herself in the breakfast nook.

"Please."

He stared at her before turning on the coffeemaker. "You look tired."

"I am a little. I don't want to go to bed now because I'll wake up in the middle of the night and not be able to go back."

As much as he wanted to make love with her, Derrick realized it could wait. "Do you want anything with the coffee?"

"No, thanks."

He brewed her coffee, set the cup with a splash of sweet cream on the table, and sat opposite her. "I called my lawyer to let her know I want more money from Alan."

Derrick slumped back in the booth. "What happened?" He listened, struggling not to lose his temper when Leah told him about her husband's offensive behavior. "What the hell is wrong with him?"

Leah peered at him over the rim of the coffee cup. "He's sly like a fox, Derrick."

"He's an asshole, Leah. It's like he's begging for someone to hurt him."

"That's what I told my sons. If they hurt him, then he can play the victim."

"I never thought about that."

"I didn't live with the man all those years not to know what he's capable of. He just retired from the bench, and he's drinking more than ever. I heard that he has hired a driver because he's crashed a couple of cars and doesn't trust himself to get behind the wheel."

"He sounds self-destructive."

"It's chickens that have come home to roost," Leah said, as she held up a hand to smother a yawn. "I'm sorry about that, babe."

"There's no need to apologize. After driving, drinking, and then driving some more you have to be exhausted."

She narrowed her eyes at him. "You got jokes, Derrick Johnson?"

"No," Derrick said, deadpan. He hadn't meant to tease her. "Richmond, Virginia, is not around the corner."

"And next time I go back I hope it will be the last time. Now that I've changed my demands it's going to be a while before I'll have to attend a deposition."

"Divorces, whether contested or uncontested, are still traumatic for everyone involved."

"Fortunately, I don't have young children, so it's just me and the judge in this cage match."

Derrick recognized a steeliness in Leah that hadn't been obvious months ago. Some women would've gone off on their husband if he'd had the audacity to flaunt another

woman in her face, and especially with his sons in attendance. And his calling her a bitch in front of them meant he
had lost all sense of decorum for himself and respect for the
woman who'd made him a father.

"I decided to revise the menu for the summer season."

Leah became immediately alert. "Why, Derrick?"

"I still want you to bake for the Café, but the cakes will be
listed as daily specials. That should take some pressure off
you to feel compelled to bake every day."

She thought because she'd been gone a week he had changed
his mind about her being responsible for the restaurant's
baked goods. "I can live with that. Maybe I'll do a couple of
marathon baking sessions and you can store them in a refrig-
erated case."

"That sounds like a plan. The cleaning company came in
while you were away and cleaned and aired out your she-
shed. I also set up the grill in the backyard and bought a tank
of propane. You have to let me know what you want to grill
before Sunday, and I'll try and have it for you."

"What are our choices?" Leah asked.

"Steak, chicken, ribs, and fish."

"You mean fish as in grilled salmon?"

"Fish as in salmon, stuffed snapper, crab, and lobster."

She stared mutely at Derrick, her heart pounding with the
blood rushing through her veins. He continued to surprise
her with his generosity. It wasn't about buying her precious
jewels, or giving her a credit card with an unlimited balance,
or even driving her to a dealership where she could select any
car in the showroom, but it was his concern for whether she
was feeling well or what he could do to make her day better.

"You just kicked the Café book club up several notches."

Derrick winked at her. "Anything to make my love happy."

"Am I?" she whispered.

"Are you what?"

"Your love?"

A frown settled into his handsome features. "What did you think, Leah? Do you actually believe I would invite you into my home to live with me if I didn't love you?"

"I . . . I don't know."

A dimpled smile replaced his scowl. "I hope you know now. I told you before that you're free to come and go whenever you want, because I don't want a repeat of what you had with your husband. When you were gone last week that's when I realized how important you've become to me, and I pray it's reciprocated."

"It is, Derrick. And as much as I wanted you to come with me to Richmond, I knew it would not have ended well. Just as I don't want my sons embroiled in the shit that I have with Alan, it goes double for you. If I didn't have you to come home to, I know the vindictive bastard would've gotten to me."

"I will never let him get to you, babe. We're in this together for the duration."

Leah got up and came around the table to sit on Derrick's lap, her arms going around his strong neck. "I love you so much," she said in his ear. That was something she'd never uttered to another man. "And I hope I make you half as happy as you've made me."

Derrick buried his face against her neck. "Happier." He slid off the bench seat, bringing her up with him as he stood. "I think maybe you'll need a little convincing."

Leah did not remember Derrick carrying her up the staircase and into his bedroom; nor did she recall his undressing her, and then himself. What she did recollect was his suckling her breasts as waves of pleasure raced through her body, and her hips rising off the bed to meet him. She dug her fingers into his biceps, trembling uncontrollably as a rush of moisture flowed down her inner thighs onto the sheets; he reached down to stroke her clitoris and continued feasting on her breasts.

Leah was losing control and didn't want to climax without

him inside her. "Please," she pleaded shamelessly, her body on fire.

Heat, followed by chills, then more heat singed her sensitive flesh. Derrick kissed her mouth, the hollow in her throat, his mouth charting a path down her body. He tasted her breasts, belly, the inside of her thighs, retracing his path as he explored every inch of her. She didn't want him to stop. Her lover had discovered erogenous zones on her body she hadn't known existed. Her heart pounded so hard she was certain it could be seen through her chest.

Derrick positioned his erection at the entrance to her sex and slowly entered her body, his moans overlapping hers. She opened her legs wider to take all of him where they'd become a perfect fit. Leah gloried in the hard body atop hers, his swollen penis sliding in and out of her wetness. A shiver of delight washed over her, a moan slipping past her lips as she felt ready to climax. She bit her lip, stopping a moan. Finally letting go, her first orgasm took over, holding her captive for mere seconds before another earth-shattering release rocked through her core, taking her beyond herself as he released himself inside her.

"You are so incredibly beautiful," Derrick whispered in her ear as her body calmed from multiple orgasms. She groaned in protest when he pulled out, lay beside her, took her hand, and threaded their fingers together. If she had doubted his love for her, he had just proved it with his unbridled love-making.

Shifting slightly, she rested her left leg over his and pressed her breasts against his muscled shoulder. She closed her eyes, smiling when Derrick raised her hand and kissed it. It was the last she remembered as she fell into a sated sleep reserved for lovers.

The weather decided to cooperate for the first meeting of the Café book club when the afternoon temperature rose to the upper seventies and no clouds meant no rain. Derrick turned on the gas grill and then left to spend the afternoon with Kayana's husband. He'd gotten up early to wipe down the patio furniture and set up the umbrella shading a round table with six chairs.

When Kayana had suggested a menu of surf and turf, he'd prepared a platter with aged steak, stuffed crab, lobster tails, and prawns. Cherie had contributed the ingredients for a raspberry lemonade virgin mojito. They had agreed to serve mocktails for the summer to not only cut down on calories but also to stay focused. Leah used her grandmother's recipe to make cole slaw, Cobb, and Niçoise salads. She'd asked Derrick to make the dressings for both salads. Cherie pointed to the platter with the Cobb salad. "I can't believe you lined up each ingredient into rows."

Leah smiled. "Rather than toss everything together, I wanted you to pick out what you like." She used diced cooked chicken, avocado, chopped tomato, crumbled blue cheese, bacon, minced fresh parsley, chives, and romaine lettuce torn into bite-size pieces.

"Nice," Cherie crooned.

"It's been a while since I've had a salad Niçoise," Kayana said, as she uncovered the platter with the prepped fish. "I made it once when I lived in Atlanta, and hardly anyone touched it."

Leah set the table with place settings for three. "I think it's the anchovies. Whenever Derrick makes the dressing for a Caesar I make certain he doesn't use too many anchovies. Even though this recipe calls for sixteen, I used only four fillets. And some traditional recipes call for raw vegetables, but I prefer cooking the potatoes and steaming the green beans."

Cherie filled tall glasses with mint leaves, simple syrup, freshly squeezed lime juice, and sparkling raspberry lemonade, and then garnished each with fresh raspberries, mint, and a lime wedge. "Hanging out with you two is like taking cooking courses. By the end of the summer I'll know how to cook enough different dishes so I can stop eating out or ordering in."

"How often do you eat out?" Leah asked her.

"At least three or four times a week. Whenever I cook for myself I usually make enough for last several days, then I get tired of eating it, so I'll order in or go out."

"Just say you make spaghetti and meatballs. Divide them into single-serve portions and put them in the freezer. You can do the same with chili, or mac and cheese. Date and label them, and that way you don't have to eat the same thing every day," Kayana suggested. "I used to do that before I got married. I'd spend the entire weekend cooking, and when I came home after work all I had to do was make a quick salad and heat up whatever I wanted to eat in the microwave. Not only did I save time but also money."

"That's a fabulous idea," Cherie agreed. "Now that I'm going back to school I have to be conscious of my time."

"Are you going full-time?" Leah asked her.

"Yes. You know that I have an undergraduate degree in early-childhood development, but I need education courses because I plan to teach."

Leah recalled that Cherie had been on leave from her position as a parent coordinator at a Connecticut childcare center when she'd come to the island last summer. "If you need some advice as to what courses you want, maybe I can help you out with that."

Cherie smiled. "Thanks, Leah. I'd really appreciate that. By the way, are you still headmistress at that private girls' school?"

Leah shared a look with Kayana. "That's a story that will need more than mocktails."

Cherie froze. "You're kidding."

"I wish," Leah said.

"Is it a secret?"

"No, Cherie. It's not a secret. I'll tell you after we eat because I don't want to ruin my appetite."

"Dam-m-m. That sounds serious."

She laughed at Cherie's shocked expression. Leah returned to the house to get cruets of salad dressing and a pot with several sticks of butter and garlic powder. She put the pot on the grill without direct heat for the butter to melt, and when Kayana placed the steaks, seasoned with salt and pepper, on the oiled grates the air was filled with the delicious aroma of grilling meat.

Leah had not realized until she sat down at the table with her book club friends that she'd been waiting all year for this moment. To reunite with women who understood and didn't judge her, and women whom she could call friends. Living in a mansion, wearing haute couture and priceless jewelry, and having servants at her beck and call paled in comparison to sitting around a table eating, drinking, and discussing books on a small island off the coast of North Carolina.

Cherie touched her napkin to her mouth. "Tell me, Red, why you're no longer headmistress at that fancy school."

"My husband got me fired."

"You're lying."

"I wish I was, Cherie."

"He beats you, but that's not enough, so he gets you fired. No wonder you want a chunk out of his ass. Don't you know any thugs that would grab him when he's getting his car and take him somewhere and fuck him up, Leah?"

"No, Cherie, I don't know any thugs."

"Even though I went to a private school and college I still know dudes in my old neighborhood I could call to have my back if I needed them to take care of a man that put his hands on me. That's what I call hood justice."

"Believe me, Cherie, if I hadn't pleaded with my sons not to lay hands on Alan, he wouldn't be breathing today. Aron and Caleb are six-three, two-thirty, and they were ready to take him apart."

"Shit!"

"Well, damn!"

Kayana and Cherie had spoken at the same time. "Had he lost his mind when he hit you, knowing his sons would come for him?" Kayana asked.

"Apparently not, because he's drunk most of the time."

"Let's hope his drunken behind doesn't come down here starting trouble, because my brother will use an illegal football move and clothesline his ass."

"Enough talk about my soon-to-be-ex," Leah said. "Talking about him is giving me indigestion."

"I really like this cole slaw, Leah," Cherie said. "It has just enough crunch and bite."

"It's the collard greens."

"Wow. I'd never think of using collards in slaw."

"Live and learn, sweetie."

"Maybe instead of going back to Connecticut at the end of the season I should sell my condo and move down here."

"What about school?" Kayana asked.

"I can take online courses to get a master's in education."

"If you decide to go that route, then I'll definitely help you," Leah volunteered.

"What say you, Cherie?" Kayana questioned.

The gold in Cherie's light-brown eyes glinted like polished amber. "I'm going to give it some serious thought. I've already resigned my position at the childcare center, so if I sell my condo that means I'll be able to make a clean break."

Leah continued to stare at the beautiful young woman with large, light-brown eyes in a flawless gold-brown complexion. It was the set of her full lips that made her look as petulant as her moody personality. She could not imagine what a man had done to Cherie to sour her on men and life.

"How are we going to top today's meal with lobster, filet mignon, and prawns?" Cherie asked.

Kayana shrugged her shoulders. "If we put our heads together we'll come up with something."

"I can make flatbread with an assortment of toppings,"
Leah said.

"I'd like that," Cherie stated.

Kayana nodded. "I agree."

"Are we going to discuss *The Alienist* out here or in the
she-shed?" Cherie asked.

"She-shed," Leah and Kayana chorused.

Twenty minutes after putting away leftovers, the three
women sat on the bed and in a cushioned rocker as Cherie
opened the meeting as the moderator for her selected title.
"What about it did you not like?"

"It was the over-the-top graphic descriptions of the bodies
of the murdered children," Leah said.

"I was bothered that all of the victims were children,"
Kayana agreed, "but it was the dark atmospheric depiction
of the seamy underbelly of New York City during the period
that left me feeling uneasy. It was as if everyone was corrupt
or deviant—pimps, police, cross-dressing boy prostitutes,
and former mental patients."

"Even when the characters lived in or visited mansions, it
was as if the darkness persisted," Leah added.

Cherie nodded. "I've read this novel twice, and each time I
felt as if I'd been transported in time where I could smell the
cooking odors coming from the apartments in the tenements,
visualize the horse droppings in the streets, and the stench
coming from the sewers where people discarded their
garbage. It was a time in New York where it wasn't safe for
decent people to venture out after dark because gangs of rov-
ing kids would shank you for your shoes as they would for
your wallet. People nowadays complain about gangs, but
New York City had more than its share of gangs from young
kids to the Black Hand that had begun to make their foray
into organized crime."

"What I did like," Kayana began, "was the introduction and development of psychological profiling."

"But remember, even though they'd employed the science of fingerprinting," Leah reminded Cherie and Kayana, "it still at that time wasn't accepted as a method of identifying the killer."

"The author got a thumbs-up from me because his characters were racially and ethnically diverse as the city was at that time period and still is," Kayana stated.

Cherie nodded. "That's what I really liked the most, because it added color and flavor to a novel with accurate historical detail. Leah, is this a novel you would recommend for your high school students?"

"Maybe for an English AP course, but not my regular students. If I taught a college course I definitely would make it required reading. What about you, Kayana? If you taught a course, would you recommend this title?"

"It would also be appropriate for psychology students. I would have them select one of the characters and analyze them."

The discussion continued with each selecting their favorite character and analyzing him or her. The sun had sunk lower on the horizon when they adjourned their meeting. Everyone decided to wait four weeks before holding the next meeting. That would give everyone time to read the next two titles. Leah had volunteered to be the moderator for *Memoirs of a Geisha*.

She was grateful they'd changed from a book a week schedule, because she'd committed to baking for the restaurant, which cut into her reading time. And now that Kayana was married she also had less time for herself.

Leah locked the shed and returned to the house when she heard Derrick pulling into the garage. She waited for him to enter the kitchen. "How was your bro-fest?"

He flashed a dimpled smile. "Great. How was your book club meeting?"

"Wonderful. We're not going to meet for another month to give everyone time to catch up with the required reading."

Derrick took a step and breathed a kiss under her ear. "Does this mean I can make plans for us to spend Sunday afternoons together?"

"Yes, it does."

"Let me know where you'd like to go or do, and I'll try to make it happen."

Leah brushed a light kiss over his mouth. "Thank you, darling."

"You're welcome, love."

Chapter 17

Leah's fairytale world shattered completely three weeks later when she answered her phone, and this time it was Caleb calling with bad news. Alan had suffered a massive stroke; and she was listed as his medical proxy. Derrick came home and found her sitting on the porch in tears.

"What's the matter, babe?"

"When am I going to be rid of him, Derrick?"

"Who are you talking about?"

"Alan. He's had a stroke and has been placed on a ventilator and I'm his medical proxy."

Derrick stroked her hair. "I can't tell you to go or stay. That has to be your decision."

She sniffled. "If it were up to me I'd tell them to pull the plug, but I don't want that on my conscience if there is the possibility that he can recover. And this definitely delays the divorce."

"Stop agonizing about the divorce, Leah. It will happen."

"That's easy for you to say because you're not married to a monster. I want to be rid of him—now!"

"That can't happen now, because the man is in a hospital hooked up to machines."

"And if I was truly the bitch he believes I am, I would sign the DNR and watch him take his last breath."

"Don't say that, Leah."

Anger and frustration warred within her, and Leah bit her tongue because she wanted to scream at Derrick not to tell her what she could or could not say. "I'm not going anywhere tonight. I'm going to call Caleb and let him know I'll drive up tomorrow."

"Is he in New York?"

"No. He's in Richmond. Aron is flying down on a redeye."

"If it wasn't the tourist season I would go with you."

"Even if it was off-season I still wouldn't want you to go with me. I told you before I don't want you involved."

"But I am involved, Leah, because I'm involved with you. You can't ask me to be there for you during the good times and shut me out when they're not. You need to make up your mind before we go any further in our relationship."

Leah froze. "What are you talking about?"

"Did it ever dawn on you that maybe one of these days I'd like for us to be married?"

Her mouth opened, but nothing came out. "But I told you I don't want to get married."

"Why, Leah? Wait. You don't have to answer that. Because you think I'll turn out like the monster you've spent thirty years with, and if he hadn't beaten the hell out of you, you'd still be with him."

"That's not fair!" Leah shouted.

"Sorry, babe. You should realize by now that sometime life isn't fair."

Leah knew she had to get away from Derrick before she said something she would later regret. Why couldn't he understand Alan Kent was a problem of her own making and she had to solve it on her own?

She went into the house to pack a bag and hoped it would be for the last time.

This time Leah did check into a downtown Richmond hotel before driving to the hospital. She found Caleb and Aron half asleep on chairs in the private room where Alan lay motionless, his head bandaged and a machine regulating his breathing. When Aron opened his eyes, she noticed they were bloodshot.

She beckoned to him. It took several seconds for him to push off the chair and join her outside the room. Leah rested her hand on his arm. "Go home and get some sleep. I'll be here when you get back."

He ran a large tanned hand over his stubble. "Are you sure, Mom?"

"Yes." She waited for him to pick up his carry-on and leave, then she took the chair he'd vacated.

"You're here."

Leah stared at Caleb. He didn't look as exhausted as his brother. "When did you get in?"

"Yesterday afternoon. Aron was in court, so he didn't get my message until late."

"How did you find out that he'd had a stroke?" Leah knew she was asking a lot of questions, but she needed to know what to prepare for as Alan's medical proxy.

"Apparently he was golfing and had complained of a headache. Someone at the country club found him on the restroom floor and called for medical assistance. One of his golf buddies called the house, and the housekeeper gave him my number. Before leaving after Grandma's funeral I gave her my card and told her to call me if Dad needed me for anything. After you left he'd begun drinking heavily until he could hardly stand upright."

"Your father needs to go into rehab, Caleb. He's an alcoholic."

"I know that, Mom, but when I questioned him about drinking so much, he nearly bit my head off."

"He can't drink now."

Caleb stretched out his long legs. "How long do you plan to stay?"

"As long as it takes, one way or the other." Leah paused. "I find it odd that he didn't change his medical proxy when he canceled the credit cards with my name."

"He probably didn't think about it. Dad always believed he would live as long or even longer than Grandma."

Leah snorted under her breath. "Your grandmother didn't drink and watched her diet, while your grandfather smoked and was a heavy drinker, and died in his late fifties."

"It appears as if Dad did not have a good role model."

Leah wanted to say to Caleb, "Like father, like son." Alan and his father were mirror images of each other in temperament and lifestyle. "Why don't you also go home and get some rest. I'll be here for a while."

"Where are you staying, Mom?"

"At a hotel. And please don't ask me to come to Kent House. If Alan doesn't make it through this and if he didn't change his will and I inherit the house, then I want to give it to you and Aron along with what he inherited from his mother."

"No, Mom. You don't have to do that."

"Yes, I do, because I'll never live there again. The house is over six thousand square feet and large enough for you and your brother to have separate apartments with a dedicated staff of employees."

"Will you come and visit if we do decide to live there?"

"Of course. I just don't intend to live there again."

"I'll think about it."

"Don't think too long, Caleb. I just might change my mind and donate it to the city as a museum."

"You can't do that. It's our home."

"It was where you grew up. New York is now your home."

Caleb smothered a curse under his breath. "I have to talk to Marisa about this. And you know you're being manipulative."

"Am I?" Her expression mirrored innocence before Leah turned her head to conceal a grin. Caleb's willingness to talk to his fiancée about possibly relocating from New York to Virginia would be a win-win for her and them. She would get to see her son and potential grandchildren more often, and they would inherit property listed on the National Register of Historic Places.

"Yes, and you know it. I suppose I could join the family practice, but aren't we getting ahead of ourselves? Dad's still alive."

"I said it is a possibility *if* your father didn't change his will. And if he did, then we'll have to wait and see."

Leah didn't want Alan to die but to recover so she could go through with the divorce and get on with her life. And she did not want the responsibility of determining whether he lived or died.

"If you don't mind, I'd like to hang out with my mother a little longer."

She patted his arm. "I'd like that."

Leah felt like a hamster in a cage running around and around on the wheel until it collapsed from exhaustion. She went from her hotel room to the hospital room and then back again. She hated herself for passing herself off as the supportive wife sitting at her husband's bedside while praying for his recovery. They did not know it wasn't for her but for her sons.

After a week she ordered them back to New York and promised to text them if there was a change in Alan's condition. It was now more than a month since she'd checked into the hotel, and she informed the front desk that she would occupy the suite until further notice.

Leah missed Coates Island, her book club friends, and she missed Derrick. She'd resorted to texting him rather than calling because whenever she hung up she was close to weeping. She called her mother and unloaded to her about Alan's assault and her subsequent decision to file for divorce. Madeline volunteered to come and be with her during her current crisis, but Leah reassured her she was staying strong and had committed to stay until there was a change in Alan's condition. After six weeks, he was moved to a section of the small private hospital where patients were afforded a personal waiting area for their visitors.

When outdoors, the heat and the summer humidity sapped Leah of her energy so she'd made it a practice to go from her air-cooled hotel suite to her air-conditioned car and the air-regulated hospital. She'd just left the hospital to return to the hotel when she got a call from the hospital. Leah reversed direction and when she walked into Alan's room it was to silence. The machines monitoring his vitals had been turned off and when she met the doctor's eyes she knew it was over. Alan Stephens Kent was gone.

Leah hadn't told Derrick she was coming back, and when she walked into the house ten days later on a Sunday afternoon he stared at her as if he'd never seen her before. She noticed his face was leaner, and there was puffiness under his eyes as if he hadn't been sleeping well.

"You're back."

She nodded. "Yes, I'm back. And to stay."

"What happened, Leah?"

She closed her eyes. "He's gone. Even if he'd been able to breathe on his own his health was so compromised that he would've required around-the-clock care."

"It's over, darling."

Leah reached for his hand, threading their fingers together. He kissed her forehead, and she struggled not to cry. She'd left the man she loved to sit vigil by the bedside of one she wanted to hate, but couldn't, while he'd continued to punish her because he refused to be a loser.

Derrick released her hand and picked her up. "You look as if a strong wind would blow you over. I'm putting you to bed, then I'm going make something for you to eat. After that you can tell me your long story."

"I need to take a shower." She needed to wash off the smell of the hospital. What she couldn't do was erase the memory of the hours she'd spent sitting at the bedside of the man who'd continued to control her when she was forced to play the devoted wife.

"You can shower later. But first you'll eat."

Looping her arms around his neck, Leah rested her head on his shoulder as he carried her up the staircase. She was aware she'd lost weight because she'd found herself eating one meal a day. She also had a problem falling and staying asleep.

"Don't put me on the bed. I want to take off these clothes." Derrick left the room while she stripped down to her underwear. She opened the drawer where he kept a supply of T-shirts and put one on. After washing her hands and splashing water on her face, she climbed into bed. The lingering scent of Derrick's cologne wafted to her nostrils, and she knew for certain that she was home.

Leah hadn't realized she'd fallen asleep until she felt Derrick tug on her arm. "Wake up, babe."

She sat up and adjusted a mound of pillows behind her back before he set a tray on her lap. He'd made a mushroom and sausage omelet, crispy home fries, and a cup of hot chocolate topped with whipped cream.

"Thank you. It looks delicious."

Derrick sat at the foot of the bed. "I'm going to watch you eat everything on that plate." The instant she put a forkful of egg in her mouth Leah realized what she had been missing: a home-cooked meal. She ate everything on the plate and sipped the chocolate, licking the cream off her lips.

"Feel better?"

Closing her eyes, she rested her head against the leather headboard. "Yes."

Derrick moved off the bed to take the tray. "I'll be right back."

Leah was wide awake when he returned, removed his jeans, and got into bed with her. "You don't know how many times I wished he would stop breathing, but then I prayed for forgiveness."

"Don't beat up on yourself, babe. Believe it or not, you are human like the rest of us."

She smiled. "I always wanted to be Wonder Woman."

"Even superheroes are vulnerable to something."

Leah wanted to tell Derrick she was only vulnerable when it came to Alan. She'd wanted to become a divorcée, but Alan had flipped the script and now she was his widow.

Epilogue

Labor Day

The summer season was over; tourists had returned to their homes, and the Seaside Café had closed, and would reopen with the fall, winter, and spring schedule of serving one meal a day Mondays through Fridays. Derrick and Kayana had decided to close on weekends to give them time to spend with their families.

Leah sat at the round table on the patio with Kayana and Marisa as Derrick, Graeme, Aron, and Caleb stood at the grill drinking beer and discussing the pros and cons of grilling. She had met her future daughter-in-law at Alan's funeral, and Aron was right. She was bright and gorgeous, and Leah looked forward to having beautiful grand-children.

Alan Kent's funeral was nothing short of a spectacle as people filled every pew in the church and eulogies droned on and on about his judicial brilliance. Leah had remained stoic throughout the service and gracious during the reception when Kent House overflowed with mourners eating and drinking while remarking on the loss of one of Richmond's native sons.

Three days later, she was summoned to the offices of Kent, Kent, McDougal & Sweeny, Attorneys at Law, for the reading of the will of Alan Stephens Kent. Her late husband had been so confident she would never divorce him that he hadn't amended his will. She inherited the bulk of his estate, including Kent House, while he'd evenly divided what he'd inherited from Adele between Caleb and Aron, making them very wealthy young men before they celebrated their thirtieth birthdays. Before leaving Richmond, she'd sat with one of the managing partners to draw up her own will.

Caleb and Aron agreed to leave New York, move into Kent House, and join the law practice bearing their name. Marisa had also agreed to relocate with Caleb to complete her internship and residency at a Richmond hospital. Leah decided to send out Christmas gifts early and used a portion of her inheritance to pay off the mortgage on her brother's house and purchase a condo for her parents.

"What are you thinking about, Leah?" Kayana asked.

"How a year ago I never could've imagined myself living here."

Kayana laughed. "Coates Island has that special magic that once you come, you don't want to leave."

Marisa pushed a pair of sunglasses atop her wavy, coal-black hair. "I never thought I'd consider living anywhere else but in New York, but this is like another world."

Leah smiled at the petite woman wearing Caleb's engagement ring. "Derrick said you're welcome to come down whenever you want."

Derrick had opened his home to her family, and she'd finally opened her heart to him with a promise that she wanted to wait a year before becoming Mrs. Derrick Edward Johnson. He'd claimed he had waited five years for her to come into his life, so he was willing to wait one more to make her his wife.

The book club was on hiatus until the next summer season when Cherie Thompson promised to return and hopefully to stay.

Connect with Us

Visit us online at
KensingtonBooks.com
to read more from your favorite authors, see books
by series, view reading group guides, and more.

Join us on social media

for sneak peeks, chances to win books and prize packs,
and to share your thoughts with other readers.

facebook.com/kensingtonpublishing
twitter.com/kensingtonbooks

Tell us what you think!

To share your thoughts, submit a review,
or sign up for our eNewsletters, please visit:
KensingtonBooks.com/TellUs.